ESCAPE

The Earthcode Quest

C N Stansfield

C N Stansfield

"Never underestimate the infinitely great power of the infinitely small."

French Chemist Louis Pasteur

I am Finn. The world that I know will never be the same. Everything that I thought was constant and reliable has fallen apart in front of my own eyes in a matter of weeks. Reports of the killer virus had been circulated by You-Tubers months ago, but world governments played them down. Life continued as normal, until I started hearing of friends and people down my street getting ill, very ill and dying. It took less than a week after for the disruptions to food and fuel deliveries to start being noticed and that's when the real panic started...

Prologue

TORCHED

~~~

It's night, the street lights are off, but the furious yellow flickers from the mob's fire torches light up the street outside their corner shop, casting terrifying shadows inside, a warning that they're in real trouble.

THUD! Against the shop display window.

THUD! Again. The rioting mob launch the trash dumpster at the window once more.

SMASH! Finally, the window caves in under the thumping weight. Glass shatters and cascades across the floor surrounding them.

Each second feels like forever. Trapped inside their own small shop, cowering behind the only sales counter, clinging to the faint hope that something will distract the mob and the nightmare will end.

Burning orange light from the lead rioter's torch flits around them as he steps over the threshold, through the gaping glass hole. He doesn't wear a face mask. He doesn't need to hide. He knows there's no one to come after him, at night especially. There's only the army now and they're nowhere to be seen. They're guarding more important buildings.

CRASH! Geo's guts churn. Poor Imp, his kid sister, huddles into a ball, closing her eyes hard. With her long frizzy wiry hair, she looks like a terrified hedgehog caught in a car's headlights. Geo holds her tightly, to let her know he's there for her. He can feel her heart pounding through her rib cage.

It was a very bad idea, returning to the shop, especially at night. They should have gone straight to the airport.

'I just need to pick up a few things,' Mum said on the way. But they'd seen the rioting on the news, seen the gangs thieving anything they could, just down the road, in the city centre... surely anyone could see it was only a matter of time before they started to widen their search for food. But Mum thought that no one would be interested in their tiny newsagent shop, tucked away, on the corner of Pleasant Street and Cranberry Road.

How wrong can you be?

She shielded Geo and Imp from the flying glass as best she could with her own body, but now her bare arms and face are splintered with sharp red slashes. Silently looking into her eyes, Geo sees her effort not to cry out in pain and reveal their flimsy hiding place. Not that the mob outside will bother much about them if they find what they want; food, drink, or maybe something they can swap for food or drink. But goods like that sold out weeks ago and there's been no new deliveries since things turned dangerous on the city streets. The mob is going to be disappointed, and then angry, that's when things will turn nasty.

Geo hears glass crunching under heavy boots nearby, each step getting closer. From behind the counter, he glimpses a flicker of the massive bulk of a man covered in a huge thick trench coat which makes him look even more terrifying. He waves his torch toward the shelves. Flaming orange fingers feel their way around the shelving revealing the bare truth.

"There's nowt 'ere!" The man's angry, hoarse voice shouts back to the others gathered outside.

The gruff but calm reply comes back, "Torch it then!"

"Waste o' time, what's the point?"

"Show people about 'ere who runs this place now, that's what! Torch it!"

Without questioning, the man turns and leaves, crunching more glass under his heavy shoes as he steps back through the hole where the shop window once was, taking the flaming light with him. The world around Geo, Imp and Mum slips back into comforting blackness, silent and still, as if holding its breath, waiting, preparing for the final blow.

A pained hushed shout into Geo's ear commands, "RUN!" Mum knows what's coming and knows they must move quickly, or risk being burned alive.

Crawling through the glass shards, on hands and knees, they use the temporary darkness to escape from behind the sales counter and shuffle down the first aisle towards the exit at the back of the shop where the deliveries are made. Geo and Imp are first. Mum guards the rear. The glass cuts into their hands and legs but they keep going. Be sliced or burned alive. In the shadows, they make it between the first two racks of empty shelves. Down this aisle would be cereals and biscuits, some chocolates opposite and magazines further down. A few magazines are still there, but the other shelves are bare and have been since the panic buying started.

With a dreadful sound like a swan's wings flapping as it takes-off, the bottle, half-full of petrol, tumbles gracefully through the gaping hole where the shop window used to be. It hits the sales counter, exactly where they had been hiding moments before, and explodes on impact.

WHOOSH! Furious streams of fire immediately engulf the counter and floor around it, flash lighting everything they touch.

Another one. WHOOSH! SMASH and FLASH! This time blasting behind them, in the aisle that they had just crawled down. Geo feels the sting of heat on the back of his neck. A cloud of thick, black petrol smoke races along the floor towards them. Geo can't help himself; he looks back to see the whole shop already crackling like a bonfire and Mum behind, struggling for air. Thick heat cuts at his own throat as he tries to breathe. He coughs and gasps but keeps moving.

"Stay low to the floor!" It's Imp's voice.

Geo drops his face to the floor and, at last, catches some less toxic, cooler air and tries to fill his lungs the best he can, still crawling forward. The back of the shop is very close now. He must be near the storeroom door now. He holds his breath, closes his eyes against the thick smoke and reaches his arm up blindly feeling for the door handle that he knows is there. The handle turns and the door opens easily. He falls in gratefully. Imp follows too. Together, they slump on the floor waiting for Mum to appear, but she doesn't.

Geo knows he can't close the storeroom door fully without her inside.

He looks back into the thick smoke, eyes streaming, and shouts for her.

There's no answer just the roaring of burning. Soon, there would be no shop left, the mob knew what they were doing, experts.

Black smoke is now pouring into the storeroom and will cut off their only escape route if he doesn't shut the door quickly. Bravely, Geo decides to crawl back to find her, leaving the safety of the storeroom behind, but the fumes and red-hot heat fiercely beats him back. Desperately he cries for her again, fearing the worst.

Suddenly Mum appears, blindly dragging herself through the smoke. Even through his tears, she looks terrible. Her skin is red and blistered and covered with sores, her clothes are charred and still alight. She is beyond screaming, but she made it! Her momentum carries them both backward into the storeroom. Swiftly, Imp closes the door in terrified silence. With her bare hands she pats down Mum's burning clothes until the smoldering stops. Together they slump there, coughing and gagging. Imp's tears leave tracks down her smoke blackened cheeks. Geo hugs Imp, trying to reassure her, but there's no time. Black smoke is seeping in, infiltrating, and poisoning the air in the storeroom, through any gap in the door frame it can find.

"Quick," he coughs, "we can't rest here! We have to get out!" Struggling for every breath, Geo pushes the fire exit door bar down and the double doors swing open releasing himself into the sweet cool night and the dark empty lane behind the shop.

Checking as best that he can through his streaming eyes, "It's OK, I don't think anyone's out here."

Cautiously, Imp too, appears out of the cloud of smoke which is filling the storeroom. "Mum's still in there! She's not coming out!"

Taking a deep breath, Geo dives back into the now smoke-filled room. He can hear the raging sound of out of control fire behind the closed door to the shop. The door won't hold for long. Smoke stings his eyes and again he tastes the acrid burning in his mouth, making him duck down for better air between coughs of black spit. He feels his way forward instinctively. Miraculously, he finds Mum's limp body, grabs her hands, and risks the thick smoke again as he stands up and attempts to drag her across the floor. She is deadweight heavy and Geo struggles to move her even a few centimetres along the floor. Desperately, he takes another deep breath and stands up as he tugs her with all his strength. His eyes are stinging with the smoke.

He can't breathe.

Overwhelmed by fumes, he falls to the floor.

He doesn't get up.

He's gone… a dream…like sinking…drowning. Strangely it feels as if *he* is being pulled sideways and dragged. The ground is hard and lumpy. It hurts. It's not a dream.

He can breathe!

He's outside lying on the ground, dazed and disorientated. Geo coughs and greedily gasps in gulps of sweet cold air between more coughs. As he regains consciousness, he props himself up unsteadily on his elbow and searches the ground immediately around him to find Mum. Imp is there, but Mum isn't.

How did he get back outside? There's no way Imp could have pulled him out.

Imp is standing just outside the exit doors, extremely agitated, looking back inside the delivery room.

Unsteadily, Geo pushes himself up off the ground and steadies himself, coughing up more black phlegm.

Stepping out of the clouds of black smoke, a tall broad figure is carrying a limp body. He hurriedly lays her gently on the ground. Mum is badly cut and burned, her skin is charred, blackened, and blooded. Her arms flop to the side as he slowly releases her. Geo recognises the familiar face of his uncle as he unsteadily stumbles closer to try to help but his head is pounding and groggy from inhaling the fumes of the fire. Imp is stood nearby and is shaking uncontrollably. In desperation, his uncle kneels beside Mum and awkwardly starts to give mouth to mouth resuscitation. There's no response from Mum when he pauses for a second, but he continues. On the second attempt, Mum coughs and splutters, her eyes flicker open and roll from side to side as if trying to focus and understand. With all her might she grabs my uncle's arm and gasps, "Go...Airport... Sarro!" before releasing him and passing limply out.

His uncle understands her urgent plea. He needs to get them to the airport. But can he risk moving her in this condition? She is right, if they delay any longer, they will miss the only flight, most likely the last flight, to Sarro and that would be certain disaster. Who knows what will happen to the country in the next few days?

The deadliest virus the world has ever known has already claimed tens of thousands of lives. Most of the developed countries misguidedly thought that they could withstand the virus like they had with less deadly viruses so many times previously. They were very wrong. The death toll is so devastatingly high that it has already caused catastrophic disruption to the national infrastructures; policing, food supplies, power supplies and waste collections resulting in disgusting piles of rat-infested heaps of rubbish on every street. The remnants of the army continue to maintain control of some government restricted areas, but for how long is anyone's guess. And now this; street mobs scaring the remaining people and burning down small corner shops.

"I came as soon as I heard what was happening. You're lucky I did too, any longer in there and you would have been fried," explains his uncle as he props up Mum with his strong builder's hands and lifts her into the back of his old van, parked a little distance down the lane. Geo's legs are still wobbly, but the night air is sweet, and each new breath slowly helps clear the shroud of confusion and the throbbing in his head as he and Imp follow close behind.

Nodding towards the van, "We've got to get you to the airport, or you'll miss your flight."

"Mum...Is Mum going to be able to?" Geo asks expecting the worse.

"She's got some bad burns, looks painful. Should really go to hospital but they're in quarantine lock down. I'd say her best chance is to keep to the plan and get on the plane. What on Earth made you go to the shop?" He asks rhetorically before continuing, "Hopefully she'll get help in Sarro. The sooner she gets proper treatment, the better." He starts the engine and immediately sets off without headlights to the airport, taps the dash board fondly and says, "I hope there's enough juice in the old girl to get us there! Probably have to walk home!"

Even though it's less than half a mile to the airport, it's still a perilous journey in the black of the night. On the plus side, the roads are deserted, completely devoid of any traffic because no one has fuel to waste. Now it's dark, they can travel unseen if they keep the headlights off. Extremely risky but using them will only invite unwanted attention. The street lights have been 'powered down' to save fuel for more important things. Traveling is painfully slow as they weave their way through the blackness.

From the front passenger seat, Geo hears Imp fussing around Mum, trying to make her comfortable in the back of the van, but it's so dark it is impossible to see how badly hurt she is. At least Imp sounds OK.

His uncle taps him on the shoulder and does one of his secret nods to the back seat of the van. Geo gets what he means. It is up to him to be strong for the others, even if he doesn't feel strong.

"Not far now... nearly there!" Encourages Geo in his best optimistic voice although he feels his voice shake a little, he hopes they don't notice in the back.

Luckily, the drive to the airport is slow but uneventful. However, the terminal building itself looks eerily deserted, like a ghost town with only a handful of dim emergency lights on, probably powered from emergency backup batteries. Geo worries that the airport has already been shut down because there is no sign of aircraft landing or taking off. The place looks abandoned. Despite this, his uncle swiftly pulls up near to the sole light marking the passenger drop-off zone and hands Geo the black backpack containing the tickets and passports.

"Be quick! You go and check in at the desk over there, there's no time to waste!" His uncle is pointing to the lone checking-in desk nearby. It is dimly lit up unlike the rest of the inside of the building which is cloaked in silent shadows. "I'll get the others over to you."

"You're very late! I was about close the shutters. Hurry, hurry!" From behind the checking-in desk, the assistant looks flustered and appalled that anyone would dare to arrive so late.

Mum, propped up by Uncle, arrives seconds later only vaguely aware of her surroundings. Urgently Uncle says his goodbyes before vanishing back into the night, he'd left the engine running. "Good luck. Take care! Don't forget…"

"They've already started boarding!" panics the assistant who quickly glances at the tickets and spontaneously decides to personally usher them through the terminal directly to the gangway and to the airplane itself while constantly reminding Geo that next time they need to check in at least an hour before boarding the flight. Geo has never seen the airport so deserted or so dark. There is no one to check the passports, in fact there is no one else anywhere.

At the other end of the short gangway to the plane is a smartly dressed air steward who looks set to seal the aircraft cabin door closed. Surprised, he halts and carefully escorts Mum to her seat. Slowly and painfully, she sits down. Geo notices him looking her over closely. Is he checking her for the virus? For the first time, in the light of the airplane cabin, Geo can see the true extent of her injuries and can completely understand why the cabin steward might be concerned. She is covered in short red slashes and her arms are blistered. Importantly though, there are no signs of any purple bruising - an obvious sign of the virus - so the steward hurriedly goes back to preparing the aircraft for take-off.

FIRST IMPRESSIONS

~~~

I am Finn. My first impression of Geo is the dirty, disheveled teenage boy who stinks of smoke and petrol with singed, frizzy hair just like his younger sister, although she also has tear streaks etched down her dirty face. Both seem completely oblivious to the annoyance and stress they have caused all the other passengers, including myself, by delaying the take-off still further. Can they not know that this is likely to be the very last flight allowed from the airport until the virus is contained or a cure found? Can they not see the fear in the other passenger's faces?

At last, the powerful jet engines roar into action and within seconds we are safely airborne. As we climb higher, the atmosphere in the cabin changes to sheer relief, and the distress of the delay is instantly forgiven and forgotten. We have escaped!

It makes me sick to think that I'm leaving everything and everyone behind. I don't like the idea that I am running away one bit. I'm not. It was my mother first, then Gramps and, finally, even my father who decided that I should leave the city immediately and go to stay with some old family friends on the Isle of Sarro. I can't remember ever seeing Gramps so animated! Normally he just sits there, staring into space as if he's re-living some distant memories but when he started to tell me about his time on the Isle of Sarro, he was pacing up and down the living room, waving his arms around like a young boy who's just discovered how to make real mud pies. He'd been evacuated to the island during the war. He told me stories that were so farfetched they were ridiculous but, in the end, I was hooked and itching to go and see the Isle of Sarro for myself. Nothing to do with escaping the virus or running away from armed vigilantes, but because I was bored of the same old same old, made worse since the internet was next to useless with all the power cuts.

The Earthcode Quest

SARRO FRIENDS

~~~

I step out of my new home in Sarro into the dazzling day. The door swings closed behind me and I halt, just for a second, while my eyes adjust. The single row of identical, stepped terrace houses snakes up the whole length of the short dusty track straight up to the twisted, tangled trees of Holdwood which completely swallows the hill on which it stands, coldly observing everything below. A sharp shiver goes down my spine, despite the warmth of the day.

Directly opposite me, is a patch of open rough grassland about the size of two tennis courts, a dumping ground, with an old three-seater sofa sat on the far-left side next to an old iron framed bed with the mattress still intact. Trampolining on the bed are two dark haired girls wearing black sporty tank tops and shorts, looking as though they've just left the gym. Stood next to them, I spot the two from the airplane although I nearly don't recognise them without their smoke smeared faces. Kicking a ball straight to me, is a taller boy. It's a good pass, the ball lands precisely at my feet and immediately starts to gently roll down the slope and away from me. Instinctively, I control the ball and kick it back to him, but it's a terrible return pass...the ball lands on the bed just missing one of the bouncing girls.

"What sort of kick was that!?" spits out the taller boy playfully.

"Sorry, I wasn't ready!" is my feeble reply, walking over to retrieve the ball from the bed.

The girls stop jumping and watch me closely. They look about my age. I feel like I'm being scrutinised with every step forward. As I approach, I start to mouth my apology but as I do the first girl picks up the ball and powerfully fires it back to me, "Looking for this?!"

"Thanks. Sorry about that."

The other girl joins in, "What's your name? I'm Genji, and this is my sister Jun."

Up close, I see Genji is the taller of the two sisters.

"Hi," I nod back trying to sound casual, but feeling awkward around new faces, "I'm Finn."

"Finn...Finn...Finn," Genji says slowly, as if she's mentally kicking the name around in her head before finally deciding,"...Finn. I like it! A good name, what does it mean?"

No one ever asked me that before, in fact I've never thought about it before and I have no idea what it means. I'm taken off guard for the second time in the space of two minutes and my answer sounds slow and stupid, "Dunno really, just my name." and trying to pull back some credibility, I try, "So what's Genji mean?"

"In Cantonese it means 'wild and beautiful' of course!" She replies with a short laugh and confidently flicks back her long black hair and smiles, holding a superstar pose, "Can't you tell?"

I am speechless. If I was back home on the street, this would not happen, you just don't connect up with newbies; even before all the trouble. Sure, I've got mates, good mates, but we never speak to new kids unless one of us knows them. I am immediately on my guard; why are they so friendly? They don't know me. I don't know them. There's another thing that's bothering me too, I like Genji and I'm not sure why or how I feel about that either; girls are trouble, everyone knows that.

I look across to the others for some sort of confirmation that everyone on Sarro is mad, but they smile back happily.

"More like 'wild and annoying'!" checks the taller boy, "I'm Charlie, we're going down the harbour. Do some crabbing maybe. Wan'te come?"

Charlie stands about 10cm taller than me although his wild, curly blond hair probably makes up most of the difference. He's the outdoor type, completely different to me, with a rugged suntanned face, ripped jeans and faded old T-shirt but he has a friendly way about him, and I warm to him straight away.

"Yeh, sounds good. What is it?"

"That's exactly what I said!" The boy that I recognised from the flight over from the mainland joins the conversation. This time I can see his round freckled face and cheeky grin, "I'm Geo, or G to my friends, by the way and this is Imp." Imp is wearing a worn-out cap perched on top of her thick wiry hair, it's blue, matching the eyes peering from underneath, silently sizing me up.

"I saw you on the plane over. You OK now? Was that your Mum with you? You looked in a bad way."

"Yeh, we're OK now. Aren't we, sis? Just a few cuts and bruises," he shows me his hands which are crisscrossed with thin cuts, "and Mum's much better too. She's resting for a bit." Geo slaps his little sister cheerfully on the back and grins, "Better for being here and not stressing about catching the..." his voice changes to a whisper," DV... Deadly Virus. A bit different here compared to back home though, don't you think?"

We walk down the lane to the harbour with Charlie carrying the ball. "How is it different? What happened to you anyway?" asked Charlie.

When he hears what happened, Charlie is appalled at our news from the mainland. Of course, he knows about the spread of the virus and he knows about some riots, but he has no idea how serious things had become. The girls are shocked too when Geo tells us what happened to him and Imp, when their shop got smashed and torched with them still inside. Imp doesn't say much and bravely holds back her tears.

It's only a short walk down the hill to the harbour wall and Genji, Jun and Charlie take us straight to their favourite spot in the sun, away from the main hustle and bustle. Within seconds, it is obvious that we from the city are useless at crabbing. I have no idea what to do; no idea about crab bait, no idea what a sinker is or, more importantly, and much to Genji and Jun's amusement, no idea how to pick up a crab without getting pincered. But with some expert tuition from Charlie, it's not long before we are catching crabs by the bucket full. In truth, it is more likely we are catching the same crabs over and over again because every time the bucket is full, we throw the crabs back into the sea, but no one seems to care. What is really surprising is that I don't care either! Back home I would be annoyed and complaining bitterly, explaining to anyone who would listen how stupid and pointless the whole exercise is, but not here, we spend the entire day crabbing, chatting, and chilling with each other.

With the high tide, we watch the small flotilla of rusty looking fishing boats return to the harbour. Each vessel with its own attachment of seagulls eagerly flapping and squawking, ducking, and diving hopeful for some more fishy morsels to be tossed overboard.

"What happens," asks Charlie thoughtfully, "if the same thing starts to happen here, on Sarro? I mean, what if everyone starts to panic and set up virus free zones here? What will happen to us?"

Genji suggests jokingly, "We should have our own virus free zone, for only us."

Jun nods her agreement, "Great idea, sis!"

There is no other reply, just a thoughtful silence. The sun starts to sink into the distant horizon and, as glorious oranges and reds paint the sky, we lazily pack up and slowly wander back up the hill, back home.

"You know, we could always build a place...like our own secret place... somewhere in the woods would be safest...no one goes there much." says Charlie.

"If we camouflage it too." continues Geo, "What d'yer think Finn?"

We turn into the short lane that I now know as my new home.

"Makes sense to me. Where are the woods? Far?" Just as I ask the question, my question is answered as I notice the unmistakable shadowy outline of Holdwood straight ahead of me, overlooking the lane.

"Meet up tomorrow for some den building then?" asks Charlie keenly and politely ignoring my question about the woods.

"Don't forget the house clearance as well!" reminds Jun.

"Yeh, Yeh... tomorrow then, see yer!" With that Charlie strides off up the hill towards Holdwood. He's the only one of us who doesn't live on our lane. The rest of us say our goodbyes and I realise I've had a great day and that I am starving!

EVIL

~~~

"**C**ome on! Hurry up. We'll be late!" Genji shouts back down the hill to us, sounding like a stressed teacher on a school trip. Sharply, she blows her long black fringe out of her hazel eyes one more time. Genji and Jun are on a mission and enthusiastically lead the way up the aptly named Hill Road. We're already late, a fact confirmed by the mocking chimes of the town hall clock striking two in the market square, far away in the distance below us.

It's a perfectly baking hot mid-summer's afternoon. Charlie, Geo, and I trail close behind, not bothering to rush. We're more interested in how long we could survive against the virus in our secret hideaway in the woods, than looking around a dead person's house. All morning we've been working slavishly in the cool shade under the tangled trees of Holdwood, rummaging for any sturdy fallen branches which would be strong enough to support the den roof and walls.

Despite the sweltering heat, the girls keep up a keen pace up the hill. They're determined to get to the house clearance sale as soon as possible just in case there are any great bargains to be had - maybe some things for our den.

At last we reach the wrought iron garden gate where the girls are already waiting impatiently. Together, we step onto the cobbled pathway which leads directly up to the impressive old grey stone house. The garden is wild and overgrown from years of neglect and the large Victorian bay windows are already boarded over, giving a sense of ending, unwanted and lonely.

I stop, briefly, under the leafy shade of the first towering oak tree which has a large roughly brush-painted sign nailed to its trunk.

'HOUSE CLEARANCE SALE
TODAY 2.00pm'

The lettering is still wet with streaks of 'Halloween' blood red paint leaking from the bottom of each letter just adding to the ghostly feeling around the place. Charlie leans over and says in a hushed voice, "You know, the night the old woman died, there was a weird electrical storm. The whole sky around here flashed with streaks of lightning. Each flash seemed to hover briefly above this place. Others say that the lightning actually came from the inside the old woman's house itself!"

I am still getting used to the natives of the Isle of Sarro. Charlie is one of the hardest of my new friends to figure out; he's a great person to know, resourceful, knowledgeable especially about Sarro but with a strange sense of humor. I never know if he's joking or not. Yesterday, I also found out that his family are extremely wealthy and own most of the Isle of Sarro; a fact that causes him much embarrassment.

Despite my increasing feeling of dread, I make sure no one else notices and stroll confidently along the cobbled pathway towards the house. Arranged on the open paved patio, in front of the house, is a selection of fine antique wooden wardrobes, chests of drawers and an upright mirror held in an intricately carved frame – none of which would look out of place in one of those old black and white films that my Gran used to make me watch.

Jun tells me that the old lady who lived here, must have been at least a hundred years old; she was incredibly wrinkly. Genji had seen her the week before she died. She was standing by the garden gate, dressed in her dirty black cloak, with her white wispy hair blowing in the sea breeze, shouting out incomprehensibly at anyone who dared to walk on the pavement in front of her house, while wildly wielding her black walking stick in the air as if she was trying to stop traffic on a busy road or trying to swat an annoying fly circling above her head. Already I know that Genji is not the type to be easily rattled, but even *she* crossed over to the other side of the road when she saw the old woman.

Earlier, Jun told me that some people say that they have seen the old lady's ghost in the shadows at night. I know that's impossible, but it all adds to the bad feeling building up inside me, making me think that we shouldn't be going near this place. Even in the brilliant sunshine, the run-down house looks stern and menacing - like trouble.

Unfazed and eager to explore inside, the girls confidently lead the way through the imposing black front door which is wedged open by a heavily varnished combination coat and umbrella stand. The umbrellas are torn and useless but there is a smart looking black walking stick with a golden handle shaped like a bird's head that Genji picks up to have a closer look.

I take a deep breath and follow them in. Immediately I feel very cold and shudder. We move silently across the black and white tiled floor into the large lobby where a group of about fifteen men and women linger, listening to a smartly suited, well-spoken, middle-aged lady. Her squeaky voice echoes unnaturally against the bare walls. She stands on the first step of the wooden stairs, recently stripped of its carpet covering. The group look up in unison as the lady directs their attention to the elegant chandelier fixed to the high ceiling.

This is our chance. As they all look up, we skillfully slip past them unseen.

Even before we go into the first room a hideous choking smell strikes me, a thick mixture of dust and moldy damp but there's something else even more pungent that cuts at the back of my throat as I breathe.

"No wonder she died! I'm choking to death myself in here. What's causing that stench?" gasps Charlie echoing my thoughts exactly, as we both scrunch up our faces in disgust.

"E-v-il, that's what it is. The smell of e-v-il!" Geo is enjoying himself, his blue eyes smiling. His real name is George, but he hates that name and insists we call him Geo or just G. He says there are already loads of Georges and he's not like any of them.

The room is badly lit by a solitary bulb which flickers as if it is about to give up the ghost. Despite this, it is obvious that, in days past, this once had been a grand front parlour but, like the outside of the house, has been woefully neglected. The beautifully carved stone fireplace mantel is hanging half off the chimney breast wall and sections of the fine Victorian ceiling cornice have fallen away with the damp.

"Why don't they open the windows? Let some fresh air in?" Jun moans impatiently, feeling annoyed and disappointed at not finding anything worth buying.

"They can't, they're all boarded up on the outside, aren't they?" answers Geo matter-of-factly, "That's why it's so dark in here."

With each footstep forward, the bare floorboards groan and creek as if complaining about being stood on. Before long, we are all walking incredibly slowly, almost on tiptoes, as if we are trying to sneak up to a sleeping guard dog and pinch its bone.

"Let's try the next room. There must be something," suggests Genji, giving up with the parlour. In unison the girls each swivel on one foot, turn around and leave. I get the impression that they both expected there would be treasures and bargains galore at this clearance sale, but they are both rapidly realising that the old lady had lived a very sparse existence.

As I too turn to leave, I notice that one of the large framed paintings, hanging on the wall, is angled as if it has just survived an earthquake while, strangely, all the other paintings are lined up and hung spirit level straight. The painting is covered in a thick layer of dust and depicts two people dressed in black hooded capes, probably a man and a woman, bending over the remains of a smoking fire. They appear to be searching for something in the ashes, but what really spooks me is that the trees and rocky outcrop painted in the background, have a striking resemblance to *our* secret place in *our* woods...exactly where *our* survival den is. I am certain it's the same place. Maybe the trees are a little smaller but...

"Hey! Check this out. Look, that's Holdwood, just where our den is!" I say excitedly pointing at the lopsided painting.

Charlie comes over to take a closer look. He's the only one who takes any notice, the others have already left the parlour. "Spooky!" he mocks with an over-dramatic voice and immediately turns away disinterestedly and heads off to join the others in the kitchen.

Feeling annoyed, I follow, not wanting to be left by myself.

It feels as if time has stopped in the Victorian era. There are two huge sinks with chunky brass taps, a large mangle in the corner and a table made from solid wooden beams, occupying the middle of the stone flagged floor.

"There's nothing any good down here. Let's go upstairs, maybe we'll find something up there," Jun suggests, her voice echoes around the kitchen. She is visibly unimpressed, as is Genji.

Again, we sneak back past the group of people still chatting in the hallway and climb up the creaky stairs, trying to avoid making any noise. In places, plaster is crumbling and breaking away from the high walls. With every step upwards the e-v-il smell gets stronger until I taste it as I breathe in.

On the landing, Geo tentatively turns the brass knob and opens the first door on the left. The door is heavy, and resists being opened as the bottom brushes against the thick piled carpet behind. Cautiously stepping inside the blackness, Geo immediately leaps straight back out, bends over and heaves - nearly to the point of vomiting. Then I get a whiff. Disgusting! The thick stench from the room is truly horrendous. This must be the source of the e-v-il smell. The others double over laughing hysterically, while desperately trying not to make any sounds that would give us away to the people in the hall below us.

"Maybe that's why it was the only door closed up here! Trust you to choose that room! I bet that's where the old dear died; she's probably still in there … decomposing!" jokes Charlie much to the dismay of the girls who stop laughing immediately.

But Geo is not put off that easily! He relishes the challenge! Undeterred he takes in a deep breath, filling his lungs to bursting, and lifts the bottom of his striped blue and white T-shirt over his nose and mouth and defiantly marches back in.

No one follows.

We wait outside expecting him to come straight back out again.

He doesn't.

We wait expectantly.

Through the half open door, the e-v-il odor seeps onto the landing like an invisible sea mist rolling ashore. The stench is worse than ever. I feel my throat complain, tightening up, forcing me to cover my nose and mouth with my T-shirt too.

From the doorway, I sneak a look into the blackness of the room. The curtains are tightly drawn, and I can't see a thing. "Geo…what's it like in there? Where are you?"

"You'd better go in and see what he's up to," encourages Jun.

"Why don't you? I don't want to get any closer to that smell!"

"Go on!" chips in Genji, her eyes daring me on.

Geo still doesn't answer so, very reluctantly, I decide to risk it.

I step inside the room.

There's a musty chill to the room which makes me shiver, it's incredibly dark inside and the thick choking smell makes it hard to breathe. My eyes take several seconds to adjust to the minimal light. I can make out vague silhouettes of an old four poster bed and a huge mirrored wardrobe up against the wall in front of me. The reflection in the mirror reveals the faces of the others, peering through the open doorway behind me, but there's still no sign of Geo anywhere. The thick pile carpet cushions each step I take, silently adsorbing all sound. Slowly I edge further into the room, I sense a floorboard underneath my foot move and softly creak but there's no echo like in the rest of the old house. This room is different to the other rooms in the house; it is still fully furnished. I think it must have been the old lady's bedroom. A terrible thought enters my head; maybe, maybe, she really is still in here... that would explain the dreadful stench and why the door was closed.

"Geo," I whisper, "Geo!" a bit louder, "Geo come on! We shouldn't be in here. Let's go!"

Still no reply.

"Where did he go?" asks Charlie who is peering in through the doorway from the safety of the landing.

Out of the corner of my eye, through the darkness, I think I see something shift on the old lady's bed, still layered with heavy blankets. I turn towards the movement. From under the blankets, something stirs and wriggles. Is it the old lady? It can't be, can it? Slowly the blanket starts to rise into the air by itself. I strain my eyes to the edge of the darkness. I see the blanket take on a ghostlike body shape. The form is still rising, now leaning forwards towards me, as if it is trying to talk to me. There's a strange croaking, wheezing noise. Still shielded behind me, the others are trying desperately to see what is happening inside the room. My heart is pounding, but I'm glued to the spot. It is incredibly difficult to make out what is on the bed in front of me.

Then from under the blanket come the words, "You took your time, didn't you? I nearly suffocated waiting for you!" Geo fully stands up on the bed and the blankets fall off him revealing, I imagine, his grinning face.

"You idiot! You great... Why didn't you answer?" I ask, annoyed.

Geo leaps across the bed and escapes back to the landing, still holding his T-shirt over his nose. He is gulping and gasping for air when I quietly close the door behind me.

"Why do you do things like that?" challenges Charlie on my behalf.

"Dunno, can't help it...just can't help it." Geo shakes his head as he speaks trying to sound sorry, but then he flashes a mischievous grin which tells a different story.

I am incredibly relieved to be back out of that bedroom, although the e-v-il stench seems to stay with us long after closing the door, lingering like an unwelcome visitor.

A little further along the landing are two more open doors close together. In the uncarpeted room on the left, there's a shabby looking decorating table, splattered with globules of old black and brown paint; the same colours as the downstairs doors and skirting boards. On the table is an array of assorted personal objects for sale. The most interesting is a hairbrush with 'Amelia' etched onto the worn brass handle, with strands of long white hair entangled in the soft bristles. I deduce Amelia must have been the old lady's name. For a moment, I feel a strange connection with Amelia the person. I wonder if she had any family, and what could have happened to change her into the wild old woman that Genji and Jun had seen?

Alongside some perfume bottles, there's an impressive collection of about fifty large rusting keys, most of them look exactly like how I imagine dungeon keys to look like. Maybe she collected them. Nothing seems to add up. The rest of the room is disappointing and the exposed floor boards do nothing to stop the echoes of the clattering keys as Genji accidentally knocks a bunch off the table.

We all freeze to the spot until the silence returns and we are confident that no one downstairs has heard.

The adjacent upstairs room is at the front of the house and has a completely different feel to it. A sharp chink of bright sunlight, from an ill-fitted window board, lasers its way across the room as if directing us to the fireplace. Resting on the elegant mantelpiece, is a large porcelain vase illuminated by the narrow beam of light. It has three, equally spaced, horizontal ochre bands painted on a faded yellow background with a detailed glazed painting filling the centre bowl. When I look more closely, I have a strange feeling of déjà vu in the pit of my stomach. It is the same scene as in the painting downstairs; the silhouettes of two hooded figures standing over the remains of a fire, but this time they are surrounded by a swirling black cloud.

"Hey Charlie! Look at this... it's the same scene as in that painting downstairs!"

Charlie takes a closer look, "S'pose so. So what?"

"Just a bit weird isn't it?"

"Mm, and...?"

"I don't know... it's just weird, don't you think? I mean, what are they doing?"

Just then the chink of light fades and vanishes, as a cloud passes in front of the sun, leaving us in the room shrouded in darkness. Awkwardly we fumble our way through the darkness, out of the room and back into the hallway and immediately bump into Mr. Taylor.

"What are you lot doing here?" Mr. Taylor asks gruffly. He's wearing a brown tweed jacket with his matching flat cap rolled up and sticking out of his pocket. He looks as if he's in a hurry and seems very surprised to see anyone upstairs, especially us.

"Oh nothing," reply the girls in unison, smiling politely as if butter wouldn't melt in their mouths.

"Not right for kids to be hanging around in dead people's houses," he moans to himself and we quickly head off down stairs.

"Not right for kids to be hanging around in dead people's houses," mimics Jun so brilliantly that we're all laughing by the time we get to the bottom of the creaking stairs.

Sunshine beams invitingly through the open front door ahead.

"Let's get out of this place," pleads Geo, then in a whisper, "there's nothing worth buying here and we've still got our survival den to finish!"

Disappointedly, the girls agree, and I'm pleased to leave the chill of the old woman's house and into the welcome warmth of the afternoon sun.

THIEF

~~~

Heavy rain thumps against the ground. Gone already are the memories of yesterday's baking hot sun and the hours we spent searching the woods for straight branches to build our survival den. The good news is that this unexpected, torrential, downpour is certainly putting our den through its paces. If it can survive this, then it can survive anything, maybe even survive the Death Virus when it reaches the Isle of Sarro. At least we'll have somewhere safe to hide, while life on the rest of the island falls apart, just as is happening back on the mainland. It helps that Charlie knows Holdwood like the back of his hand as it is part of his family's estate. The trees might have even been planted by some of his ancestors, who used to be boat builders, amongst many other things. He knew exactly where we should build the den, far from the well-used pathways and bridleways, away from prying eyes.

We are extremely fortunate that we decided to finish attaching the roof just as it was getting dark yesterday. Genji and Jun were all for leaving it, but Charlie insisted, so we hastily attached the 'borrowed' tarpaulin sheet between the four elm saplings that are the den's main supporting posts.

When we returned early this morning, we stood back and admired our handy work with pride. However, no sooner had we laid down an old thick plastic ground sheet that Charlie had found in one of his parent's sheds and emptied the meagre goodies from our carrier bags, the heavens well and truly opened. The only option we had was to wait inside our den and hope that the tarpaulin roof held out.

An hour later and the rain is still falling thick and heavy as if it is determined to demolish all our hard work in one fell swoop, but our den stands solid, firm, and resolute. Much to our huge relief, not one drop of water enters our survival den. It is incredibly gloomy outside, and the clouds overhead are more black than grey. It's even darker inside, but with a green tarpaulin tinge. Despite this, there's a real sense of success and optimism when we all sit comfortably dry, peering out at the intense rain splashing hard against the ground outside. Briefly I relax and think of home, back on the mainland; our back garden, Gramps moaning about his aches and pains, the smell of freshly baked bread and playing with my friends down my street. I wonder what they're doing now, if they're still alright. Deep down I doubt it. Then I remember my Mum's brave face as she waved me off at the almost deserted airport, Dad gave me the biggest hug ever; it felt like they were saying goodbye forever too, as if they didn't really want me to go...but it was their idea.

High up in the trees a bird screeches, breaking my thoughtful silence, but rain continues drumming on the tarpaulin roof; the thick heavy thuds just adding to the excited atmosphere in the den, nearly drowning out the crunch of twigs nearby. Someone is close to the den.

Everyone looks up at each other.

We all know who it will be.

And it is!

"I've brought more supplies and this." Imp pokes her head through the den opening. In one hand she has a plastic bag bursting with everything you would ever need to survive in a secret den in the woods and, much to Geo's horror, a chunky necklace in the other. The necklace has several large stones of random colours and shapes bound together by a thin leather strapping. She hands the bag to Jun who immediately starts to organise and disperse its contents around the den.

Imp hardly gets under the tarpaulin roof before she rounds on her brother and holds up the necklace accusingly at Geo who looks mortified, "Where did you get this?"

"How did you find that? You have no right to go rummaging around in my room!"

"Where did you get it?" Imp persists, her bright blue eyes accuse her brother from under the brim of her cap.

The rest of us spectate in stunned silence. I thought Imp was the quiet type.

"How dare you go through my stuff!" Geo's cheeks flush red, a combination of anger and embarrassment.

"I was looking for the family photo to put in Mum's room," upset, she concedes and pauses before looking straight into Geo's eyes, "If you've stolen this from Auntie, you're gonna put it straight back!"

Now it is Geo's turn to be upset. Since they arrived on Sarro their auntie had treated them like royalty and made sure Mum was being well cared for.

"From Auntie?!" he protests in disbelief.

Immediately, and with some relief, Imp knows she's guessed wrong, but she also knows her brother very well and continues, "Well then, where did you get it?

Turning away from the accusing faces Geo tries to explain, "You remember the house clearance sale? You remember that room upstairs. Well, when I hid under the blanket on the bed, trying not to breathe in that e-v-il smell, while I waited for you to come and find me, I felt something hard under the pillow. There it was. It was really dark in there and, without thinking, I put it in my pocket. I didn't even know what it was...then Finn came in. Anyway, it's just some old stones tied together, useless junk I reckon."

"Well, you can take it back now!" Imp continues, "What will Auntie say if she finds out? Why couldn't you just keep your hands off it?"

Imp is upset but not angry with her brother. She knows what he's like; acts first then thinks about it.

Charlie takes the old necklace, holds it up to the tarpaulin roof like an expert jeweler valuing rare diamonds, and agrees with Geo, "Looks homemade to me, probably not worth much."

"Even so, better take it back. It might belong to someone, it might be a family heirloom or something," Jun chips in wisely.

"Not much point, is there? The house is empty now... locked up... s'pose I could post it through the letter box... but who will be checking for post?" says Geo.

He has a point.

BLACK MIST

~~~

G eo's penknife scratches against something hard at the back of the survival den, probably another stone. Undeterred, he keeps digging. He's determined to bury the necklace somewhere in our survival den to keep it safe, just in case he can find a way to return it to the old lady's family one day.

He scratches against stone again.

It's a much bigger job than he expected, and he begins to doubt that his small pocket penknife is going to be up to the job.

Stone again.

This time he uses his free hand to sweep away the loose pebbles, soil, and twigs so he can see more clearly exactly what is causing the problem. Just beneath the surface he has been working, he uncovers the top of a massive stone - much too big to dig out - so he decides to shift across and dig a hole for the necklace at the other side of the den.

Awkwardly, Geo crawls over to the other side of the den, being careful not to accidentally dislodge the tarpaulin roof. He starts digging again at a more hopeful looking spot but again the knife prods something solid. He brushes away more dirt. By now we are all watching him, wondering what he's up to.

Soon there's a good-sized collection of smaller stones, twigs and soil scattered in the middle of the den floor.

"Will you stop it, you're covering everything!" says Charlie, still very protective of the new survival den.

"What are you up to anyway?" It is still gloomy under the tarpaulin, under the black cloudy sky, so Jun shines her torch light towards the back of the den to see what Geo's up to. She sees that he has revealed a slab of flat smooth black rock about an arm's length from side to side. It had been hidden just below the surface of the ground.

"Oh, just cover it back up, there're leaves on the biscuits now!" Genji adds as she too flicks her powerful torch light in Geo's direction making him squint. Her beam flashes over a circle of markings etched into surface of the slab that Geo hadn't seen in the poor light even though he is directly above it.

"Hey, look at that," Genji says, pointing to the unusual circular dents in the rock.

"Did you make those Geo?" I ask.

"No. With this?!" he waves his small penknife in the air. There's no way he could have made the marks on the rock with it.

"It looks like the ... well, a bit like ... it looks like ... an imprint of that old necklace if you ask me. Look even the holes are the same shape as the stones on the necklace!" remarks Imp, moving closer.

"Don't be silly, just looks a bit like it, that's all," says Geo, wishing that everyone would stop talking about the necklace.

"That's what I said *'looks like'*..." defends Imp who does not like being told she is silly. Defiantly, like a dog with a bone, she continues, "It matches ... see." Grabbing the necklace, she places it exactly on the imprinted markings carved on the slab of rock.

Everyone can see that it's a perfect fit. Exact. Stone for stone.

But there's no time to think about it. Immediately, the slab starts to glow orange and then yellow and then bright white, getting brighter and brighter until it's too bright to look at. The air around us is hot and smells like it's burning. There's a sharp crackling noise then the whole slab vanishes as if it has evaporated into thin air along with the old necklace.

Gloomy darkness returns to the back of the den except for the Genji's torch which is fixed on the spot where the slab of rock and the necklace had been. Her beam reveals a black hole, the same size as the rock slab that had covered it. The ground around the edge of the hole continues to bubble like orange molten lava briefly before cooling and solidifying into a crusty black ring. Suddenly, there's a stirring of air deep in the hole below us, gushing and hissing, as if immense pressure has been released from a tyre. A whirling thick cloud of Black Mist gasps out and fills our den, surrounding each of us, sending a cold shiver down my spine and making me want to pull away - but there is nowhere to go. We are instantly hit by the strong thick smell of e-v-il, the same smell as before in the old lady's house. With another cold rush, the Black Mist swirls above our heads, like a swarm of miniature black locusts, before escaping from under the tarpaulin into the freedom of the surrounding trees, ripping straight through any green leaves in its wake, slicing a tubular channel to the sky, leaving only the bare branches behind.

"Wow! Bet you can't do that again!" Jun exclaims excitedly.

I cough away the foul air once more, "What was that?"

"Whatever it was, it was desperate to get out! I think we did it a favour," suggests Geo, trying to take it all in.

"Where's the necklace gone?" quizzes Genji, fascinated by what had happened.

"Just disappeared, along with that slab of rock," replies Imp who had been the closest and is still right next to the black hole in the ground. Her hair is stood up and she looks as if she's just had a powerful electric shock.

Ignoring the lingering stench from below, Charlie leans over the hole and peers into an impenetrable blackness, "Here. Pass the torch. I can't see a thing!"

"I'll hold it, you look," suggests Imp, bravely trying to control her shaking hands as she aims the beam into the hole.

"It's still too dark... I can't see a thing down there! Phew! Smells just like that old house though!" Charlie waves his hand in front of his nose, "Gross!"

"Uggh! Smells like someone's died down there!" complains Imp who was the only one of us who was not at the house clearance sale yesterday.

"How would you know? How many dead people have you smelt?!" challenges Geo recovering back to his old self.

Imp dutifully ignores the dig from her older brother.

"I still can't see a thing! You'd think you'd be able to see something... it must go down miles." says Charlie, straining his eyesight to the limit.

"I know. Drop a stone in and listen for when it hits the floor... here." I pass Charlie a fist sized stone.

He drops the stone. We all wait in dead silence.

"It must be bottomless!" says Charlie in disbelief.

"Wish I could say the same about you, I can't see a thing... MOVE over!" jokes Genji cheekily pushing her way through so that she can see what's happening.

Then it happens, a cold dull *plop*, as if the stone has landed in water.

In reply, as if being awoken from a deep sleep, a very faint, almost fluorescent, blue glow appears from the deep depths below.

I can't resist looking into the hole despite the smell. The light is so faint that it is impossible to make out any details of what might lurk in the blackness. Next to me, Charlie squints to force his eyes to adjust. He thinks he can make out a ledge just below the top of the hole.

Turning to face me, he says, "I'm going in!"

He flips around and then he lowers himself onto his front and slowly backs into the hole, feet first, probing for the ledge below or for something solid to rest his foot on as he drops. He's already half way in before anyone has a chance to say anything.

"What're you doing?!" asks Jun not believing what she was seeing.

"I can see a ledge, just down here, I'll get a better look if I can get onto it."

"Who cares what's down there... what if you fall in and break your neck!" continues Jun, her face full of concern.

"It's just..." with all his strength Charlie gradually lowers himself and tries to locate the rock ledge with his dangling foot, "almost got it…No… can't seem to reach it…Ah ha…There!"

His hair disappears completely below ground level leaving just one hand in view, gesturing for the torch. "Quick, pass me my torch and I'll have a look down!" Already his voice is sounding muffled.

I rummage in Charlie's rucksack for his torch and place it carefully in his outstretched hand.

"Sees a hole in the ground that appears from nowhere and thinks he has to jump right in it! I thought he was the one *with* the brains. How wrong can you be?" Jun is annoyed at Charlie's stupidity although also impressed by his strength and agility.

"Damn!" Charlie curses angrily, "I've dropped the torch!"

Jun sucks in air and tuts loudly.

There's a dull thud as the torch immediately lands, safely, on another hidden rock outcrop only a metre or two below Charlie. It is a good thing the torch is encased in a solid rubbery outer, otherwise it would have smashed into pieces.

"Come back up here before you fall in yourself! Leave the torch," beckons Jun.

"I reckon I can reach it." Charlie is undeterred.

"Who cares about the torch. *Leave it!*" shouts down Jun once more.

"It's just there… hold on," ignoring Jun's protests, Charlie jumps further downwards and lands precisely on the rock outcrop next to the torch. As he jumps, he disappears into the darkness; if it was not for the torch light, we would not know he was even there.

"Got it!" he shouts jubilantly, his voice now echoing around the vertical stone walls of the tunnel shaft. He shines the torch light straight back up into our amazed faces above him, blinding and dazzling us, before turning the beam back down into the dense darkness of the hole below him.

"I reckon I can get all the way down if I had a long enough rope."

"Well we haven't, so get back up here quick! How do you

know that ledge won't break?" Jun is worried.

"No, it's fine," he tests the ledge by jumping up and down on it, "See?"

At that Jun loses her temper. "Now, get back up here! Finn tell him!"

"*OK! OK!* We'll have to get a long rope or something before I can go down any further," chimes back Charlie, oblivious to how annoyed Jun is.

"Whatever, now you'd better climb back up...here grab my hand," I lie flat on the ground, dangling my upper body over the lip of the hole. Reaching over as far as I dare, I try to grab Charlie's outstretched hand. Straight away, I realise that I can never stretch far enough to reach him.

"That won't work! You're gonna have to climb back onto the first ledge," I suggest with a hint of concern creeping into my voice for the first time.

"Erm, just a minor problem with that. Didn't you hear? I think it broke off when I jumped off it," Charlie replies matter-of-factly.

Jun joins us still peering into the dark hole.

Taking control, Imp turned to Geo, "We need a rope, quick!"

"Where from?" Geo looks at her, already knowing the answer.

"No idea... what about where the tarpaulin came from?" she suggests.

"Got'ya!" he doesn't need to be asked twice... within seconds he's gone, rain or no rain.

"It's alright, hang in there! Geo's on the case, he's gone to get a rope. Hang on!" Imp encourages optimistically.

BLUE LIGHT

~~~

E ven though he's only a few metres below ground level, a strange feeling of remoteness sweeps over Charlie as he takes stock of his predicament; standing on a small rocky ledge suspended between a hole of light above filled with unseeing faces peering down at him, and below in the distant darkness, a faint tinge of blue light staring up at him like an invitation. Charlie awkwardly shuffles backwards and sits down.

He shouts up towards us staring down at him, "I'm gonna switch off the torch – save me having to keep winding it up."

Resting against the cold dark rock wall of the shaft, he closes his eyes. His arms still ache from carrying all the heavy branches they had needed to build the survival den yesterday. He moves his head from side to side, as he always does, as if he is stretching his neck. He opens his eyes. Opposite him, staring straight at him, he sees a pair of red and yellow eyes hanging in the blackness ... then they are gone. He blinks and takes a second look. Nothing!

He waits a second and checks again. Still nothing.

Hesitantly, he shouts back up to Genji who is the only face remaining at the surface, "Did you see that?"

"See what?" She clearly had not seen anything.

"Oh, nothing," he replies, thinking that he must have imagined it.

He settles himself for a long wait, uncertain if the heavy darkness is making him hallucinate. He stretches his aching legs out in front trying to find a more comfortable position. With no warning, there's a silent rush of stale air directly behind him; the rock his back is resting against, abruptly shakes and then disappears revealing a gaping hole, and leaving Charlie leaning on thin air. Gravity takes over. Like a rock falling down the side of a cliff, he helplessly tumbles backwards and downwards, into another vertical tubular shaft. It happens so quickly, he has no time to call out or react in any way. He is propelled, ever faster, by the jet of rushing air which bubbles around him as he is finally thrust, head first, deep into a pool of bluish water, disorientated and unable to breathe.

He is underwater. Upside down!

He doesn't have time to panic although he knows he is in serious trouble. Through the wall of bubbles caused by his crashing into the water, he can make out a faint blue light, although this time it hangs above him, above the mirror of the water's edge. Kicking his legs hard, he swims urgently upwards, toward the dim bluish light. His lungs start to complain as his arms and legs demand more oxygen for their effort. Desperately, he hopes he must be near the surface and the air that he so badly needs, but then he realises he isn't moving. His foot is tangled in something! Whatever it is, is holding tightly to his foot. Urgently, he kicks his foot and wriggles free. With huge relief, he finally feels himself moving upwards, upwards ever closer to the surface and the blue glow. At last, his head breaks through the water's surface. He gasps and gulps in the cold stale air – it feels good as his lungs fill up to capacity.

Charlie finds himself clumsily splashing to keep afloat rather than swimming. After recovering his breath, he starts to regain some control of his arms and legs. He starts to tread water and look around him, but it is difficult to see much. He's inside an underground cavern, the size of a tennis court, with a low jagged roof lit only by the reflected bluish glow, the same glow that he had seen at the entrance of the tunnel. Charlie wonders what it was that held his leg back as he tried to swim up to the surface. It felt like a hand had grabbed his leg, holding him down. He peers down beneath the water's surface, but he can't see anything.

The deeper he looks into the pool, the darker it gets. He has no idea where he is and no idea how to get back to the others.

Still breathing deeply, he swims over to the outcrop of rocks at the other side of the cavern, where he hopes he will be able to climb up and pull himself out of the water. There's that unpleasant smell again; it's not the odor of stagnant water but the same e-v-il smell of the old lady's house. Finally, he swims across to the jagged rocks, which jut out of the slippery cavern walls surrounding the pool. He tries to grab hold of one. He has to duck under the water first and then spring upwards to try to reach it. Already tiring, Charlie knows he needs to rest soon. He fails the first attempt and tries again. This time he manages to get a firm grip on the rock with his right hand and quickly flings his left arm even higher, finding a useful crack in the rock to cling on to. His feet are still dangling in the water. It feels like all his energy is being drained, sapped away into the water. With an enormous heave, he twists and pulls his lower body completely out of the water and, luckily, his shoe locks itself snuggly onto a tiny ledge. From there he wriggles and claws his way over the edge before finally finding safety on the smooth flat horizontal top of the rock ledge overhanging the water below.

For a few minutes, he lies on the cold rock breathing heavily from the exertion. Then he notices he has a deep cut on the side of his hand, most likely from the sharp stone edge when he had pulled himself onto the ledge. As he sits up to look over the edge, a single droplet of blood drips from the wound. Charlie watches the globule of blood as it falls and lands on the now still surface of the pool below. It causes only a slight ripple but, as it mixes with the rest of the water, instead of dissipating and disappearing to nothing, it seems to become contagious, as if infecting the water in a ripple, turning the entire pool black. The water starts to move and swirl with a life of its own. The whole pool begins to gurgle and spins with increasing ferocity into a mass of whirling black. In the centre, a revolving, whirring funnel of darkness appears like an inverted tornado. The deafening roaring of rushing water grows louder and louder until it is unbearably painful, and Charlie is forced to cover his ears with his hands. Without warning the black water starts to drain away downward, as if a massive plug has been pulled deep within the Earth's crust below.

Charlie tentatively stands up on the rock ledge in an eerie empty silence and looks down from his new vantage point. It appears to be giddily higher up than it had done before when the water pool had filled half the cavity below. He can also see, for the first time, the newly exposed expanse of wet rock of the cavern floor and, exactly in the centre of the space, a glowing blue stone! The stone is hanging in mid-air, suspended in the grip of two huge black rocks shaped like giant hands. They are tall and twisted together in a vertical embrace, as if they are reaching out to shake hands with each other from below and above.

INSIDE

~~~

Returning with a grin, Geo stands panting and rain soaked at the entrance to the den. He is leaning backwards to counterbalance the weight of the rolled-up rope ladder he is carrying. He can only just see over the top of it. No wonder he'd been gone for so long! It must have taken all his effort just to carry it.

"Cool! That's perfect. You're a genius!" I say, meaning every word.

Peering over the edge of the hole, I excitedly shout down to Charlie, "Geo's found a massive rope ladder. He's tying the end to the big tree and we'll roll it down to you in a second. Switch on your torch so we can see exactly where you are."

There's no reply.

"Charlie, did you hear me? Wake up! We've got a rope ladder. Switch on your torch so we can see you!"

No answer.

"There you go… sorted, one rope ladder… secured. Am I the best or what?! Don't be shy, you can say it …" chirps Geo very pleased with himself.

"Sshh! Charlie's not answering. Maybe he's hurt himself," Jun is full of concern.

"More likely he's asleep," answers Geo as he joins us at the hole opening and shouts down into the darkness, "C'mon! Wake up lazy bones! Stop messin' around. I've found a rope ladder for you. Put the torch on, we can't see you."

Nothing.

"Maybe he fell down the hole," panics Jun again.

"Oh, you're a joy, aren't you?! Anyway, I didn't hear anything. Did you? We would have heard the plop or something, I've been right here all the time!"

"I know, let's roll the rope ladder down anyway. Then we can go down and wake him up ourselves," whispers Imp.

There's no choice. I roll the rest of the rope ladder carefully over the edge of the hole opening and hear it clatter against the side of the shaft wall as it unravels itself deep into the darkness below us. Finally, there's the echo of the splash as the ladder hits the water at the bottom of the shaft. With a feeling a deep foreboding, I slowly edge myself backwards on my stomach until my feet are dangling over the edge of the hole. Gingerly, I search for the first available rung of the ladder with my foot.

"Don't worry, you won't fall, the ladder's tied to that huge oak tree, Geo's seen to that. C'mon you're wasting time, Charlie could be hurt!" says Jun with an unusual sense of urgency in her voice.

At last my foot connects with the solid bar and I ease more and more weight on to it until I'm sure the rope can take it. Only then do I completely let go of the rim of the hole and hold tightly onto the rope ladder itself. It wiggles and wavers from side to side as I move to look down for any sign of Charlie but it's difficult to make anything out. Only the faint blue glow indicates that there is something way down below.

Tentatively I edge down another rung reluctant to let go with my hands. Rung by rung, step by step, I gradually descend to the level of the ledge where Charlie should be. The only reason I know for sure the ledge is there is because I scrape my leg on it as I climb down.

"Charlie!" I only whisper but my voice echoes around me. "Charlie! You OK?" I repeat in vain.

"I've found the ledge here!" I shout upwards at the worried faces peering down above me.

"Be careful! Can you see Charlie? Is he OK?!" shouts back Jun.

Dangerously, I lean over towards the narrow ledge, reaching

out with one hand and clinging tightly on to the rope ladder with the other. I feel the cold dry rock ledge. My fingers walk across the reachable parts of the ledge, searching the darkness, until at last I touch something solid that is definitely not cold rock. Whatever it is, rolls further away as I touch it but then I feel it again; the torch! With a lurch and a swing, I grasp the torch and hold onto it desperately as if my life depends on it. I steady myself on the ladder again. I flick the torch switch. For a second, the brilliance dazzles my eyes which are now accustomed to the darkness of the hole, despite this I instantly see that the ledge is empty. There is no sign of Charlie.

"He's not here! Nothing!"

I continue clinging on to the rope, the torch, and my courage but I am concerned for Charlie's safety. I search again, directing the torch beam downward, more in hope than anything else. The torch light seems to get soaked up by the deep hole like water by a sponge. I see nothing, just the same blackness with the dim blue glow coming from the very bottom of the shaft.

"You'll have to go further down and see if he's fallen! I'll come too!"

"I'm not sure that the rope ladder will hold two of you," Imp says, holding Geo's arm gently, with concern in her voice.

"It's wobbly enough with just me on! Better leave it to me," I reply, clinging on, sounding much braver than I feel.

Slowly, I continue descending towards the faint blue glow. I begin to feel dizzy. Then I remember that I need to breathe!

"Breathe!" I instruct myself. A few moments later, the dizziness and panic subside, "One foot, then the other...one foot then the other..."

I talk myself down the ladder rung by rung. After a while, I dare to look upwards; the tunnel opening has already shrunk to the size of a football. I can no longer make out whose head is whose. Now I can see the blue glowing shimmer on the surface of the water not far below me. "Not far now." I convince myself feeling more confident.

At last, I reach the pool of water which covers the bottom of the shaft. There's no way of determining how deep the water is. Instinctively, I dip the toe end of my boot in the water; immediately it seems to react violently to the rude intrusion and starts to hiss like a steam engine, exploding into a life of its own turning black. The water bubbles and leaps upwards towards me. Quickly, I scramble back up several rungs of the rope ladder. The water continues churning and spluttering from side to side, spitting jets like geezers, reaching ever closer to me even as I climb further back up, frantically grabbing at each new rung. The bubbling hiss turns into a roar of moving water which echoes up the shaft and alerts the others at the surface.

"What's happening down there?" shouts down Geo urgently.

I don't have time to answer. I just keep climbing higher, back up the rope ladder, expecting to be swept up by the jets of water which continue to chase up just centimetres away from my feet. The rope ladder is lurching, turning, and swinging forcefully; influenced by the ripping currents that seem to have complete control of the bottom of the ladder still gripped by the tormented pool below. I crash painfully into the hard rock face and then I am thrown to the other side, nearly losing my grip, as the ladder thrashes me again from side to side.

Then, with no warning, the water below mysteriously halts, gurgles, and drains completely away as if someone is sucking the last of a fizzy drink from their glass with a straw, leaving only a bone-dry rocky floor below me.

"What's going on down there?" It is Geo's voice echoing again from the lofty opening above.

I shout back in shock, shaking and still clinging on to the rope ladder now several metres above the shaft floor, "The water's ... just ...gone! Hang on. I can hardly see. I need to wind up the torch!"

I reach over a ladder rung and tightly hold it between my upper arm and my bruised rib cage. At last I can hold the torch and wind the handle at the same time with my free arm, without losing grip of the ladder and plummeting down the shaft to an untimely end. The winding seems to take forever and the ladder twists and wiggles with every revolution. Finally, I have light but still can't see anything below me. I climb slowly back down the ladder and, as I near the bottom again, I search for any sign of Charlie.

Still nothing.

Sweeping the torch beam over the rocky floor surface, I check if the ground is safe enough to stand on - and decide to risk it. Planting both boots firmly down, I am relieved to be back on solid ground even though it is a small cramped space at the bottom of a dark deep hole, no more than a metre wide.

'Where has Charlie gone?' I think to myself, 'There's nowhere else he could be. It just doesn't make any sense.'

The rope beside me starts to move and twist. Geo's excited voice echoes down the hole, "I'm on my way!"

I shine the torch upward and am surprised to see how far down the rope ladder he has managed to climb already.

As I point the light upwards, the space around me turns eerily black and my legs and boots are swallowed up by the darkness. Previously undetectable in the bright torch light, I notice the glow of the blue light again. It is coming from the side of the shaft wall, level with my waist. I move towards it and shine the torch light at it. I find a circular tunnel opening, slightly smaller than the entrance high above, although this one is horizontal. I peer into the opening. Intuitively, I flick off the torch light; there it is, the blue glow from the other end of the short tunnel.

"There's an opening down here and I can see that blue light again!" I call up to Geo as he is nearing the rocky bottom of the shaft, "There must be something in there!" I say excitedly.

"Oi! I can't see a thing! Turn the torch back on!" Geo's reply echoes around the space.

"Oops, sorry!" Flicking the light back on.

I'm amazed at how speedily he has managed to climb down the rope ladder.

When Geo joins me at the bottom he puffs, slightly out of breath, "That's one long way down, that is!"

"Look!" Keen to show him my discovery, I point the torch to

the tunnel opening in the side of the shaft wall.

"Maybe Charlie's in there!" He climbs in as he speaks.

"Hang on, you don't know what's in there! You can't just…"

"We've come this far, we might as well go all the way. Come on, where's your sense of adventure?"

I know he's grinning even though I can't see his face. I stand at the entrance of the tunnel opening and try to light his way from behind. Using his elbows, he shuffles along on his front until all I can see are the soles of his boots, disappearing down the short tunnel.

"Wow!" he sucks in his breath and said, "you've got to see this!"

"What is it?"

"Come 'n see!" his boots disappear completely, "Come on!"

Reluctantly, I climb into the tunnel opening and follow, scuffing my elbows as I creep through the narrow gap. It's not very long, just uneven. I poke my head out and look in disbelief at the sight of Geo grinning from ear to ear with Charlie standing right next to him!

SKELETONS

~~~

Meanwhile up in the den, Genji and Jun decide to take things into their own hands. They've seen the torch light disappear down at the bottom of the shaft and no one is answering them when they call down. They want to know what's going on down below. Why should they miss out on all the excitement? But there's no torch to light their way down.

Then Jun has a brainwave; "Why don't we use the flash lights on our mobiles?" she whispers to Genji as she pulls out her mobile, "I can't believe I didn't think of it before!"

"Might as well, haven't had any signal since we've been in the woods," replies Genji.

Thunder continues to rumble menacingly and another flash of lightning spears across the darkening sky overhead. The rain intensifies, falling thick and fast. They look at each other and shiver.

"You'd better stay up here just in case. You can get help if we don't make it back," says Genji turning to Imp who scowls back, unimpressed, but, nevertheless, she knows it's the right thing to do.

"It was my idea, I'll go down first!" claims Jun.

She clips the mobile to her belt and backs herself easily into the hole. She locates a rung on the rope ladder straight away and climbs on fully, allowing the rope ladder to take all her weight.

"Whoa! It wobbles!" she warns as the rope ladder ripples and sways with her on it.

"I can see the ledge here!" she says as she squeezes past where they had last seen Charlie.

Carefully but determinedly, she continues downward until she finally reaches the rocky floor of the underground shaft. She shouts back up to her sister who is waiting impatiently at the top, "Your turn!"

Within seconds she spies Genji's feet at the top of the shaft already searching for a secure footing on a ladder rung. She can hear the echoes of the boys' voices through the short tunnel next to her in the side of the wall.

Flashing her light across the entrance and into the short tunnel she calls to them, "Hey! Where are you?!"

"In here!" they reply, "climb in and see for yourself!"

"What is it?" she can hear the excitement in their voices.

"You need to see for yourself!"

"I'll just be a second, I'll just wait 'til Genji gets down. What's in there anyway?"

"It's like a great cave," replies Charlie.

"Charlie! Is that you?! What happened to you?" she asks surprised to hear his voice and trying to disguise her relief.

At last, Genji makes it to the bottom of the ladder and stands next to Jun. She heard Charlie's voice too, "My turn first now, I think!"

Genji nudges Jun to one side and climbs into the tunnel. As soon as her feet disappear from view, Jun follows leaving the lonely blackness of the deep shaft behind them.

"How did you get here without a rope? It's miles down!" I ask Charlie just as Genji's head appears out the opening of the tunnel.

"Dunno really, I just leant back against the wall. The next thing I knew I was falling backwards and then I landed in deep water, just where we're standing now, I guess. Thought I was a goner! Nearly drowned. I saw the blue light and swam towards it, but something grabbed my foot. I couldn't get free at first but, somehow, I pulled loose. I climbed up there onto the rocks," Charlie points high up to where he'd been standing at the other side of the cavern and continues his story excitedly, "Then there was a massive whooshing noise and suddenly the water turned black, and then it all drained away like someone had pulled the plug on it!"

"Same sort of thing just happened to me!" I chip in, "I was almost at the bottom of the rope ladder and, without warning, the water hissed and seemed to be trying to grab hold of my legs, then it turned black and was gone a few seconds later! Weirdest thing ever!"

"I cut myself on the rocks over there when I was trying to climb out of the water, a drop of my blood dripped into the pool... that's when the water changed colour!" Charlie says but then realises that what he was saying sounded a bit farfetched, so he added, "or at least that's what *seemed* to happen. It was quite dark."

"Oh gross! Look at that! There's another over there too!" says Jun pointing to the second human skeleton lying sprawled on the rocky floor. Headless. The nearest skeleton is complete with its arms outstretched. They are too big to be children's skeletons which is some sort of relief. The torn fragile remains of a hooded cloak are still wrapped around the white bones of the first skeleton. I feel a strange sense of recognition but think no more about it.

"Maybe that's what grabbed your foot! Maybe its arm got tangled, see, the hand looks as if it trying to hold onto something," I suggest to Charlie.

Jun walks over to the middle of the cavern and looks up at the blue stone suspended between the finger grasps of the intertwined black rock hands.

"So that's where the light's coming from. D'you think it's the blue stone from the old lady's necklace?" she wonders out aloud, "Who could have put it there? Have you tried to reach it?"

"I don't think we should stay here. What if it floods again? Let's get back up to the surface, quick!" interrupts Genji nervously, not impressed by the skeletons either.

"What do you mean? *This* is the best survival den ever!" replies Geo in complete disbelief at what he's hearing, "Who's ever had such a brilliant den like this? There's no way anyone will find us, and we'd be safe here until everything's back normal above ground!"

"I don't like it." says Genji, unconvinced, "What if the water comes back?"

"All it needs is a few chairs - a bit more light and hey - the best den in the world!" Geo keeps going as if he is not hearing a single word Genji's saying.

"I think Genji's right, how do we know the whole cave won't flood again? And anyway, what do we do with the skeletons? Can't just leave them there, can we? Who do you think they were?" says Jun supporting her sister.

"Who knows?" replies Geo incredulously.

"Don't *you* think that the fact that there *are* skeletons here is a bit of a *clue* that *maybe* this is not a great place to be?!" I add sarcastically, completely agreeing with the girls.

"I reckon it'll be cool!" says Charlie forgetting his near death-by-drowning experience in an instant.

"Says the person who jumps into a strange hole, which appears out of nowhere," continues Jun unsatisfied, "and then vanishes without a trace!"

"Look, it's getting late anyhow, why don't we go back up to the surface and see *if* the water comes back tomorrow? *If* it doesn't then maybe we could set up a den here," I try diplomatically, fully expecting the water to flood back especially considering the amount of heavy rainfall we've already had today.

"OK, but everyone agrees not to say anything to anyone! Keep it our secret, no blabbing.... agreed?" argues Geo reluctantly, "We want to keep this place under wraps. We don't want *anybody* else down here, do we?"

We all agree to keep our new discovery a secret.

Whatever our misgivings, it is impossible not to be impressed by our amazing find and we definitely need to come back to investigate further tomorrow, if it's not flooded out.

I quickly wind up the torch one more time preparing for the ascent back up the rope ladder. The girls leave the cavern first leading the way with their rapidly dimming mobile phone lights. One by one, we crawl back through towards the bottom of the vertical shaft. That's when I notice something strange. At first, I think it is just my imagination. I'm not one hundred per cent sure but I think that the blue light held between the tall twisted fingers of rock faded slightly when Geo left the cavern. To test my theory, I call to Geo and ask him to come back for a second. His questioning face obligingly re-appears, and I ask him to stand back in the cavern and, sure enough, as soon as his feet touch the rocky ground, the blue light brightened slightly.

"Wow! That's odd!" exclaims Geo.

"I thought so! It went darker when you left, and it goes brighter when you came back!" I announce triumphantly as if I had discovered sliced bread, "It's like it knows you are here!"

"No wonder Charlie said it was darker and he found it difficult to see. That's because it *was* darker!"

THE GATHERING.

~~~

T hud! Thud!

There's another knock on the grand Holdwood Manor door. The heavy wrought iron knocker is working over-time tonight. Normally Mr. and Mrs. Boyd, Charlie's parents, have very few visitors but this evening five people have arrived in the last five minutes, making nine altogether.

Charlie is responsible for greeting the guests and escorting them to the large parlour at the front of the huge mansion. The room is decorated to impress; it has six large sash windows inserted into painted paneled walls which reach up to a high, decorative ornamental plaster ceiling. Each window is framed by substantial rich, ruby curtains, currently closed, giving the room a misplaced warm ambience. Charlie always feels that this is the coldest room in the whole house and usually avoids it but, on this night, the strange chill seems to perfectly match the solemn atmosphere of the gathering taking place before him. Awkwardly, he stands in the middle of the front parlour com-pletely unnoticed by the guests, he feels as if he is invisible. He recognises most of the guests from around the town but knows only a few by name. There's Mr. Taylor, who is stroking his short goatee beard thoughtfully, sat by himself on an old cane chair, which creaks every time he moves on it. Also, Genji and Jun's parents, who have just arrived - their father, Mr. Chen, is politely admiring the grand painting above the stone fireplace.

For the first time Charlie also looks closely at the painting, it looks strangely familiar. He has passed the painting many times, he had grown up with it, but never bothered to look at it properly, until now. It is an impressive landscape painting of Holdwood; in the foreground, just off centre, are two hooded figures. They seem to be looking for something in the burnt-out embers of a fire. With a start, Charlie suddenly realises that he is looking at another, albeit far grander, version of the lopsided painting that hung on the wall, back at the old lady's house clearance sale. To Charlie, close up, the smoke from the fire now looks more like the swirling Black Mist that had escaped from the shaft earlier today. He notices that the two hooded figures appear to be forcing the Black Mist into the hole in the ground somehow. This painting is also different because in this one, there is a third person holding a wooden staff with a ball of light, fizzing at the end of it.

Meanwhile Vincent Boyd, Charlie's father, paces up and down on the thick pile claret carpet, clearly irritated about something. Near the walnut veneered writing cabinet in the far corner of the room, Charlie's mother, Carmella, is huddled with the Genji and Jun's mother in a secretive looking conversation. Finally, his dad stops pacing and stands facing the guests and waits for them to somehow notice that the meeting has started.

"Everyone's here. Now, let's get down to business," he says with an air of authority, then he realises Charlie is still in the room and continues, "Thank you, Charlie. You'd better leave before you get bored to death!"

He is trying to sound humorous but actually Charlie is relieved to remove himself from the cold parlour, although he lingers behind the door a while to listen in, to find out what all the fuss is about.

BEHIND CLOSED DOORS

~~~

"**I** take it all of you received the letters from Amelia?" Vincent Boyd enquires in a hushed voice.

Everyone in the room nods back a secretive acknowledgement.

"Vincent, before we start, shouldn't we make a toast to our departed friend?" challenges a lady's haughty voice from the opposite side of the room, "After all without her, we'd have had to do this much sooner!"

"You're quite right, Jennifer, well said," chirps in Carmella Boyd calmly, trying to reduce the obvious tension in the room whilst moving closer to her husband's side. She raises her glass and solemnly leads the toast, "To Amelia, who gave herself, to delay this day, for as long as she could! Amelia!"

Everyone in the room raises their glasses and repeats back, "Amelia!"

Jennifer is placated for the time being, although her frown never leaves her face. She sinks down in a huge leather armchair and, with an air of aloofness, smooths an imaginary crease from her designer outfit.

Without further delay, Charlie's father restarts. "We received our letter the day after we heard she'd died, I assume everyone did. She must have known her time was running out."

"Taylor, did you get the necklace as instructed?" Charlie's

father asks urgently.

"It wasn't there! I was there only minutes after the doors opened but it had already gone!" replies Mr. Taylor clearly distressed.

"What!?" pipes up Jennifer in disbelief, "All the preparations in the world won't count for anything, if we don't have the necklace. We might as well forget it!"

"Typical, run at the first sign of a problem!" retorts another voice.

"That's not what I meant, and you know it!" she spits back bitterly, her green eyes flashing an evil look across the room.

"Look, there's no point in us fighting amongst ourselves, we must stick together!" coaxes Charlie's mother, wishing that these gatherings were less stressful. However, she knows that everyone here would give everything they could, even their lives, to protect and keep their secret. After all it was a collective decision to keep the stones hidden until their Holders were ready, a collective decision to imprison the Black Mist and a collective decision to charge Amelia with the responsibility for the necklace, the key to the prison. "Remember, we all agreed that the key should not be held here, we all agreed this would be the first place he'd look. Amelia did her job well."

"Who was there, at the house clearance? Did you recognise anyone or see anything strange?" Charlie's father asks Mr. Taylor hopefully.

"No one special, just the usual second hand and antique dealers that you'd expect." Mr. Taylor answers impatiently, not comfortable with the idea that he is in some way to blame for the necklace's disappearance. He has either completely forgotten about bumping into Charlie and his friends in the upstairs hallway or does not think it worth mentioning.

"I went straight into her room and looked under the pillows as the letter said - but there was nothing there. I searched all over the place - you would not believe the smell in that room - but I couldn't find it anywhere!" then pausing for breath, he adds, "I didn't want anyone to get suspicious and suspect that I was searching for something, so I left and went back that night. I had to break in the kitchen window at the back of the house although the glass nearly fell out on its own, the window frame was so rotten! I searched all over the house and I mean *everywhere* but zilch, zero, nothing. Maybe the old dear changed her mind and hid it somewhere else?"

"Amelia would have found a way to let us know if she had!" points out another voice, "She was old and a little eccentric, but you know full well she would have found a way."

"So where is it then? If that necklace falls into the wrong hands there will be no end to the trouble we will be in," says Mr. Chen calmly.

A tangible cold shudder sweeps through the already chill room.

"All we can do, is hope that whoever has it also has no idea what it is! We *must* find it! Taylor, please make me a list of everyone you saw; we'll start there," Mr. Boyd starts to pace around the room again emphasising the sense of urgency.

Outside, there's a rumble of a car pulling up the long gravel driveway up to the Holdwood Manor followed quickly by the sound of tyres crushing against loose stone chippings as a car grinds to a halt. Next is the familiar, 'Thud! Thud!' of the wrought iron door knocker. Charlie, who is already in the hallway, opens the huge door, only to be rudely brushed aside, nearly falling over backwards, as the unexpected guest forces his way past him. The mysteriously hooded stranger storms into the parlour and is met by eleven completely startled and disbelieving faces.

"Thought you'd start without me, did you?" the hooded figure says as he sweeps into the front parlour. His deep hoarse voice is instantly recognizable to all, except Charlie.

"I...we...had no idea you were..." starts Charlie's father in surprise.

"...alive?!" replies the hooded figure.

"Yes, we thought you'd surely been killed in that South American incident. You never came back!"

"A long story - maybe another time - now which one of you has the necklace?" getting directly to the point and touching a deep scar on his left cheek as if he was remembering something.

"Alfide! It's great to see you again!" says Charlie's father warmly as he shakes the man's hand vigorously as if welcoming a long-lost friend, "Bad news. The necklace is missing!"

CHARLIE'S NEWS

~~~

The next day Charlie is late. It's a wet and chilly morning. We wait for him in our cozy dry den, under the tarpaulin, armed with three windup torches and three fully charged torches. Apart from Genji, we're all extremely keen to climb down to investigate our newly discovered cavern below. She still needs to be convinced that the cavern has not flooded again overnight but the rest of us are convinced it will still be dry.

Charlie charges in to the den, bursting with news of the mysterious meeting that took place last night at his parent's house. "You are not going to believe this!" he blurts out, "It's the necklace from the old lady's house - there was a weird man with a cloak and hood, he nearly pushed me over when I opened the door, he wanted the necklace. Taylor was there - that's why he was at the house clearance - and your mum and dad too!" says Charlie breathlessly turning to the girls.

"What on *Earth* are you talking about?" I can see Charlie is excited, but he isn't making any sense.

"OK!" he takes a deep breath, "My parents had loads of people come 'round last night. I was helping with coats and showing them to the front room. My father was pacing up and down the carpet. I've never seen him like that before! When everyone'd arrived, I had to leave the room, but I listened by the door, to see if I could find out what all the fuss was about. Well, they were talking about someone called Amelia, sounded as if she was dead. I think it's the old lady from the house. Then they were talking about the necklace! Mr. Taylor said that he'd searched everywhere for it but couldn't find it. You remember he was at the old lady's house too. I bet he was looking for the necklace you found! Just after that a car screeched outside and this hooded man with a scar on his cheek pushed straight past me when I opened the door for him. I'd say you don't want to mess with him!"

We all listen intently, not daring to miss a single word.

"The first thing he wanted to know was where the necklace was. Then the door was closed on me. I don't know if they knew I was listening or not, but I didn't hang around. It must have been really late when they left. I fell asleep." Charlie stops for more breath and then says, "We've got to get the necklace back somehow before they find out who's got it otherwise there'll be real trouble!"

We are stunned into silence. For a few seconds, the only sound is the familiar pattering of the rain on the tarpaulin den roof.

Geo breaks the uncomfortable silence, "Well, they *can't* have it back because we don't have it. It's vanished, hasn't it?"

Genji and Jun don't say anything but are both secretly wondering why their parents were at this strange meeting.

Abruptly reality dawns. Not only have we stolen the necklace, but it has vanished leaving behind a deep hole in our den, which, itself, leads to an underground cavern with a strange blue light and two skeletons.

"You know, things don't just vanish, do they? Maybe the necklace is still nearby, maybe in the cavern? Maybe we'll find it down there, if we have a proper look." suggests Imp moving towards the hole opening, "What about that blue stone, didn't you say that looked like a stone from the necklace?"

"Come on then. Let's get going!" chivvies Geo already heading towards the opening to the dark shaft.

"How do you know it's not flooded again?" checks Genji blocking the way to the hole.

"Look for yourself, the blue glow is different to last time

when the water was there." I answer but I can see she's not convinced, "I'll drop another stone in and test it, should I?"

Without waiting for a reply, I find the nearest pebble and drop it into the mute darkness.

We all wait in hushed silence, hardly breathing.

When at last the sound echoes back up to us, it is the clatter of stone against stone, not the plopping of a stone in water.

"There...there's your proof! Come on, let's get going!" Geo moves forward again and confidently starts his climb down the rope ladder.

"Hang on G', I want to try something," Charlie says as he picks up his rucksack which is heavily loaded with supplies from home. He lowers it gently down to Geo who is already several rungs down on the rope ladder. "Here, put this on that ledge where I was sat yesterday. Can you reach it? Make sure you lean it right up against the wall."

"Why?" checks Geo warily.

"I just want to see what happens."

"What...do you think the same thing that happened to you might happen to the rucksack?" asks Geo as he puts two and two together.

"Who knows? I just want to know how I ended up in the cavern. One minute I was resting on the ledge, leaning against the wall, the next I was flying backwards!" says Charlie a little embarrassed at his experiment and not really expecting his rucksack to move.

Geo climbs further down into the dark shaft and reaches for the ledge. With his torch light he searches the ledge for anything that might explain what happened to Charlie yesterday. There's nothing obvious. With difficulty, he lifts the heavy rucksack onto the ledge. Nothing happens.

Charlie watches from the surface opening, shining his powerful torch down. "Push it up right against the side there." He points to the spot with his beam.

Geo has to swing on the rope ladder to push the rucksack right up against the side of the shaft.

Nothing happens.

"Sorry, doesn't look as if anything..."

Without warning, there's the sudden whoosh of cold air that makes Geo feel as if his hair is being blow dried and the rucksack's gone.

"It's gone!" Geo's voice echoes as he shouts up to Charlie who's looking down from above, "Just vanished!"

"Keep going down, see if it's down in the cavern!" returns Charlie's voice excitedly.

~~~

Expectantly, Geo pokes his head out of the opening of the short tunnel into the cavern. Everything looks exactly as it did yesterday except there, right next to the decapitated skeleton, is Charlie's rucksack tipped on its side. He climbs out of the tunnel opening and stands firmly on the rocky ground. Simultaneously, the glow of the blue light intensifies as if acknowledging his presence.

Charlie arrives next, feeling vindicated, and checks his ruck sack for any damage. "Shame we can't get things back up as easily!" he grumbles, thinking of having to carry everything back up the rope ladder to the surface, at the end of the day.

This time, Imp comes down with us. We decided that it's unfair to expect any one of us to miss out on all the excitement, so we agreed to leave a handwritten message, to say where we are, pinned under two rocks next to the tunnel entrance in the den - just in case.

She pokes her head through the tunnel opening as Geo is circling around the vertical base of the massive gripping fingers of stone. They surround the much smaller blue stone, the size of a whole walnut, with an invisible hold, suspending it in midair, well out of our reach.

Charlie walks across and shines his torch directly at the captive blue stone, "It looks like it could be a stone from the necklace. Can't tell. But how did it get up there? I wonder if I can climb up and reach it?"

DEAD WEIGHT

~~~

I t's easily mid-morning. Everyone is frustrated and annoyed. We've been trying to reach the blue stone since we arrived in the cavern. True, it is difficult to reach but even when one of us manages to climb up the spiraling arm, there's no way to reach inside and grab the blue stone and, adding insult to injury, we keep slipping back down! The surface of the beautiful shiny black rock is so smooth, that it's impossible to get a firm enough grip to hold position for more than a fraction of a second. When I touch the rock, it feels as if it is trying to push me away, repelling contact, like identical magnetic poles being pushed together. Genji found a collection of smooth rounded pebbles, probably left behind from when the water had been here. She tried throwing them at the suspended stone, but they just bounced off the spiraling arms, never getting close enough to knock it free of its perch, despite her best efforts.

Even ever resourceful Geo is stumped and looking dejected. Charlie is also at a loss. He'd tried the hardest to climb up the spirals and his face is red with his effort and annoyance at his lack of success.

"This is a complete waste of time. Anyway, I'm starving," Charlie complains hopelessly. He sits down on a large boulder and pulls his heavy rucksack towards him. Unzipping the top pouch, he pulls out a stack of bread rolls, plastic water bottles and several packets of biscuits; a feast in the making! We are all hungry. We've all brought our own sandwiches that we'd hurriedly prepared in the rush to meet up this morning, but

Charlie's is like a banquet in comparison. Much to Charlie's huge embarrassment, his mother packed him off with enough food to feed the five thousand, which is a good thing from our point of view - our own meagre portions hardly make a dent in our appetites. He flattens a large plastic bag on the ground and generously spreads his feast out for us all to share. We all gratefully tuck in.

"I think I know who the skeletons are," I muse as I munch on a sandwich, "or were. See the hoods, I reckon that one is one of those hooded figures in the painting at the old lady's house."

"How d'you get to that?" quizzes Charlie, remembering the huge painting hung above the stone fireplace in his own parent's front parlour.

"I dunno, I just *feel* it," I say, still munching, "I reckon that they must have been looking for something down here. The painting must be showing when they first found the entrance, then somehow they got down here and drowned trying to get back."

"S'pose it could be," agrees Charlie adding to the story, "it does look as though they were standing right at the same spot where our den is." At first, he doesn't mention the painting in his parent's front parlour but, after a few chews, he thinks that he should, "We've got the same painting hung up above the fireplace, never really noticed it much before last night."

I am pleasantly surprised at Charlie's unexpected support for my theory.

He continues, "In that one there's another person holding a wooden pole with a light on the end. Strange thing though, you know that Black Mist that escaped from the hole yesterday?"

We all nod, remembering the cold chill as the Black Mist swirled around us, and the smell.

"Well, it looked to me as if they were forcing it into the hole. Like a trap." explains Charlie.

"Or prison." I add.

Genji and Jun both listen intently, eyes wide open. They hadn't noticed the painting hung at the old lady's house but were imagining the skeletons with flesh on, in black hooded cloaks, alive and climbing down the shaft...only to end up as bones sprawled out on the cavern floor.

"That doesn't explain why they're down here, though." questions Jun, "I mean, if they trapped the Black Mist down here, why come back again?"

"Maybe they needed to check it was still here, maybe they thought it had escaped. Who knows?" suggests Geo.

"Why would they want to trap the Black Mist? How many more people, do you think, know about the necklace?" Genji asks.

"It looked really old," Imp joins in, between chews.

"How long do you think they've been down here? Why has that one got no head?" Jun points at the headless skeleton.

"Probably ages, the painting shows the trees were not as big as they are now - could have been painted a hundred years ago - maybe more!" answers Charlie as if he is now the world authority on the painting, that I had discovered.

"I wonder who closed off the entrance to the hole with the slab of rock?" Genji asks thoughtfully, "Why did they block it off?"

"To keep that Black Mist trapped inside here, forever," suggests Imp and adds thoughtfully, "and we released it. We let it escape!"

"Maybe who-ever-it-was knew that it was flooded and didn't want anyone to drown down here!" speculates Charlie.

"Maybe that's what happened!" I say, "Maybe they were trapped in here and couldn't get back out because someone else had shut off the entrance. Maybe it's the only way out."

"That's horrible!" exclaims Genji putting her bread roll down in disgust.

"What if someone saw them go into the hole and didn't want them to be able to climb out. They'd have died trying to escape!" Geo joins in, enjoying the gruesome speculations.

Absent-mindedly, Geo starts to blow over the top of his water bottle, making a musical note that echoes around the cavern. The sound hangs in the air eerily, longer than you would expect. Noticing this, he blows again, only harder. Charlie decides to join in with his bottle, his note is higher and so he has another mouthful of water and blows again. This time both notes sound very similar. The echoes seem to combine and resonate and reverberate around and around the cavern. Suddenly, the cavern walls start shimmering impossibly, moving, and vibrating with the notes like a great tuning fork. Simultaneously, tremendous shudders shake the ground from deep below us and the roof of the cavern above. The twisted spiraling hands which are closed around the suspended blue stone, slowly start to slide apart, unravelling, one twisting left and upwards like a screw, the other twisting right and downwards, both disappearing centimetre by centimetre, being swallowed into unseen holes in the cavern floor and roof rock faces, revealing the now uncaged blue stone still suspended and held by an unknown force in mid-air by itself, glowing.

I feel an undeniable urge to run, jump and grab at the stone.

It is still annoyingly out of my reach by an arm's length height easily. Immediately, the girls take up the challenge too. Since they are both much more athletic than me, I think that they will easily reach it but, frustratingly, the suspended stone seems to hover, mockingly, just millimetres higher than their highest reach.

I notice that part of the black rock pillar has not receded completely into the cavern floor and is still exposed directly below the blue stone. I stand on the top of it gaining an extra twenty centimetres or so above the cavern floor and jump one more time, but it is useless. At that moment, the top of the black fingers of rock under my feet starts to rumble and tremor. To my dismay, the great twisting hands of rock move, slowly reversing as if the spell had been broken, heading back to their original position. If we don't act very quickly, the twisting arms of black rock will interlock again around the blue stone and there is no guarantee that we will ever get another chance to release it. I hold my balance and stand firm on the moving rock as I'm slowly lifted upwards, turning as the twisted arm edges higher, ascending ever closer to the suspended blue stone. Finally, I am only just out of reach of the blue stone. I make a grab for it, but mysteriously it drifts even higher, further away from me, as if it's taunting me. Simultaneously, the other twisting arm has been descending from the lofty cavern roof. I know I will be crushed between the two hands if I stay too long and it also dawns on me that I am now uncomfortably high. Out of the corner of my eye I see the others are watching helplessly. Ever closer, the twisting arms move together threateningly – the blue stone is still suspended between them and I'm balancing desperately on the rising lower pillar – then I notice that the blue stone appears to hesitate as the influence of the upper arm begins to have more downward force like a repelling magnet. Now the stone is being pushed downwards as well as upwards by the opposing twisting hands as if pinned between them.

My palms are sweating, and my heart is beating hard. I am in a very precarious position, now raised several metres above the cavern floor. I don't dare stay any longer. With a huge final effort, I leap up and at last feel the blue stone in my hand. I try to land firmly back on top of the lower rotating hand but completely miss my footing and crash off centre. With my spare hand, I lunge to grab hold of the smooth side of the black rock pillar, urgently trying to avoid my impending fall. There's nothing to hold onto, to slow my fall, except the cold smooth black rock which offers no resistance. Nevertheless, I wrap my arms around the pillar as much as I can and desperately cling on. As I tumble, I'm swung around with each twist downward like a high-speed helter-skelter ride with no soft landing. I fall to the ground with a heavy bump and the blue stone clatters on the surface, bounces and slides across the floor, landing directly at Geo's feet.

The cavern walls respond with a shudder and a jet of cold, foul air blasts through the cavern creating an icy whirlwind around us. Then comes the most terrifying sound of all, the sound of gurgling gushing water rushing up from the depths under the trembling ground below our feet. I look down only to see the cavern floor is already covered in a thin, but fast rising, carpet of water. Our worst fear is realised, the water is returning to the cavern. Fast.

We are all galvanised into action.

Geo grabs the blue stone and helps Imp up to her feet. Genji and Jun leap up and climb toward the highest raised rock ridge they can find. It is the very same ridge that Charlie had swam to and found safety the day before. Charlie pulls on his rucksack. I regain my breath and balance and, now already knee deep in water, wade across to join the others.

Only a few seconds pass, and the water is already waist high and still rising. Charlie is struggling to climb onto the raised ledge with the rucksack on his back.

"Take off the rucksack, pass it to me," I yell to be heard over the rushing water, "I'll pass it up to you! Quickly!"

Charlie hands me his rucksack, quickly climbs up and leans over the edge to grab it back off me. The girls have already pulled Imp up to safety and are in the process of heaving Geo up over the edge and onto the ledge. The water continues rising rapidly. I have to swim now. Swirling currents are forcing me towards the jagged wall below the ridge, making it more and more awkward to reach out and hold on to anything solid. The power of the water suddenly propels me further away from the others. They are shouting for me to grab onto a protruding rock in the cavern wall; I can see it, but I can't reach it as I am swept straight past it. Before I know it, I am pulled back to the middle of the cavern almost exactly where the stone had been suspended but now it is me who is suspended in racing water, being dragged, turned, and pulled further away from the others, the ledge and safety. I know I'm in deep trouble. The water keeps rising and I am flung across to the opposite side of the cavern. It feels as though the water has a tight grip of me and will not let me move despite all my efforts.

In the distance Geo shouts, "Swim!"

"Can't!" I gulp back, "It won't let me!"

"Try!"

"I am...it won't let me! It's like the water's holding me!" I know it makes no sense and I am tiring fast; even though I'm not moving, it is taking all my energy just to stay where I am. In the end, I have no more energy and stop fighting the water. Instantly, I'm slammed against the nearest rock face about half way up the cavern wall, but instead of being splattered, I am spun back around again towards the others by an even stronger rip current.

That's when I must have faded out of consciousness.

Through my unconscious haze I imagine that, over the roaring and whooshing of the water, I can hear the single musical note, identical to the one Geo and Charlie had made with their water bottles earlier. The raging currents around me seem to calm.

I limply bob in the water, slowly being drawn closer to the raised ridge where the others are standing. Charlie and the girls manage to grab my shirt as I float in front of them. Together they drag my dead weight out of the water. For several minutes I lie in a heap on the rocky ridge, recovering, unaware of the strange circumstances of my timely rescue. It was Imp who saved me. It was Imp who blew the musical note and held it, unwaveringly, until the others were able to rescue me. No one else would have thought of doing that but, to her, it just made sense.

While I recover from my ordeal, the others stand at the edge of the rock ridge looking down into the dark murky water that now completely fills the cavern below.

"That's what it was like when I had to swim up here yesterday," Charlie confirms, "except everything's churned up now too."

Geo holds up his glowing blue stone in front of his face. Its cold glow lights up his face. He passes it to Genji, and the glow dims slightly as if it knows that Geo has gone. She hands it back to him and immediately its brightness returns. They look at it in wonder. One thing is certain, it is definitely a stone from the necklace but where are the other stones? How did it get down here?

"How do we get back up to the den now?" asks Jun already knowing the answer.

"We don't!" Charlie sighs as he too grasps our desperate situation; stuck on a high ridge above a swirling, impenetrable dark pool of water which conceals our only escape route back to the safety of our den up in the woods, "There's no way we'll be able to swim all the way down to the tunnel, let alone swim through it *and* get back into the hole shaft without breathing!"

"It's a good thing we left the rescue note in the den," Jun says positively, "how long d'you think until someone comes looking for us?"

"I said not to come down here, didn't I? I said it might flood!" sobs Genji to herself.

"I'm sure they'll start looking for us soon," replies Charlie trying to sound more certain of a speedy rescue than he really believes.

I remember that we had all agreed not to tell anyone about our discovery of the tunnel *and* that Charlie had purposely chosen to build our den off the beaten track, means that it is very unlikely we will be rescued soon. I keep my mouth closed, Jun already looks as if she's about to burst into tears.

"Unless someone covers up the hole like before," teases Geo, "then we could end up like those skeletons... der da da de dah!"

"Oh, stop it! You're not helping!" snarls Imp.

As I recover my strength, my eyes lazily wander around the cavern. I notice the colour of the rock of the wall behind us changes abruptly half way across the rock face. I see a second, tall curtain of rock in front of the main cavern wall rock face which blends in so well that it creates an optical illusion giving the appearance of a single rock face and not the two overlapping walls of rock that are there in reality.

Imp, who is still nearby keeping a watchful eye on my recovery, follows my eyes. She sees it too. She calls to the others, "Shine a torch over here!"

She walks up to the first curtain of rock and walks behind it and vanishes from view, completely shielded from our viewpoint.

"It looks like a tunnel!" Imp shouts back excitedly to the others from behind the curtain wall of rock.

Immediately, the others race over to see what the fuss is about. They see a large tunnel opening although it is totally impossible to see if it leads anywhere.

"This could be a way out!" says Charlie optimistically.

Still slightly shaky, I stand up and join the others at the tunnel entrance and peer into the blackness. The beam of Imp's torch light hardly penetrates more than a few metres in. It is only then that I realise that we are down to only Imp's battery torch, all our wind-up torches have been washed away or lost in the panic to reach the safety of the ledge. In addition to Imp's torch, we now also have the gentle blue glow of Geo's stone which he lifts up to illuminate the inside of the tunnel directly ahead of him. Geo steps forward, moving into the tunnel, to investigate further.

ESCAPE

~~~

"I still think we should go back," whispers Genji nervously and holds Jun's free hand tightly.

We left the flooded cavern at least half an hour ago but the passing of time is impossible to judge precisely in this shadowy underground and none of us ever bother to wear watches. Each new footstep on the uneven tunnel floor holds the risk of tripping, falling, or bumping into someone or something. Imp's torch light finally flickers, dims and dies leaving us with only the glow from Geo's blue stone, which he holds out on the palm of his hand. Visibility is down to only a few metres ahead of Geo although it's obvious that the tunnel is gradually dropping deeper, sloping steeper and, ominously, falling further from our den at the surface.

"Go back where exactly?" whispers back Jun.

"I wish we'd never come down here, I said it might flood again...I told you!" Genji is right but there's no real choice left now. Behind us, the cavern is flooded with no way of escaping. Forward is the only way.

The air is gradually turning icy cold and dry, making me shudder and shiver. There is no sense of water nearby – that, at least, is some comfort. Onward, forward, and still downward, we descend deeper into the heart of the hill under Holdwood. The echoes of our slow deliberate footsteps are the only sound that accompanies us, apart from the occasional ricocheting rattling of a loose pebble, unexpectedly kicked against the rock wall of the tunnel, making us jump and freeze on the spot, until the noise eventually dies away.

Onward, forward, and still downward we continue.

The roof of the tunnel unexpectedly dips so low we find ourselves crawling along on our hands and knees for a short time. Then, without any warning there is an abrupt right hand turn as if to avoid some hidden object ahead deep in the rock. In front is Geo and Imp who suddenly stop dead in the darkness. I walk straight into the back of Geo. Charlie walks into me and the girls into him…each time bumping Geo further forward at the front of our line. His face now only centimetres away from a vertical solid rock wall.

We are at a dead-end.

Geo puts his free hand out in front to steady himself and tries to push himself away from the rock face in front. The wall looks solid but as his hand touches the rock it shimmers, and his hand disappears into the rock face as if it had turned into liquid. Quickly, he pulls his hand back and checks it for damage. Being Geo, he can't resist trying again.

"Wow!" Geo says, "Look at this, my arm…"

The rest us are already tightly bunched up around Geo and, in the dim blue light, have already seen what is happening. I reach out to test it myself, but the rock stands solid and unyielding to my hand. I am disappointed. The others follow, trying for themselves also with no success. Meanwhile Geo decides to see if he can shuffle gradually further and further sideways into the wall of rock, until all that is left of him is his other arm holding the dimly glowing stone. Then he reverses and rejoins us.

"I think there's another tunnel or cave on the other side, but I can't see much, I'll have to use the stone's light," Geo comes back excitedly.

"But then *we* won't have any light!" points out Genji uncertainly, "You'd better be quick…I don't like it in the dark!"

"We'll be fine… we can hold on to each other like this," suggests Charlie bravely, "be quick though G', just a quick look and straight back yeah?!"

Geo is already halfway submerged into the rock and then he is gone.

An unbalancing blackness engulfs us all, when both he and the blue stone disappear into the rock. We wait in deafening silence, hardly daring to breathe, listening intently for any clues to mark Geo's return.

Time silently slips by. Still there is no sign of Geo returning. Nothing.

Genji's shaking voice expresses what we all are thinking, "What if...what if he can't get back!"

"Don't be silly. G'll find a way... you know what he's like...he always finds a way...you know that," says Jun trying to sound convincing for her sister even though she's not completely sure herself.

In the silent blackness, the dawning that Geo's plan has gone wrong comes upon us.

Geo is not able to get back and we are stuck at a dead-end.

"What are we going to do now?" I ask, trying desperately to disguise my increasing feeling of panic. I can hear my own heartbeat.

"We can't go back, we'd never find the way with no light. We can't go through the rock like Geo. I still don't see how only he could get through? Why can't we?"

"I think it was the stone. He was holding the stone!" Imp says.

Dark silence greets her suggestion that the stone might have had something to do with it.

Then I agree, "A blue necklace stone that glows, that's pretty weird and unusual, so why not? But why isn't he coming back?"

Again, we wait together in the blackness trying to figure out our options; there is only one – to crawl back the way we had come, this time with no light to guide us. There is no guarantee that we will ever make it back and, even if we did, we would still be stuck in the flooded cavern with no way out.

"If he can't find his way back to us, what's happened to Geo?" Imp asks full of concern for her brother.

"Geo always finds a way!" I remind her, sounding much more

positive than I feel. It is impossible to tell how long we have already been underground. I begin to wonder if anyone on the surface has even noticed that we were missing yet. Would they ever find our den? Would they even notice the note we left under the two stones by the entrance to the hole? The more I think about it, the more unlikely a rescue seems. Then I think about the two skeletons back in the cavern. Is this what happened to them? Did they get stuck here and blindly crawl back through the treacherous tunnels all the way back to the cavern only to die there, unable to escape?

Not a second too soon, there is a scuffling scratching sound straight above our heads, followed by huffing and puffing and, to everyone's total relief, the faint blue glow of the stone and Geo!

Geo is above us, looking directly down from an opening in the rock just above us, grinning.

"Sorry about that, couldn't find the way back...next time I'll mark it out. I found this passage way and nearly fell down this hole!" Geo was bravely trying to disguise the fact that he too had thought he had lost us for good.

"What's on the other side of the wall?" Charlie begins to fire questions excitedly at Geo, "Is there a way out?"

Geo replies, "Difficult to see much but I bet I've just found another stone from the necklace...I couldn't get to it but there's a red glow to one side of the cave. Here," stretching out his arm and offering a hand, "can you reach up here? If you can climb up here, you can see for yourselves! Charlie, if you lift Imp up first - she's shortest, I'll pull her up then Jun..."

Before long, we have all climbed up and joined Geo in the high tunnel above except for Charlie who can't climb up with no-one to help lift him up from below.

In frustration Charlie says, "However you looked at this, one of us gets stuck here!"

"I've got an idea!" replies Geo and jumps down next to Charlie leaving the others in darkness in the tunnel above, "Here, I'll help you up...then I'll go through the wall again and go back through the tunnel to guide you!"

With Geo's help, Charlie climbs up easily. We all look down at Geo's grinning face.

"Just wait there. I'll only be a few minutes - just wait there," he says as he plunges his arm deep into the rock face below us followed by the rest of his body, again.

Silent darkness engulfs us for the second time.

"Oh great! I can't see a thing again...great...just great," Genji complains feeling uncomfortable back in the black silence.

It seems like another eternity before we can hear the scraping sound of Geo approaching, although it is probably only a matter of minutes.

"Sorry about that, I needed to mark the opening in the rock wall, so I know where it is if we need it again," Geo apologises unnecessarily.

"Maybe it only works one way," Imp suggests in her matter of fact way.

In his enthusiasm, Geo scrambles ahead leaving Imp and myself in near darkness at the back. We are very careful to avoid falling back down the now near invisible hole that we had all just climbed up through as we try to keep up with the others.

"Wait for us!" protests Imp, "Wait for us!"

Geo stops and turns apologetically. We quickly catch up. It's a strange short tunnel. Unlike the others, we are walking in a circular loop with only a shallow decline. We follow Geo into a huge spherical, smooth walled cave with wide spiraling ledges etch into its walls, leading from the ground upwards as far as I can see, into the roof of blackness. It feels like we are inside a massive snail shell. It is much bigger than the first cavern. Across, on the opposite side, I spot the faint red glow that Geo had mentioned. The gulf of darkness between the two glowing stones makes it impossible to see whether there is solid ground between them or if there is a deep gaping chasm.

"Careful that there aren't any more holes where you walk," warns Geo, still unsettled by the 'nearly falling on top of us' experience.

Charlie takes the lead and steps out uncertainly on the unlit cave floor. There's a crunching noise from under his feet and Charlie quickly pulls back his foot.

"What's that?" Genii asks just as Charlie cautiously crouches, reaches down and blindly tests the ground with his fingers. It feels rough and uneven like a stack of thick, dried branches piled up on top of each other. They are wobbly and move easily against each other, but there's something else.

"Geo, give me some light here, can you? Feels like loose branches - not sure what it is!"

Geo moves closer to where Charlie is kneeling and holds out his glowing blue stone on the palm of his hand, dropping closer to the floor surface.

"Here, is that any good?" he asks, trying to see for himself.

"I can't see, feels like dried out branches but it can't be. Not all the way down here," explains Charlie.

"We are under Holdwood!" Jun says as she comes over to look for herself.

"Yeah but ..." his voice trails off.

Geo lowers his palm further until his own hand is testing the ground and the blue light reveals what Charlie has stood on.

"Bones! The whole floor is stacked with old, dried out bones!" Geo exclaims as he realises what he was touching, "Could be human bones!"

"What makes you think that?" asks Charlie interestedly.

"Look for yourself, what do *you* think?!" Geo holds his stone so that we can all see for ourselves.

"Yeah, but how did they get here? There must be thousands here, maybe more! It's like a huge grave with everyone just piled on top of each other!" Charlie investigates further.

"I've heard of places like this. When there were plagues, like the Black Death, loads of people died at the same time. There were too many bodies to bury in single graves and those left alive didn't want to hang around in case they caught the plague - they just flung them on top of each other in a big hole in the ground," I inform the hushed silence.

"That's gross!" Genji exclaims, breaking the spell.

"I wonder if we can catch the plague...by being here, too close to the bones?" asks Jun in a whisper.

"I think the plague dies when it has no more flesh to live off," answers Imp, "I don't think it can live on dried out old bones."

"What if you're wrong?" Jun says, not convinced.

"Then it's already too late!!" replies Geo. Then he picks up the largest leg bone he can find and waves it around above his head, trying to lighten the mood, "Ugg! Ugg!" Trying to impersonate a caveman. Badly. Although Jun is unimpressed, she can't help smiling at the ridiculous shadowy sight.

Just then, there's a rustling noise from over on the other side of the cave, near the red glow.

We all turn on the spot and, standing motionless in the darkness, listen intently. Geo slowly lowers the large leg bone to his side.

There it is again, as if someone or something is moving at the other side of the cave, unseen.

Silence.

We all listen not daring to move or breathe.

There it is again - there is no doubt, there is definitely something in the cave with us.

Charlie is the first to react. He nudges Geo and motions for him to shine the dim light of his stone over in the direction of the sound. That's when we all see the red and yellow eyes hanging in the blackness staring right at us.

Charlie whispers "I've seen those before!"

"When?" I ask him.

"At the entrance by the den, on the first day."

"Why didn't you say anything about them?" I press him further.

"I forgot!"

"Forgot? How can you forget something like that?" I continue in disbelief.

"Well the fact that I went flying backwards, landed upside down in a pool of water and nearly drowned might have something to do with it!" Charlie answers defensively.

The strange eyes vanish just as quickly as they appeared, exactly like they had before.

Geo relaxes his grip on the leg bone but quickly tightens his grip back again when we hear the familiar scratching noise again, this time to our left. I wheel around to face more darkness with the red glow to my right.

"Grab a bone!" Geo urgently commands as he raises his blue stone higher trying to expose whatever it is that is making the noise.

"Maybe it's rats!" suggests Genji.

I slowly kneel down and rummage through the bones below, feeling for any large bone that will make a good weapon, without taking my eyes off the darkness ahead just in case something happens. The others do the same.

More scratching. Then crunching - now I know what the noise is. It is the sound of walking on dried bones - getting louder and closer.

Still I can't make out anything in the blackness ahead of us, but there is definitely something there and what-ever-it-is is moving nearer with each creepy crunch. The hairs on the back of my neck are stood up and my eyes strain to see what is out there.

Still I can see nothing.

Bravely, Geo moves forward, towards the crunching noise.

"Careful!" cautions Jun, almost unable to get the word out.

My heart is pounding hard as I decide to join him, leaving the others behind. It is tricky to keep my balance on the uneven cave floor. Moving silently is not an option; each footstep is amplified by the crunching of more dry bone against dry bone. I can hear what direction the what-ever-it-is is but, likewise, it can hear where we are too - not that we are trying to hide. The crunches continue coming closer and, finally, are straight ahead of us. Geo and I stop dead and stand our ground ready to face the what-ever-it-is. By now, it sounds so close, we should be able to touch it, let alone see it!

What is going on?

82

It is Charlie who spots it first. Against the cave wall in front of us, he spies a shadowy outline of a human shaped figure.

"There!" he shouts and points to the wall excitedly, "On the wall. Look! See the moving shadow!"

I glance towards the cave wall further ahead of us and just make out the faint silhouette of a thin hooded figure, slowly getting larger and more distinct as it moves closer to the light of Geo's blue stone. The shadow fills nearly the whole cave wall before halting, directly in front of us. On the ground, I can just make out the two boot size gouges where white bones have been pushed out by the shoes of the shadow.

It feels like a stand-off, neither of us wanting to move any closer, afraid of what might happen.

The shadow stands silently, unnervingly, and unmoving.

Geo turns to me, then back to the others and shrugs his shoulders and whispers, "What now?"

No one has an answer. This is unexpected. We stand face to faceless wondering what will happen next.

Imp fearlessly takes control, "Who are you? I can see you're not going to hurt us - you could have done that already. Who are you?"

Imp's confidence and understanding of the situation impresses me. The tension in the cavern reduces significantly although none of us dares relax completely, and I still hold tightly on to my dried leg bone, just in case.

At first there is no reply, then a husky, choking but oddly quiet voice replies. Each gasped phrase sounds as if it requires a massive and exhausting effort, "We have guarded... against the evil mist... we drowned... we have battled ... in these caves .... there is no escape."

As it speaks, the shadow on the wall slowly moves away from us and towards the red stone. The slow crunching of bones underfoot fills the intervals between each gasp. Our eyes flit between the moving shadow on the wall and the vanishing trail of moving bones on the floor, our ears follow the eerie voice and the footsteps until it finally comes to rest behind the red stone.

"This is what... you seek... is it not?" The harshness of the voice is less husky and awkward with use.

It is only then that I realise we have not said anything, spellbound by the movement of the shadowy figure and the strange haunting voice.

"Yes, we need to return the necklace," says Imp with authority.

"I know nothing...of a necklace."

There is something about the voice, almost indiscernible - it is a woman's voice.

"We think the red rock is part of it," Imp explains honestly, much to the dismay of Geo who is clearly unimpressed that she should be telling anyone else about the necklace.

Imp asks calmly, "Madam, who are you?"

"You don't know?!"

"No, I don't, Madam."

"Then how are you here?" the woman asks, shuffling backwards uncertainly.

"More by accident than anything," replies Imp.

"There are no accidents here. I am Jess. We have guarded tirelessly. How did it escape? There is nothing... only this cave.... not even a way out! There is black evil here blocking the way. Then you arrive. Beware the Black Mist!" Her voice cracks and hisses angrily but the anger is not directed at us, more in frustration.

Undeterred Imp expertly continues, "How long have you been guarding these caves?"

"Time has no meaning here."

"You say *we* but there is only you, Madam. Who else is here?"

"We are three. The others guard elsewhere."

The silence is thoughtful and awkward. She pauses as if collecting her thoughts together, "Yes. What of the others?" Jess asks herself with concern; her shadow starts to lose its shape as though she is struggling to even exist.

"Others, what others?" Charlie is thinking of the meeting back at his parent's house the other evening, the paintings, the rude hooded stranger, and wonders if there is some sort of connection between that and this shadowy figure but nothing makes sense.

"We set off as a guard of three, I passed through, but the others did not." Jess is clearly struggling to speak, heaving heavily, and sounding distraught.

That explains the skeletons we found!" interrupts Geo without thinking.

"Skeletons, what skeletons? Where?" Clearly shocked, Jess's shadowy figure backs towards the wall of the cave, shrinking and fading as the shadow falls away from the red stone light and Geo's blue light.

"I think your two friends didn't make it. I think we may have passed them in the first cavern," Geo tries to be tactful but fails dreadfully.

There is a quick scuttling movement and Jess's shadow is completely gone.

"Well done Geo!" says Imp annoyed at her brother's unbelievable insensitivity, "You certainly have a way with words don't you? We need to find out where the other stones are, and you've just freaked her out! Good work Geo!"

"Phew!" says Genji beginning to swelter, "Is it getting hot in here or what?"

She pulls around the neck of her top as if she is trying to let steam out.

"I was thinking that," agrees Jun, wiping her forehead.

Our attention switches away from poor Jess to the red glowing stone. Unwittingly, as we moved with Jess, we also moved closer towards the red stone which seems to be reacting to our presence by glowing brighter and, until now unnoticed, there is a definite rise in temperature in the cavern. The red stone is spinning, suspended above a cone shaped stone pillar about two metres in height, and the air around the stone is shimmering as if it is being cooked inside an invisible oven. It is just too high to reach, even if I was on Charlie's shoulders.

"What if we pile up the bones and make a ramp up?" I suggest.

"Sounds like a plan!" encourages Geo enthusiastically already kicking the bones into an uneven pile with his feet.

"I'm not so sure that we should be disturbing the bones, after all they are human bones. How would you like it? It feels wrong," doubts Jun.

"Oh, come on! We are underground, probably miles underground by now, there may be no way out, and there's a weird person who says there's evil down here that we can't even see sharing the same cave as us!" I exclaim with dismay.

"I see your point!" says Jun quickly overcoming her concerns and starting to help.

The temperature continues to rise as we stack the bones on top of each other, higher and higher.

While our attention is on reaching the stone, there's no sign of Jess. I suspect she is still nearby somewhere in the darkness, upset.

"Don't bother with the skulls, they just role straight back down the ramp!" advises Geo.

Quickly, I discover that the rib bones are quite sharp at the one end and require careful handling, but they do a good job of holding the other larger bones in place if you use them like pegs. Every so often, Geo decides to test the ramp. Each time he does he gets stuck because his legs start sinking into the bones, knee deep. Charlie suggests that Imp should be the one to test it because she's the lightest, but the same thing happens to her. Unbelievably we start to run out of decent sized bones, and we are still only about four fifths of the way up the cone shaped column which, frustratingly, would be high enough if Imp didn't keep sinking back down into the bones.

"What we need is a way of stopping us sinking," says Genji stating the obvious but the rest of us are now too hot and too tired to react.

"I have an idea. What if... what if we tie some of the bigger bones together and make a cross shape and tie them on to the bottom of someone's shoes? Like snow shoes!" Charlie suggests with a flash of inspiration.

"We've got nothing to tie them with," says Genji dismissing the idea.

"We *could* use our own shoe laces!" Geo is enjoying himself again and rising to the challenge.

It's not long before Charlie is wearing a new pair of cross-bone shoes each spanning about 40cm which will, we hope, spread his weight much more evenly than his normal shoes. He stands up unsteadily, wobbles and very nearly falls over - it is only his incredible counterbalancing skills that allows him to stay upright. As he walks, he looks comical, heavy, and uncoordinated like an old-style robot. I would laugh if I wasn't so exhausted in the roasting heat.

Holding his hands, Genji and Jun help Charlie to keep his balance as he walks towards our ramp of bones. Taking a deep breath, still held up the girls, he takes his first step onto the ramp of bones - it's awkward but the cross-bone shoes hold up well. The second step, then the third step. The angle of the ramp is very uneven despite our best attempts. Charlie overcomes this by stepping up sideways like a crab even though he finds this tricky at first.

"Hold on to your shoes and get ready to run for the ridge, you know what happened last time we got near a stone!" he announces, confident that he will be successful and pointing to the bottom of the spiral ridge. It is the only possible way out, unless we want to go back the way we came.

We are ready - expecting the cavern to flood at any second. From our viewpoint at ground level, it looks as though Charlie will easily be able to reach the spinning stone but when he stretches out his arm the stone spins off his hand leaving a stinging burn mark on his palm.

"Ow! It burnt me!" Undeterred, he calls down to the ten eyes watching, "Imp, pass me your cap, I might be able to use that to catch it!"

Cap in hand, Imp moves forward to Jun who is still standing closest to the ramp of bones - she hands her pride and joy over to Jun who reaches upwards and passes it to Charlie, who is crouching and stretching downward, as much as he dares, to avoid tumbling back down the bone ramp.

Charlie rights himself once more at the top of the ramp and in one sweeping motion scoops the spinning red stone out of the air, straight into the cap at the first attempt. Success! Making sure the scorching stone doesn't slip out of the cap, Charlie awkwardly scuttles his way down to the bottom of the bone ramp as fast as possible, expecting the cavern to start flooding at any moment. As soon as he reaches the bottom, he shakes off the cross-bone shoes and is ready to run to the ridge. Urgently, I grab each of them before running with Charlie, to join the others already safely at the bottom of the upward spiraling ledge, ready to escape.

This time, there is no sign of any flood water.

At the bottom of the spiral ledge, Charlie unravels Imp's cap to get a closer look at the red stone. It is no longer spinning and, daring to touch it again, Charlie finds that it has lost much of the heat that burnt him the first time he touched it. In the palm of his hand, the red stone glows warmly in the forgotten darkness of the cavern. Geo moves his blue stone closer. Together the stones glow even brighter as if they recognise each other. Meanwhile, I am busy untying the shoe laces that were holding the cross-bone shoes together and quickly pass the laces back to their owners.

"What happened to Jess?" asks Genji scanning the darkness around us for clues.

"She just vanished," I answer, feeling that maybe we can do more for her.

"How can she *just vanish*?" quizzes Jun.

"No idea, but she did!"

"Jess...Jess!" calls Imp.

"What are you doing?" Genji asks.

"Trying to find her, she might need our help."

"And exactly how can we help someone who we can't see?" Genji challenges sarcastically.

Imp's cheeks glow red with a mix of anger and embarrassment. Fortunately no one can see her reaction in the poorly lit cavern, they don't need to - the silent reply is enough.

To put Imp's mind at ease, Charlie and Geo decide to risk it and search the cavern for Jess. Initially they search together, but then they split up to cover more ground more speedily. There is no sign of Jess or any shadows on the cavern wall nor do they hear any more crunching bones sounds.

"Wonder what happened to her?" Geo whispers to no one in particular.

"I think she was shocked by the news we gave her. It took a huge effort to speak to us. Maybe it was too much for her," Imp sums up what the rest of us are thinking, as she adjusts her slightly scorched cap back on her head.

With all our shoe laces tied we are ready to crawl up the spiraling ledge leading into the black roof of the cavern - our only hope of escape.

"Well, we can't stay here forever, let's go!" Geo says looking upwards. He seems to be looking forward to the challenge of the climb.

"Not all the way up there!" gasps Genji in horror.

"No choice from where I'm standing! We can't go back, there's no other way out...so..." Geo replies, nodding his head upwards.

Genji knows he is right, unfortunately.

GREEN STONE

~~~

U neasily, Charlie leads the way, in a single file, with one hand holding his stone lighting the way ahead with a warm red glow. Genji and Jun follow him closely trailed by Geo with his blue light. I follow Imp at the back of the line just in case Jess returns, although I have no idea what I am going to say or do if she does. Our escape route quickly becomes too awkward to walk upright along so we are forced to crawl. From a distance, we must look like a line of ants heading off to forage for food. The rock ledge is jagged and uneven but feels solid and sturdy enough, it is securely attached to the cavern wall, dispelling my initial fears.Within ten minutes my knees are already complaining. We have only managed to crawl one full turn of the spiral, 360 degrees, so that we are now directly above the start of the ramp but approximately five metres higher. I notice that from this point onwards, the ledge starts to get more angled than before, tilting slightly downwards away from the cavern wall so that my left knee is slightly lower than my right knee as I crawl. This unsettling tilting gradually worsens the further we crawl up the ramp. If the angle of tilt continues to increase, it won't be long before we will have to stop or face the real possibility of slipping off and tumbling onto the sharp bones on the cavern floor below us.

We continue crawling painfully along.

Forwards and upwards.

Before long, it is difficult to work out exactly how far up we have climbed because the ground below has already faded and disappeared back into the dark shadows.

"Watch out here, it's very narrow!" warns Charlie from the front.

Doubt begins to enter my mind once again. The crawl is getting more and more precarious, but my real unspoken worry is what if, in the end, the ramp leads nowhere. What then?

Genji calls out from behind Charlie, "Hey! Stop a second! There's a gap in the rock wall here."

It is a thin, vertical opening not much more than 20cm wide at its widest point and about a metre high. Charlie was concentrating so hard on making sure the ramp did not unexpectedly stop or narrow again that he completely missed the crack in the wall as he passed it. We all halt in our tracks but can't really do much other than let Genji explore the gap while we wait. She presses her shoulder tight up against the rock and, with her arm at full stretch, delves into the space behind the gap as far as she could but, after a few minutes, it becomes obvious there is nothing there except she notices the rock inside is wet, with water streaming down the walls.

No way out and water - not a good combination!

We continue crawling on although Geo stops briefly to see if the rock wall will shimmer like before to indicate that he might be able to pass through it but there is no change, nothing but a cold lifeless rock face.

"Worth a try!" He says, sounding much more optimistic than I am, "We must be half way up the cavern wall by now."

That is the sort of news that the rest of us are not too happy to hear – it means we still have plenty of climbing to do but are still high enough up to be in real trouble if we slip off the ramp!

Bravely we keep going until, about half a turn further up the spiral, Charlie stops and says "There's a decent sized opening here. It's easily big enough to crawl through but I can't see anything from out here. You wait here and I'll slip inside for a better look."

"Be careful, remember what happened the last time you just went in!" Jun remembers Charlie climbing into the black opening back at our den.

"I will, don't you worry!" is Charlie's cheerful reply and he cautiously squeezes himself through the opening taking his stone with him, leaving the girls at the front in near darkness.

"What's it like in there? Is it high up? Is there anything to hold on to?" Genji rapidly fires questions nervously.

"It's like... there's a flat section right here. I'm going to try and put some weight on it before I step fully onto it...there...it feels like another cave, but I can't quite stand up. I can't see anything else here and there's no way out that I can see. If there's a way out I can't see it, and the walls are soaking wet...must be water nearby." Charlie gives us a running commentary as he surveys the space. "We could all just about fit in here, but that's about it! I can't see anything else...no stones."

I can sense the disappointment in his voice and another mention of water nearby fills me with dread. What if there's another flood? I am keen to keep crawling despite my aching knees.

While he is inside, using the light from his glowing red stone to investigate further, Jun notices a faint green tinge reflecting off the wetter rock directly above her head. It's so faint that the glow of Charlie's red stone must have swamped it as he had passed by. Now, she can just see it.

"I can see a green glow up there!" she says excitedly hoping she has found the way out and, maybe, another stone from the necklace.

Charlie sticks his head out of the opening and looks up into the darkness along with the rest of us.

"Let's keep going then!" I encourage from the back, with a sense of urgency and feeling that I'm missing out on all the excitement at the back.

"OK, OK, what's the rush all of a sudden?!" said Genji, who is far less keen to hurry especially as we gain more and more height.

"My knees are killing me!" I groan, "I'm sure their bleeding too! This ledge is rougher than sandpaper and the slant is just making it worse!"

"I know what you mean - not much further now!" Geo joins in, still optimistic that we will soon find the way out as long as we keep going. Imp is unusually quiet. Maybe she's still thinking about Jess; what it must be like to be trapped underground for years on your own, not knowing where your friends are.

Quickly Charlie re-joins us, and we continue painfully crawling onwards and upwards. The tilt of the rough ledge gets ever more dangerous and is compounded by a distinct narrowing of the ledge which worries me further. This section of the crawl seems endless. I grit my teeth. Salty stinging sweat runs into my eyes, but I can't wipe it away. I daren't lift my hands from the rock. From the hush that descends on us, I am in no doubt the others are feeling the same.

At last, much to everyone's relief, the ramp unexpectedly widens and flattens out beside what appears to be the entrance to another tunnel. There is just enough room for all of us to peer through the opening and investigate. From behind the others, I can make out a faint green glow, but it is deep down in the blackness below us. Jun was right! It must be another stone. It's impossible to make out anything else without stepping deeper inside the tunnel. Unsure how solid the floor is inside, Charlie and Geo slowly edge further forward to investigate. Standing on the very top of a wide flat rock, they hold their stones close together to maximise their combined light but even that does not penetrate the blackness; the gulf between us and the green stone.

One by one, we crawl deeper in and crowd together. We know we are very high up, almost in the roof of the new cavern, towering above the green glow. Moving further forward, with great care, Geo and Charlie notice a smooth dip in the rock ahead. From the top of the dip they notice it falls away very sharply so that only the very top section of the edge is visible, and the rest quickly disappears into the darkness of the main cavern below.

I feel a strange chill cold from behind me, turn my head and glance behind us to see a pair of yellow and orange eyes staring right back at me. Then they are gone.

"Look those eyes!" I shout out to the others, pointing at nothing - the eyes have already vanished. The others turn towards me and look where I am pointing only to see nothingness staring back at them, but they all know exactly what I'd seen.

"I wonder what those eyes mean, who do they belong too?" poses Imp. No-one has an answer for her.

Meanwhile, Jun daringly moves close to Geo and Charlie who are at the brink of the dipping ledge. Though impossible to see very far, she looks down and running her hands over the surface says, "Reminds me of the death slide at the park. The rock here feels smooth, but the drop is vertical!"

Genji joins her and adds, "What if it really is a *death* slide! *Death* being the key word."

"There's only one way to find out! Who's going first?!" asks Geo grinning and treating it like a fairground ride.

"You are joking. I'm not going down there! We can still continue on the spiral ramp, we don't know where that leads to, yet."

Charlie joins in, "We might find the way out or even another way to reach the stone. Looks too risky to me!"

"That ledge outside is getting more and more dangerous!" I remind them rubbing my knees and elbows.

"Oh, and I suppose jumping off this ledge because Jun says it looks like a death slide is less dangerous! Look! You can't even see the bottom of it. You don't know if it goes all the way down or what else is down there!" Genji isn't keen at all to continue climbing but is in no doubt that Geo's idea is worse.

"I know, why don't I lean over the edge with you guys holding my legs and see how far it goes down?" suggests Geo as a compromise.

"Worth a try," I agree, still keen to avoid the ramp again if at all possible.

"I vote we continue going up the ledge - at least, if the ledge doesn't go anywhere then we can always come back and risk this," Genji argues but it's too late.

"OK. Ready when you are!" shouts Geo who is already lying

flat on his belly with his face staring over the chasm edge. With arms stretching out in front he holds his blue stone tightly hoping that he will get a better view of whatever is down there. Together, Charlie and Jun grab one leg while Imp and I hold the other. Geo squirms and shuffles forward as far as he can until he's being held completely upside down by the four of us.

"Keeps dropping all the way down as far as I can see, I reckon you can slide down," Geo huffs back to us. "Can you ... let me down any further?"

"That's ... about ... it, I think!" replies Charlie under the strain.

"I'll just…Oh! No!"

"What?! What's up?" asks Charlie who, like the rest of us, can't see over the ridge because we are holding tightly onto Geo's feet and legs.

It sounds to me as if a piece of the rock face has broken away and is clattering and rattling as it bounces rock on rock and rolls to an eventual stop on the cavern floor far below. But it isn't.

"Pull me up. Pull me up! Quick!"

We all tug hard and pull at Geo's legs. Within seconds he is back on his belly on the ledge with a red face caused by the blood rushing to his head.

He lifts himself up, turns over and sits facing us. He grins.

"I have some good news, and some bad news."

"What is it?" asks Genji impatiently, "What's happened?"

"The good news is that I'm sure the rock goes all the way down, but it looks really steep and I don't know what's at the bottom."

"That's not *so* bad." says Jun cheerfully.

"*That's not* the bad news. I dropped the blue stone and it's down there too - it just slipped out of my hand. Didn't you hear it?"

"That's what that rattling was!" I say checking his hands to see if it is one of Geo's bad jokes but there is no sign of his stone anywhere.

"Idiot!" says Jun crossly. "You are such an idiot!"

A thoughtful silence falls over us as each of us assesses our new situation. We need to get all the stones if we are going to remake the necklace. Now the blue stone and quite possibly the green stone are out of reach down below us.

"Well, at least that makes our decision easier!" I say, "Now we *have* to go down there and get both stones. Geo says we can slide all the way down to the green stone. I say we go down."

"There is one other thing," says Geo thoughtfully, "once we go down. I don't know that we'll be able to get back up. I can't tell for sure, but it looks too steep and too smooth to easily climb back up. We'll have to find another way."

"What if we split into two groups? Imp and I can keep going up the ramp and see if it leads anywhere, and you can go down there." suggests Charlie who could see that Imp is not keen to go down any 'Death Slide'.

"I don't think splitting up is a good idea." disagrees Genji, "What if you get into trouble?"

"We should only go down, one at a time so that there'll be someone up here if we need help. I'll go first...I don't mind," Geo is very keen to get his blue stone back, "there's probably another way out down there anyway."

"You don't know that. And how can they help from up here? There's no rope or anything!" Genji is not impressed.

"It's not about who goes first, is it? It's about getting the stones isn't it? We *have* to get them," reminds Geo.

"There, you see, we have to go. Geo reckons it goes all the way down. I bet there's a way out too. Let's do it!" I am already persuaded.

Charlie and Imp are the least convinced. Jun isn't very happy either and argues once more, "We can still all go up the ramp ledge and see what's up there... we can always come back if it doesn't lead anywhere."

"Yeah, but what if we can't turn around...you know how narrow it's getting...we'll be stuck there forever." I voice my concern about the worsening narrowing and tilting of the ledge. Looking at the faces around me I can see that everyone else is worried about that too.

"And we'll be down to only one stone and one light... it was bad enough before with two!"

Charlie repeats, "There's no choice - we must split up. We'll go up the ramp! You go down there, if you want to, you'll have two stones...if the ramp doesn't lead anywhere, we'll come back here and try to help. Who knows, there may be a way out down there!"

"How will we know that you're OK?" asks Genji.

"We'll be fine," says Charlie confidently, "it probably doesn't go anywhere anyway."

Charlie, Jun, and Imp wish us good luck and return to the spiral ramp leaving us in darkness with only the faint glow from the distant blue and green stones far below. It isn't much but it is enough.

QUAKE

~~~

Having the only stone, Charlie leads their crawling procession up the narrowing and increasingly tilting ledge; Jun follows with Imp close behind. The red glow of the light seems to be dimmer than they remembered, now that they are apart from the others, especially away from the blue stone.

Charlie stops suddenly.

Something has changed.

He can feel a faint cool shifting of the air ahead of him.

"What is it?" asks Jun.

"Not sure, something feels wrong... I can feel..." Charlie starts to answer but trailed off.

"It's Jess," says Imp, "she's showing us the way."

"How can you be sure?" asks Jun, "Why should she want to help us?"

A rasping voice shook the air around them, "You must leave this evil place immediately, or you will end up like me - follow!"

"We are still searching for the stones of the necklace, we can't leave yet!" answers Charlie defiantly.

"And the others are still in the other cavern. We have to get back to them!" adds Jun.

"You have no choice! It is already too late!" Jess replies hurriedly, "The evil is upon you!"

As she speaks, there's a low rumbling from far down below followed by earth trembling echoes. Rocks from high above us, fall past and crash down on the cavern floor, crushing the old bones. The rumbling gradually grows louder and louder until it becomes a painful, deafening crescendo, filling and vibrating the dome shaped roof and the ledge where they are crawling.

Looking down, they can hear the spiraling ramp ledge is starting to break away from the cavern walls from the bottom upwards in large chunks of rock, each collapsing heavily on top of each other in the darkness below. Gradually their narrow escape route is being destroyed as if being eaten and spat out by some force intent on destruction. There is no turning back to the cavern below now but, more urgently, there will be nothing to crawl on, no ledge at all, within minutes. Jess is right, there is no time left for discussions. Finally understanding their danger, Charlie urgently starts crawling upwards. The rest follow immediately behind.

"This way! Follow!" rasps Jess trying to help.

Charlie huffs under the new exertion and mutters to Jun, "Would be easier to follow her if we could see her! Anyway, I thought she said there's no way out."

Jess makes sure that, even though Charlie cannot see her, he at least can hear her by maintaining a running commentary as she expertly leads the way. "The Black Mist has gone...it hid the way out from me. That's right... over this dip...past this jutting out rock...nearly there...now...turn in here..." Her straining voice is gradually being drowned out by the increasing volume of noise of the falling rocks behind them.

Imp and Jun scramble close behind Charlie. At last Charlie sees the opening Jess is guiding them towards, it is not far ahead but the roaring sound of cracking stone behind them sounds like a train rushing towards them, getting louder and louder, making them panic and fumble as they crawl urgently upwards.

With relief, they fall into the relative safety of the passage-way where they steady themselves against the rock walls to avoid tumbling and falling over as the whole cavern shudders and shakes violently around them.

"Go with God's speed!" Jess rasps her farewell.

"You're not coming with us?" notices Imp as she clings on to the shaking rock face in the passageway.

"I cannot leave this place…go before the same is true for you!" Those are the last words they hear Jess utter, before the thundering and crashing rocks drown her out completely. Splinters of rock and dust fill the tunnel entrance. Then silence.

When the dust settles about them, they realise that large boulders have sealed the way back into the cavern.

Now there is no way back to save the others.

DOWN THE DEATH SLIDE

~~~

"Ok then, decision made!" says Geo getting himself ready to go down the death slide.

A second later it he is gone.

"Whoa - oo – ah - ahh!!!" His shrieking voice echoes upwards as Geo speeds downwards and is completely engulfed by the darkness.

Before he knows it, Geo has slid down to the bottom of the cavern.

Although I can't see his face, I know he is grinning and that he has his blue stone back because there's a blue light hovering around in the air as if someone has picked up a torch and is waving it from side to side.

"Phew! Now that was a death slide and a half!" Geo's excited voice reverberates back up to us, still at the top.

"Right, I'm ready!" I shuffle forward and sit on the edge of the darkness, heart racing and the palms of my hands sweating.

"Hold on! Before you come down." shouts up Geo urgently trying to explain, "The green stone is hanging in mid-air, suspended somehow, just before you get to the bottom of the slide... here...you might be able to grab it on the way down! You can't reach it once you get all the way down."

"He is joking, isn't he?" I ask Genji who is next to me looking down over the edge.

"Say that again!" I shout back.

"You'll have to grab the green stone on the way down, otherwise it's impossible to reach," Geo gathers himself together and explains, "When you come down, you pass under it, close enough to touch it but you'll only have a fraction of a second to grab it!"

"He isn't joking," whispers Genji in my ear.

"What else is down there?" I ask, not sure if I am delaying the inevitable or genuinely interested.

Silence answers my question, but the blue light continues moving around below. "Looks empty down here!" shouts up Geo a minute later.

"What about a way out?" I ask, still delaying.

"Can't see anything! There's no way you can climb back up, that's for sure, the rock's too steep and too smooth... there's nothing to grip onto!" echoes back Geo's answer.

"We can't leave him down there on his own, can we?" points out Genji as if she can read my mind.

"Right here goes!" I push myself off the edge and aim for the green light below in the darkness using what very little control I have to steer my fall. I reach out to grab the green stone as I slide underneath. I touch it with my fingertips but can't close my hand around it before I zip passed and land in a muddled heap on the cavern floor, empty handed.

Meanwhile the green stone smoothly glides diagonally away from its initial position under the force of my contact but, as if attached to an elastic band and on the end of a pendulum, starts homing back. It continues to smoothly move gently to and fro, around the spot where it was suspended, before finally coming to rest in its original position as if nothing has happened.

"Sorry Geo," echoing my disappointment.

"Hey, no probs... you watch, Genji'll get it!" replies Geo as he offers his hand to pull me up, "C'mon Genji you can do it!" he shouts up to her confidently.

It is true that Genji is more agile than me; that might go in her favour.

"You might need to use both hands; it seemed to move away from my hand as I reached for it!" I advise from the darkness down below.

Seconds later there's a swish and a whoosh of air, then the sight of the soles of boots quickly followed by the rest of Genji flashing into view. At the very last moment, she arches her body and pushes herself away from the smooth surface of the slide and glides in mid-air, easily clasping her hands around the green stone and gracefully landing with a tumbling roll on the floor of the cavern.

We have the third stone!

Suddenly, from high above us, we can hear the thickening rumbling of falling rocks like an earthquake; the whole cavern starts to shake violently, and we are swept off our feet, falling onto the cavern floor, unable to stand back up.

"Whoah! What the...?" exclaims Geo as he struggles to stay on his feet. His voice is drowned out by the thunderous noise of the shaking movement all around us.

Expertly, Genji regains her balance and stands up holding firmly onto her green stone, only to be shaken off balance once again by another, even more powerful, shock wave. As she tumbles, Genji nearly loses grip of her stone as the ground violently shudders again and again. She is brutally bounced against the rough stone wall of the cavern. From the look on her face, I can see that she is hurt. This time she stays down, nursing her left shoulder. I can't stand up to go and help her.

The cavern fills with thick dust from high above us as the whole place rocks wildly for what seems like an eternity, before the tremors finally weaken and gradually fade to a halt.

I check myself for injuries. My whole body is caked in grey brown dust but, much to my relief, I am only bruised on my left side where I fell.

Geo stands up, unsteadily at first, checks himself over too. Stood up, he looks like a stone monument. As he moves, layers of dust tumble off him.

Genji remains exactly where she had been thrown, unmoving, covered in her own blanket of dust.

Although the shaking has stopped, I still feel unbalanced and breathing in the dust makes me cough and splutter. With care, I cross the cavern floor to Genji. She still has the green stone clasped in her right hand, but her left arm is dangling limply at her side. Immediately, I think it is broken.

"Genji... are you OK?" I ask, concerned but already knowing the answer.

"I can't move my arm!" she chokes tearfully, "Look!"

She tries to move her arm, but it remains completely stationary.

"Can you stand if I help you up?" I suggest, trying to sound as though there's nothing to worry about.

"I guess so," she answers bravely, clearly in a lot of pain.

Gently and slowly, Geo and I help her back onto her feet. She fights the pain through clenched teeth. In silence we turn and look upwards toward the cavern entrance high above us, where the awful noise and falling debris had originated; gathering our thoughts. What could have happened to the others? We sense that there is no possibility that they would have been able to safely cling onto the spiraling ramp ledge throughout all that violent shaking. If they fell, it was a long way down into the darkness below. Are they even alive? At the very least, they will be badly injured.

To take his mind off these dark thoughts, Geo starts to look around the cavern walls for an exit. Every so often he checks the unyielding cavern walls, secretly hoping that a section of the wall might shimmer like before, allowing him to pass through again and, maybe, even get some help. Meanwhile Genji determinedly straightens her back, lifts her head up and stands tall before joining Geo in the search for the way out. The new green stone is brighter, as is the blue stone, as she nears Geo, but this makes little difference to the cold gloom that descends over us.

We search the cavern; everywhere the light can reach. I try to climb back up the death slide, but it is useless - even if I manage to reach the top, the entrance will most likely be blocked by the fallen rocks.

Eventually the cruel enormity of our situation begins to sink in.

No way back up.

There is no way out.

The others are not going to return to save us and we can't save them.

The cavern is now our prison.

DISLOCATED

~~~

Refusing to be beaten, we frantically search every nook and cranny of the cavern again and again, but it is no use. We are surrounded by tons of rock in all directions. Genji's arm is still causing her discomfort but she continues to put on a brave face. I admire her for that and wish I could help her in some way. I rip my sleeve off at the shoulder and make a sling for her but when we try to put her arm in the sling, it just makes it even more uncomfortable. In the end, she is relieved to simply sit down and rest for a while.

Finally, we slump down together in silence.

Finally, out of ideas.

Finally, out of hope.

From out of nowhere, as if answering our silent desperation, there is a quiet crackle to the left of us. Another louder crackle follows, this time joined by an incredibly bright electric blue flash with the strong smell of burning in the air...but there is nothing to burn. I try to shield my eyes from the stinging light but before I can, it vanishes leaving nothing except an orange glow on my retina like a sparkler on fireworks night. I try to blink the line of light away, but it seems to be burned forever in my brain.

An instant later it returns, this time burning and crackling more intensely. The intertwined bright lines of electric blue flashes, like metre length bolts of lightning, twist and turn around each other, growing until they become a person sized shimmering shape of a squashed hexagon, taller than it is wide.

The fizzling shape takes on a life of its own and slowly shifts closer to where we are sitting, fading then flashing back brighter than before. As it deliberately moves along the cavern floor towards us, it hums and hisses but then even that noise is drowned out by the crackling and fizzing of the sparks electrifying and ionizing the air around us.

I hold my hands half in front of my eyes to shield them from the powerful brilliant bursts of the pure energy. The shape comes to a halt two metres away from us and holds its position, fizzing and crackling. I can feel the welcome heat for the first time, but half expect it to burst into flames at any instant, so I stay back.

From within the centre of the shape, a face appears and then another. At first, the faces are looking away at something to the side of them and are unrecognizable. Then, as if realising they are 'on air', both faces turn and stare directly at us. It is Mr. and Mrs. Boyd, Charlie's parents! At first, they look at us blankly as if they are unseeing then, as if a fog has lifted, they seem to see and recognise us.

"Charlie!" calls Charlie's mother, looking from side to side, with concern, "Charlie!"

"He's not here," I reveal, "he went with the others."

"We don't have time Carmella, we must act quickly!" Charlie's father interrupts urgently and points to the centre of the strange flexing fizzing frame.

"Listen, I want you to jump into the middle of the shape, straight towards us. Quickly! We're running out of time!"

All three of us stare back at Charlie's father's face in complete disbelief. Mr. Boyd clearly had not thought this through; we will surely get electrocuted or burned alive if we even touch the shape.

As if he can read out thoughts, Charlie's father calmly continues, "Make sure you don't touch the shape frame itself and you'll be fine…get as close as you can and then jump in – aim at the middle and you'll be safely here before you know it!"

Both Charlie's parent's faces back away as if they need to give us space and we get a glimpse, a flickering image, of the darkened room that they are stood in; they beckon us to come to them.

"C'mon! Quick as you can. There isn't any time to waste!" repeats Mr. Boyd.

At first none of us move, but then Genji boldly edges forward and, without a word, gets as close as she can and leaps directly at the middle of the burning shape. As she does, she is completely engulfed by a terrific orange flash that seems to spin around between her and the frame of the shape. Despite the raw blinding brightness, it's clear she has vanished. Blackness returns to the centre of the burning shape which is swiftly replaced by an image of the room; this time with Genji too. She has fallen and is pushing herself back up with her good arm. Mrs. Boyd rushes towards her to help her stand up.

Regardless of this heartening sight, I am still reluctant to move any closer to the crackling shape.

Geo turns to me and asks, "What are you waiting for? Go on!"

"You go!" I challenge.

Geo, seeing that I am worried, turns to me and says, "We'll jump together...c'mon!"

He grabs my arm and pulls me closer to the bright heat of the shape.

"C'mon! What have we got to lose? Let's do it...can't be any worse than another earthquake!"

We both move cautiously forward.

Geo counts, "One. Two. Three...Go!"

We jump.

As we move through the air it feels as though our surroundings have lost all substance, as if we are falling through thin yellow jelly that hasn't quite set. Everything slows down and strange sepia coloured objects float past us or us past them; it is difficult to tell. Then, abruptly, we land awkwardly, cushioned only by the thick carpet in Charlie's parent's parlour. For a few seconds Geo and I lie there as a bundle of legs and arms staring up at the ceiling with a circle of stranger's faces staring straight back down at us.

I turn to look back in the direction we had jumped from. Hovering only centimetres above the carpet, is an identical replica hexagonal shape fizzing and crackling with electric blue flashes to the one we left behind in the cavern. Looking back through the fizzing shape, I can only see the blackness of the cavern which had become our prison. It lasts for another few seconds and then is suddenly gone, only the bitter burning smell remains with us in the room.

Hurriedly, Charlie's mother and father help us both back onto our feet and look us up and down for any injuries. Shakily we stand, stunned, struggling to comprehend exactly what has happened. One good thing was clear - we have escaped the cavern but now we have some very serious and worried faces staring at us.

"Well done! Good work Shadrack, how long before we can start searching for the others?" asks Mr. Boyd.

The reply to Charlie's father's question is a silent, exhausted, red-faced glare from a stranger sat at a table at the far side of the room. Shadrack is a strong stocky solid man but evidently, whatever his part in the search for us was, it demanded a lot of effort and had taken a huge toll on him.

"Great work! I know you'll do what you can!" Charlie's father encourages.

Charlie's mother comes over to me and asks about Charlie, "You said that he'd gone with the others...where did he go exactly and who are the others?"

"Charlie, Jun and Imp..." as I speak, I notice the room is silent and everyone is listening intently to my every word. It is very unnerving, but I continue, "... they decided to go further up the spiral ledge to see if there was another way out."

"Where is this spiral ledge? Do you know if they found a way?" asks Charlie's father in quick succession.

"It's hard to say exactly," I reply cautiously careful not to mention the massive shaking of the earthquake and the awful sounds that we had heard from the direction the others had gone, "I'm sure they will have found a way!" I lie.

"Why didn't you stay together? You would all be here now, safe!" chips in Mrs. Boyd, visibly concerned and upset.

"Now, now, I'm sure they did the best they could under very unusual and trying circumstances!" soothes Charlie's father putting his arm around his wife's shoulders to comfort her.

Charlie's mother turns away to hide her tears. Another person, I have never seen before, hands her a handkerchief, beautifully embroidered with a red rose.

"You were very brave...all of you!" reassures another woman's kindly voice noticing Genji nursing her sore arm, "Here, let me look at your arm."

The large woman gives the impression that she knows a thing or two about injuries to arms. She moves confidently towards Genji who is still clutching the stone in her hand, the faint green glow concealed by her fingers.

"Does this hurt?"

She pinches Genji's fingers and then her lower arm. It is obvious that it does hurt.

"Mm...can you lift your hand?" she continues.

Genji can't move it a centimetre without moving her whole upper body.

"Do you mind?" It isn't really a question. The woman expertly feels the top and back of her shoulder.

"Ah ha...thought as much... dislocated shoulder...."

She pauses as if in thought but, with amazing strength and surprising speed, she quickly yanks the arm down across Genji's front and in a sharp lifting and twisting motion she pushes the elbow upwards and back. As she does it there's a cracking sound and a dull popping as the shoulder relocates itself back in its socket.

"There! Put some ice on it and you'll be fine...might ache for a while!"

During the process Genji is a model patient but is hugely relieved to have her arm relocated; gently at first, she tests the range of movement of her arm. Just then Genji's parents arrive and make a huge fuss over her although also wanting news of Jun. When they ask about Jun, Genji has no useful answer and chokes back the tears.

When Charlie's mother returns with the ice pack, it is obvious that she is very agitated about Charlie's whereabouts. She checks with Shadrack one more time, but he has no news but then her attention rests on the green glowing stone in Genji's hand.

"My darling! Where did you get that?!" she quizzes and points to the green stone.

Genji quickly clenches her hand back firmly over the stone and withdraws her hand from view as everyone in the room spins round to look. Reluctantly, Genji changes her mind and holds the green stone out for all to see. Each adult in the room appears surprised, even in awe of what Genji is holding in her hand.

"It's one of the stones! How is this possible?" asks one.

"My child, where did you get this?" enquires a haughty lady's voice from behind us.

"From that last cavern, where you found us," answers Genji, surprised and wondering why the stone is causing so much interest.

"Then that's where it belongs!" storms another voice fiercely.

"Calm...calm! Jennifer," replies Mr. Boyd who had remained silent up to this point, "I think we need to take advice on this new turn of events. Genji, you hold on to the stone and keep it safe, will you?" He smiles and gently closes Genji's fingers around the green stone. Genji drops her head and looks down at the object that has caused so much commotion and nods 'yes'.

Geo is not sure if now is the right time, but he can't resist the limelight, so he stands next to Genji holding out his hand with the blue stone in his palm.

"We found this one first, just after we found Charlie!" he says excitedly not thinking about what he was saying.

"Found Charlie!" Charlie's mother interrupts, "Where was he? Was he lost?"

"Oh! He went into the first cavern and nearly drowned, but he was fine, we found him at the bottom of the hole," answers Geo, too quickly again and without any thought.

"What hole?!" asks another voice.

Suddenly, we are inundated by a flood of questions from all sides of the room.

"Wait! ...Wait everyone! Wait! These young people have had an exhausting time. Maybe, if we give them some space, and time, they will tell us what happened from the beginning," Mr. Boyd reassures everyone and saves us from the onslaught.

Mrs. Boyd finds some comfortable upright chairs for us to sit on.

Severely shaken but hugely relieved to be safe, we sit down and tell the attentive audience what had happened to us. We sense that this is not the time to leave out any details. The rights and wrongs of what we have done would come later.

Unfortunately, what we have to say does very little to comfort Jun's and Charlie's parents. As we speak, they keep a constant eye on Shadrack in the hope that he might have located the others. Shadrack looks totally exhausted. Both sets of parents begin to fear the worst as, yet again, he looks up and shakes his head despairingly. He takes another swift drink from his glass, grumbles to himself, as if he is missing something; an important fact, the key to the puzzle, which he can use to find the others. Why can he not find them? He knows he has searched everywhere below Holdwood - where could they be? Unless they are dead...he wouldn't be able to find them if they are...but he refuses to believe that...he would have sensed that but there is something strange down there. He can sense that too.

NO TURNING BACK

~~~

C harlie climbs out of the cave tunnel into a cloudless moonlit night followed closely by Imp and then Jun, panting from the exertion but extremely relieved to be breathing fresh air. At first, the chill breeze is refreshing against the cheeks, but their dust covered, sweat soaked shirts offer no protection against the cold and they start to shiver.

Even though they are desperate to find help for the others, it is much too dark and dangerous to risk moving far away from the cave entrance despite the bright silvery light of the near full-moon. Exhausted and in need of a rest, they sit down and huddle together in the safety of the cave entrance, eventually falling into an uncomfortable, restless sleep.

In the hazy early morning light, they immediately see that they had made the right decision not to venture from the cave entrance. They discover that they are extremely high up, look-ing down on a small, lonely, sea-filled cove with impossibly steep cliff walls to the left and right. The rocks ahead are uneven with deep black cavernous gaps between many of them, even in the light of the new day it looks like a perilous descent.

From their lofty vantage point, the choice before them is simple: impossible ascent or dangerous descent; they stand up and stretch their aching limbs and, with few words, start their climb downwards. Every so often, they come up against a series of tall column rocks that jut upwards as if they have been shot out of the earth forming a barrier, like prison bars, forcing them to change direction each time they stumble across them.

They continue the awkward downward trek. Every step is painful but after the previous day's crawling through low roofed caves and tunnels, it is a tremendous relief just to be stood completely upright. Eventually, they manage to weave a route down to the rocky water's edge. The sea smoothly rolls innocently inwards, almost reaching the rocks on which they stand, before gently rolling back into the vast sea.

Charlie surveys the rock bay and steep cliffs that surround it, in the forlorn hope that there might be an obvious pathway to walk or climb to the next bay along the coastline which he thinks he vaguely recognises. If he is right, they could get back to safety and get help, but he'd only ever seen the coastline from the sea when he'd sailed alongside his father.

As they continue to search around them, Imp notices that the sea level is rising and that the tide is coming in. Each new wave slithers a little further onto the rocky shore with certain, relentless inevitability.

"If we are not careful, we could be trapped!" worries Jun.

"We can always climb back up the way we came down," reassures Imp, disappointedly thinking that once more they have come so far, just to be thwarted again.

"I can't see any other choice...we're going to have to swim for it! You wait here... I'll go first, I bet the next bay will be just around that rock!" Charlie points out in the direction of the last few rocks jutting out into the sea on the right.

"There won't be enough time!" answers Imp full of concern, "If we wait for you, the sea will already have us pinned back up against the cliff edge and we'll get thrown onto the rocks... we'd be better off going now, all of us...at least we can help each other as we go!"

Jun nods her agreement. She is a strong swimmer anyway and, even against the tide, knows that she can cover the short distance.

Surprisingly calmly, they bravely swim out against the incoming thrusts of the writhing waves. Making good progress, they swim confidently, bobbing up and down slowly at first, but just as they near the edge of the rocks they are aiming for a set of fierce waves swiftly drags them all off course, wrenching them backwards. They swim even harder. Imp's arms begin to tire under the extra workload. She starts to noticeably lag behind, but her gritty determination shines through and she keeps going.

The three swimmers manage to get back on track and make good progress despite their aching limbs. Then, one by one, they start drifting steadily backwards against the direction of their stroke. They are gripped by another, even more powerful, rip-current which sucks them outwards into the open sea, further and further away from the rocks that they are aiming for. Desperately, they try to fight the strong rip-current before realising it is useless. They are caught in its grip. Relentlessly, they are propelled further and faster towards a tall circle of huge grey-black, monolith-like, stone columns. They appear similar to those that had barred their way as they had climbed down to the water's edge, but these are jutting vertically from out of the sea depths in a closed circle like an immoveable massive towering Stonehenge. Each tremendous column looks rooted to the spot, unflinching against the constant onslaught of the powerful sea waves crashing against them. Absentmindedly, Imp thinks it looks like the old wooden crab trapping cage she noticed back at the harbour-side but, if this is a trap, this one would be for ancient sea monsters! If she wasn't so exhausted, she would have laughed at herself.

Luckily the rip-current drags the three closer together, but simultaneously and perilously, towards the towering stone columns. Before they know it, they are trapped inside; caged by the circle of jutting out columns of rock, some are smooth while others look razor sharp with jagged edges.

They search for a way out, but they are in a precarious position and completely at the mercy of the rip-current and the strong waves of the incoming sea.

Gradually, centimetre by centimetre, they are drawn towards the open middle of the cage. As they are dragged closer and closer to the centre, they find it harder and harder to swim. As if realising it has won, the sea changes around them. The water feels thick like syrup. The air above them falls quiet and eerily still. The sea clings to their clothes and skin making any movement difficult. Attempts to break free and swim to safety are sluggish and ponderous; slow motion. The three are sucked even closer together while simultaneously the clouds in the early morning sky respond by darkening thunderously above their heads leaving them gripped in a strange half-darkness. Seconds later, they are surrounded in swirling vale of darkness, a Black Mist.

From within the unnatural stillness, they hear a single sea-gull squawk menacingly from its high perch on the top of one of the rock columns, like a warning. All around them the fierce waves are crashing against the rock columns, but in the middle the water stays calm and thickly serene about them.

They sluggishly hold out their arms and reach out to steady each other. In his left-hand, Charlie still holds his red stone as well as Imp's hand. Together, they make a ring of their own inside the outer ring of encircling rock columns, supported only by the treacly water, suspended like flies in a spider's web, unable to escape the deadly grip of the venomous sea.

Imp is shattered and gratefully receives the support from Charlie and Jun but still manages to gasp out between desperate breaths, "Great idea!" she continues and mimics exactly Charlie's words, "It'll be just around that rock…. Now what genius?!"

Charlie doesn't reply.

He has no answer.

There is no escape.

Black storm clouds rapidly approach, gathering ominously all around them. It is as if the Black Mist has been lying in wait for this moment, hunting them out, and now they are completely trapped, it is ready to unleash its angry hatred on them. Rain starts to fall heavily and is drumming hard on the thick water about them. Imp's head briefly dips under the water, Charlie, and Jun struggle to pull her back up but in doing so, they both sink themselves, deeper into the syrup as if they are being swallowed in quicksand. The storm crackles with hard thunder above them as if it too knows that this is the end.

Just for an instant the three spontaneously think the same thought, as if they are one. It's the image of dry land, somewhere where they can stand on terra-firma. Instantly, the air around them starts to swirl, slowly at first but then with increasing force like a whirlwind. As the air spins, it sucks up the sea water around them like a vertical spinning tube. From inside, the spinning walls take on a solid appearance as both water and air compress together becoming more densely packed with each second under the extreme centrifugal pressure, like thousands of marbles in a high-speed spin. The eerie silence returns. Engulfing them, blocking out the thunder still raging high above them.

The syrupy water that grips them, is slowly but steadily, being sucked towards the spinning wall surrounding them, draining away.

It is Jun who is first to notice that they are slowly dropping downwards, like in an elevator to the ground floor, and the dark sky is drifting up away from them. At last, she senses something hard beneath her tiptoed feet. She is standing, with the others, on solid rock! They stand still, bound together, hand in hand, ring within ring, silent.

Charlie is the first to react, seizing the opportunity he quickly breaks the circle and moves carefully toward the spinning wall of water where he has spotted a slim opening between two rocks at its base. He threads himself through being careful not to lose his footing. Imp follows, easily slipping under and calls for Jun to hurry. Leaving the whirling tube behind, they find themselves instantly exposed to the sharp claws of the ice-cold rain scratching at their skin and the blast of the whipping west wind piercing through to the bone. Trying to find the least dangerous route, Charlie continues over the slippery rocks towards the nearest cliff face which will offer them some shelter, checking every now and then that the others are close by.

As she joins Charlie at the cliff face, Imp gasps exhaustedly, "What's going on? What just happened? Where are we?"

"No idea!" replies Charlie trying to take it all in himself, "It was when we held each other, that's when it started!"

"We're *here*... I mean... it's the *same* place!" chirps in Jun, "Look! It's the same place *but* the water's gone... *all* the water. Look, there's the cave entrance, way up there!"

"It can't be," says Charlie, "you'd never be able to get up there...it as if the sea level has dropped...way down!"

Imp glances around her, he's right... it is as obvious as it is impossible!

Like a wakeup call, the biting wind gnarls, and snarls around them once more. It is as if the storm is challenging them saying 'Get back to where you belong! What have you done? You shouldn't be here! Get back!' as if it knows that this is all wrong. Unbalanced.

In silence, they huddle and shiver together.

"We can't stay here for long, we'll freeze!" declares Charlie. "I know..." he pauses to gather his thoughts, "if we are where we were, we can make it 'round to the other cove! We'll be able to get there by foot now!"

"Yeah! Haven't I heard that idea before?" replies Imp sarcastically with a little mischievous, Geo like, grin.

"Good idea!" says Jun backing Charlie up, "Better wait until this storm calms down a bit though."

They all peer out from the meagre protection of the cliff face. As they do, thunder cracks once more in the dark sky above them and the heavy rain continues to thump hard on the rocky ground splashing their feet with freezing water.

"Oow! What was that?" Jun jumps up quickly shaking her foot, "That crab just pinched my foot!"

"Our den is much better than this!" adds Imp fondly trying to raise spirits, "And a lot dryer! What we need is Geo to get some tarpaulin for us!"

Jun and Charlie smile thinly but struggle to join in, besides the thought of Geo just reminded Imp how concerned she is for her brother.

"Might have to wait here for days for this storm to stop! We're *already* wet...let's just go! We need to get help for the others," suggests Jun impatiently.

"Yeah, but it's freezing! That wind's evil!" Charlie is reluctant to leave the protection of the rock shelter.

They sit huddled together for a few seconds longer before Charlie agrees in desperation, "OK, let's get out of here! C'mon!"

They squelch through seaweed as they climb over the wet rocks. Surprisingly, it only takes them a few minutes to move passed the rocky point that they had so desperately struggled towards and failed to swim around moments before.

Disappointingly, as they round the point and get their first good look at the new bay. There is no visible escape route to be seen, as Charlie had hoped. Just more cliffs with another rocky outcrop jutting even further out from the shoreline than the one that they had just come around.

Again, they fight onwards against the bitterly cold wind; biting and pushing them backwards. Each step forward is hard won; an elemental battle. With grit and determination, they finally round the awkward outcrop of rock leaving the previous bay behind them and reaching the next cove along the coastline. By now Imp is being dragged along by Charlie and Jun.

The towering, rugged cliffs before them are cold and uninviting. The storm winds continue to howl their disapproval. Above them the thick black clouds still hang low and the freezing rain continues to heave down on them as if they are still being stalked by the Black Mist. The rock they are currently standing on should be completely submerged and hidden by the sea. It is only exposed by the unnaturally low sea level.

Imp is bitterly cold and starts shaking visibly. Despite this, she is the one who first hears the distinct rush of tidal water from the seaward direction.

"The tide's coming in!" she exclaims, "We'll be trapped here if we can't find the way out! Quick!"

Charlie turns towards the sound of rushing water. The tide is coming in. Fast. So fast that it threatens to cut them off completely, leaving them stranded and at the mercy of the crashing sea once more. It is as if the sea is trying to return to its rightful level, where it knows it should be; moving towards its own equilibrium, to be in balance, fighting back against the strange unnatural forces that recently disturbed it. In the distance, the spinning tube of water is noticeably slowing and losing its powerful grip on the ocean around it; gradually sinking back into the sea, allowing the water to return, refilling the rock beds around it, and taking away their only means of escape.

Already the rising sea is devouring the exposed seabed behind them, soon they will have no rock to stand on. Instinctively they run towards the higher rocks on the shoreline and closer to the cliff face. The sea water seethes and swells again already swallowing the ground that they had walked across just minutes before, completely cutting them off from the other cove.

They are blocked off, sealed into the new bay.

There is no turning back.

With each second, more and more low-lying rocks are engulfed by the irresistible rising rushing sea.

"We'll have to climb, there's no other way! We'll be safe on one of those ledges up there!" Charlie points upwards and drags Imp along with him.

Several metres up the cliff face twist a series of ledges, carved out of the rock by the relentless pounding of rolling waves over the centuries.

"I can't reach that ledge!" shouts Imp urgently over the noise of the incoming crashing waves.

"Here, I'll lift you up!" bellows back Charlie as he reaches out and grabs hold of her arm.

Jun helps too. With a hasty shove and a firm push, Imp is hauled up onto the first ledge followed swiftly by the others. Just in time as the first wave washes over the rocks nearest to the cliff face where they had just been standing below. A sense of relief sweeps over them.

The ledge they are standing on provides an extremely narrow route upwards. There are several short-stepped ledges which rise higher up the side of the cliff face although it is not clear if they will lead anywhere.

With their backs pressed against the cliff rock face, they slowly continue to edge upwards. Daring to glance downwards, Charlie notices that the first ledge is already submerged, covered by the continuing, fast-rising sea water. Urgently, they inch onwards and upwards, the icy rain still pelting against their faces, but their cheeks are so numb they hardly feel it.

"I think we're high enough now!" huffs Jun panting from the exertion.

Still clinging to the cliff face, they briefly rest and hope she is right. It's difficult to believe the sea water level will rise any further up the cliff. It is a relief because, worryingly, the next ledge is completely engulfed in shadow, so it is difficult to be sure what is ahead.

"I think we should keep going as far as we can!" encourages Imp even though every muscle in her body is screaming for her to stop and rest, "What if the water keeps rising?"

They know she's right, they can't afford to risk it. They climb even further on, into the shadow, uncertain where it might take them.

Fortunately, just as quickly as the sea water had flooded the cove, it recedes by a few metres and then settles at its natural level...the level it was at before the waters sank, before they were trapped in the circle of stone columns, before they left the safety of the cave...back as it should be – balanced.

As the waters settle so the black storm eases; the wild wind and rain cease pounding at them. Gradually the skies brighten, and their spirits rise only to fall crashing down as the full enormity of their new situation dawns on them. They were so busy avoiding the onslaught of rising water that they had not considered the danger they have put themselves in. Every new ledge had taken them higher and higher. Far from moving out-of-danger, they are now precariously perched on an extremely high, narrow cliff ledge up the side of another rocky cliff in a cold shadow wondering what might be around the next corner.

"C'mon, can't stop now!" chants Charlie yet again, this time more for himself than the others, "Got 'a keep going...there's bound to be a way up! C'mon!"

At last Charlie sees what is around the corner. For once he was right, not only right, but *really* right.

"There's a way out, up to the fields above!" Charlie relays back to the others unable to disguise his relief.

In front, is a narrow pathway but, even better, there are steps hewn in the rock face leading upwards to the grassy surface at the top of the cliff! They look steep and slippery, but they are still steps! They are well worn and wet with a thick covering of spongy green moss-like growth indicating that no one had used them recently.

"I wonder why someone would go to the trouble of making steps here of all places? They don't lead anywhere!" Imp asks as she stops and clings close to the cliff edge for breath.

Her concern is drowned out by Jun's exuberant celebration.

"Hooray! We've made it!" then she pauses thoughtfully, "My parents are going to be *really* mad!"

"They'll be fine when you tell them what happened, don't worry!" cheers Charlie, for the first time himself, daring to believe that they may be able to reach safety, "We'll have to take it easy ... those steps are really slippery."

"What's this?" asked Jun touching the cliff face next to her.

In their excitement, Imp and Charlie missed the thin jagged vertical crack in the rock face as they shuffled past, it is about a person high and just wide enough to squeeze through sideways if you breathe in.

Braking away from their celebrations, they eye it up, then eye up the inviting steps and the way out.

Carefully pushing her head through the opening in the rock face, Jun can't make out any details except for a distant faint purple shimmer and she only notices that when her eyes have fully adjusted to the oppressive darkness inside.

"There's a purple light right at the far end, it's difficult to be sure but the cavern seems to open out a bit, but I can't see much..." she whispers excitedly as she leans her head back out of the crack in the rock. She turns to the others, "I bet it's a stone!"

Imp's tired and dismayed face tells Jun exactly what she thinks. 'Forget it, let's go home...come back tomorrow *if* you have to.'

Jun has to investigate; it's as if she is being drawn towards the purple glow. "We can't just ignore it – I'll only be a second!" she pleads.

"You know what happened last time; we were lucky to get out in one piece!" protests Imp in desperation glancing towards Charlie for support.

"And very nearly didn't!" Charlie continues, backing her up.

"What about the others? We might be able to save them!" Jun says, grasping at straws, she knows there is no way to help them from here. She also knows now it is up to them to raise the alarm and the quickest way to do that is to get home fast.

"We could always come back tomorrow," suggests Charlie as a compromise.

"Oh c'mon! I'll go in...you wait here for me!" Jun is determined and already pressing herself, shoulder first, back into the narrow opening. Breathing out, she squeezes through the crack to the other side. Straight away she sniffs the air in the cave, it is dry and stale, tinged with a dreadfully unpleasant smell which reminds her of the dark upstairs room at the house clearance sale. Quickly, she puts that memory out of her mind and focusses on the distant purple glow ahead of her.

Uncertain of the lay of the ground in the cave, Jun warily places her left foot forward feeling for a firm footing in the darkness. As she moves slowly forward, she realises the floor is smooth, but like the steps to the top of the cliff outside, worn with use. She moves forward again cautiously; the floor is rolling and uneven. The dim shaft of daylight which manages to pass through the crack in the rock face from outside, hardly touches the darkness inside the cave. The faint purple glow is only a direction guide, too far away to help her see her immediate surroundings in the cave. She now knows from recent experiences that she can easily step straight into a chasm or trip up on old bones or tumble down a death slide. Her heart beat quickens as she takes a deep breath and continues purposefully forward. She's being drawn to the purple glow, each step taking her further and further from safety and her two friends who have both, reluctantly, squeezed through the crack and are standing at the entrance behind her - ready to help if needed.

There's a 'snap' as Jun places her foot down on a thin dried twig, or is it a bone? The sharp sudden noise pierces through the dark silence of the cave and echoes vibrate around the rock walls. Gradually, they fade only to be drowned out by a flapping and a rustling. High above Jun, the whole roof of the cave is alive, a heaving black mass, hardly visible but definitely there. All three look upwards in dismay, but the rustling quickly calms and then ceases, returning the roof to a quiet restfulness.

"Must be bats or something!" whispers Imp to Jun, her tired voice is hoarse.

With huge relief, Jun treads steadily towards the purple glow, certain it will be another stone.

The undulating rock floor unexpectedly dips down sharply making her topple forward, nearly losing balance, before gently rising again.

Like a lioness creeping up unseen on her prey, Jun steadily moves closer and closer. Now, finally within her reach, she sees the purple stone clearly, it is just like the other stones. Holding her breath and with arms fully stretched she deliberately takes one last step forward. Strangely the floor beneath her briefly gives way. She is standing on a wide flat stone slab which has sunk a few centimetres into the floor under her own body weight. Her heart skips a beat. She stops still, frozen to the spot directly in front of the purple stone. It is resting on top of a rock about waist height. In the purple glow, Jun notices that the cave walls nearby are plastered with strange intricately carved patterns.

In one smooth swooping motion, she grabs the stone off its perch. She wastes no time. Holding the stone tightly in her fist, she immediately swivels round and leaps off the stone which, like a lever, springs back to its original position. As it does so, she is surrounded by a screeching siren of sound that shakes the previously silent empty stillness into a vibrant swirling black mass of movement. The roof of the cave comes alive with an army of swarming black bats. Bats of every size swoop from their lofty roost in waves like swarming locusts, dive bombing Jun. Quickly, she awakens from the shock and launches herself back towards the others who are still stood, still stunned and still motionless at the cave entrance.

Instinctively Charlie holds up his stone, its red glow seems to warn off the encircling mass of black swarming bats by the entrance; most keep a short distance away, only a few of the larger bats dare to brave the glowing red light from his stone.

As she runs frantically back towards them, Jun also holds up her purple stone to protect herself. The angry swarm swoop towards her but then flap and screech away to avoid the purple stone. She continues running, nearly tripping again on the uneven ground as she goes.

Imp is already squeezing herself back through the opening back to the cliff ledge as Jun approaches the crack in the rock face. Charlie stays by the exit and bravely waits for Jun waving his stone high above his head.

As the two stones become closer together, they both shine even more brightly, as if gaining strength from each other; working together in some way.

Jun inches herself back through the crack in the wall and Charlie swiftly follows her, leaving behind the screeching swirling black cloud of bats to their domain of darkness.

From the ledge outside, they pause for breath and hear the screeching gradually fade back into an uneasy silence.

"We did it!" pants Jun triumphantly.

"You idiot!" says Charlie more in relief than anger.

"What? Now we've found another stone!" replies Jun still catching her breath but very pleased with herself.

Imp is already making her way to the bottom of the steps which ladder their way sharply upwards and to the very top of the cliff edge. She is too cold and exhausted to care anymore. With a huge effort and aching limbs, she climbs upwards being careful to avoid slipping on the wet green slime covering each step.

As she reaches the top of the steps, Imp peeps over the top of the cliff edge and through the tall grass shielding her exit, she spots three silhouettes against the sunlight in the lush green field above. The three hooded figures are facing each other in a black huddle as if holding a secret conversation. Hopefully, at first, Imp thinks they might be part of a search team looking for them and is about to call out to them, but there is something curiously sinister about the strange way the figures are moving.

She stops and watches them...to be sure.

After a few seconds, they separate from their huddle and start waving their hands in the air while moving around in a circle about each other.

Imp signals to the others, just behind her, that there is danger. Charlie and Jun stop climbing, each freeze to their step, feeling the cold slippery green slime squelch between their toes as they stand like posts in the protective shadow of the cliff only a few metres from the top.

They wait.

Without provocation and with no warning, all three hooded figures break from their circle and turn menacingly towards Imp, who remains hidden from view.

'Can they see me?' she thinks.

They begin to sway, rising higher and hovering above the grassy field. Together, still in a line, facing Imp directly, they release a terrifying, wild, screeching sound just like the bats in the cave below.

They float across the field, alarmingly, straight towards her.

Surprisingly quickly, they move over the tall grass, closer to the edge of the cliff where Imp crouches, with her face now pressed flat against the rock and field top soil.

The others are still hidden in the cliff's shadow, behind her.

Despite her desperately aching muscles, Imp clings as close to the cliff edge as she can. She scrunches her eyes closed, not knowing what will happen.

The three figures hesitate as if they aren't certain about something, yet some inner sense is drawing them towards the cliff edge and Imp. Simultaneously, both Jun and Charlie reach in their pockets for their stones.

In response, the volume of screeching increases again, becoming unbearable, and they float again toward Imp's position. Abruptly, as the three hooded creatures loom over the edge of the cliff directly above Imp, the screeching stops.

'They must have seen me!' Imp presses herself harder against the cliff face.

Charlie and Jun wait below; motionless on the steps, hidden only by the shadow of the cliff face.

Without warning the three figures propel themselves high into the sky with one last screech and howl. They launch themselves upwards into the clouds where they are engulfed and vanish from view, leaving the cliff edge behind in stunned silence.

Still clinging to the cliff edge, Imp dares to open her eyes.

All is still.

When she is sure they are not going to return, Imp shakily crawls quietly over the ledge, followed quickly by the others.

In the warm glow of the sun, they sit together by the edge of the field at the top of the cliff, with a huge sense of relief knowing that this time they *have* made it!

They have no time to relax, within seconds Charlie finds his bearings. He knows exactly where they are. Tired or not, they must raise the alarm to save the others – there is no more time to lose!

THE ERUKE'S MESSAGE.

~~~

Oceans away, Afide's brother, Maulum, stirs menacingly, sensing an awakening and potential escape from his long-suffering imprisonment. His thin purple lips tighten, and his brow hardens. He has already perceived disorder in the order of things; a change finally confirmed by the arrival of his howling Eruke messengers from the distant Isle of Sarro. Entombed deep within the thunderous mountain, Maulum slumps on his oversized stone throne which has been sliced out from the black volcanic walls. His ghostlike appearance ripples as his shadowy hand flexes, tightening its grip on the cold armrest. Slowly, he leans forward and straightens his back, revealing a grey, weathered embattled face with a single scar on his right cheek. Maulum is a faded dull reflection of his sibling, his brother, his antagonist, and his rival; Alfide, for whom he harbours a cancerous loathing and overwhelming hatred.

Maulum's slow but deep and powerful voice vibrates out, "So, my friends... at last... it begins. The Black Mist is released, and the stones are lost!"

"At last! My lord! At last!" echoes another voice with excitement.

"Shall I call back the watchers?" asks another voice from within the darkness, keen to please.

"Have them focus on the Isle of Sarro. Find out where the stones are. DO NOT let them escape us again!"

"Vengeance will be yours, my lord Malum."

"GO!"

A scattering of strange, dark looking beings of all shapes and sizes, flood out of the massive stone throne room, leaving an icy cold stillness behind.

"At last! My lord! At last!"

"More essence! Quickly!" he coughs and gasps as if he has massively over exerted himself.

"Here... here you are my lord." The shriveled being before the throne tenderly passes the stone goblet of essence. It is only half full.

Maulum drinks deeply and, feeling his strength returning, orders forcefully, "Another!"

"My lord, no, we must conserve our supplies! Our supplies are running low, extremely low. They have not been replenished for some time."

"Then we must find another supply and quickly!" he commands.

"But from where?"

"I need more! Round up more people, I will drain their Earth essences. We must find some more long-liveds!"

"But my lord, they are nowhere to be found!"

"You must find them! Their Earth essences have much more potency... When we regain all the stones, I will use their power combined, to return to normal... Then I will destroy the one who opposes me!" he pauses breathlessly, over exerted, "and those that dared to do this to me, will pay with their lives!"

THE CALLING.

~~~

"**B**ad news! I sense we have been discovered." Shadrack huffs with disappointment, "We are out of time! I am sure the watchers know we have lost the stones."

"How can they know?"

"That I can't say," he replies, "but I can sense it. I can feel *his* awakening anger!"

"Then no more delays! Put our plans into action immediately – we must not allow *him* time to regain his strength and return. NEVER!" The harsh voice comes from a hooded man with a scar across his left cheek, Alfide.

"Yes, and we must not let poor old Amelia's death be in vain!" says Jennifer speaking through gritted teeth.

"And the countless others! All their deaths through history, will count for nothing if Maulum is allowed to be free. My friends, we have fought long and hard to put off this moment but now the time is upon us – we have no choice - we cannot delay!"

"Call everyone together. Warn them all. We will meet here again tomorrow. Go! Waste no more time! Go!"

HOME!

~~~

C harging through the back door, followed closely by Jun and Imp, Charlie crashes straight into his mother. She is getting a new ice pack from the refrigerator for Genji's aching shoulder.

"Mum! Great you're here! We need to call the lifeguard, mountain rescue and the police. We need a rescue team to find Genji, Geo and Finn. They're stuck underground in a cave below the woods...it flooded and there was no way out. Quick!" says Charlie urgently and out of breath, having run all the way. He tries to explain their predicament, but his mother seems incomprehensibly unconcerned.

"Charlie dear! You're OK!" she gives her son a big motherly hug, much to his embarrassment.

"But... the others! They need help! They're stuck in a cave under the woods..." he repeats even louder, "They need our help!"

"Don't worry darling, they're all fine. They are here waiting for you! Although I must say, we've all been very worried about you three. Now, go through to the drawing room and see for yourself," she replies happily, "and I'll bring you all a nice hot chocolate. You look dreadful!"

Charlie looks at her as if she has gone mad, "What do you mean they're here? How can they be? How did they...?"

"Just go and see for yourself, darling. I'll be along with some towels and hot chocolate presently. Poor Imp, you look absolutely shattered my darling."

She gives Imp a hug and gently ushers them down the hallway toward the drawing room.

"Go on! Go in!"

~~~

Genji, Geo and I are deep in discussion about what might have happened to the others, when Charlie opens the drawing room door and they all step in. We can't believe it! He looks worse than I feel, even with all my cuts and bruises! They all look in a very pitiful state! I quickly realise that they have been through some dreadful ordeal; much worse than ours.

"I thought you must have been buried alive in that awful earthquake!" Genji stood up and warmly hugs her sister with her good arm.

"What happened to your arm?" enquires Jun, full of concern.

"Oh! Nothing much...just dislocated...it's fine now really," she dismisses Jun's worries and leads her to a comfortable chair close to the huge open fireplace, "What happened to you? You look terrible! How did you get out?"

"Thanks! You don't look so good yourself!" jokes back Jun, but she is clearly shattered by her experience and incredibly relieved to be back safe. She makes the most of the warmth of the burning log fire.

Imp is barely able to stand up by herself and tears of relief roll down her cheeks. Geo reaches out to hold his sister, just in time, breaking her fall as she collapses to her knees, totally exhausted.

"It's OK sis', you're OK now."

Geo holds her close, mortified at how icy cold she feels and immediately grabs a thick woollen throw and wraps it around her. Her trembling lips are purple and blue with cold.

"What on earth happened to you?!" I ask.

"A nightmare, Finn! That's what happened... a nightmare!" replies Charlie dramatically - he has no other way to describe it.

After a long, thoughtful silence Charlie returns the question, "Anyway, what happened to you? I take it you found the way out. We should have gone with you!"

"Well, not exactly," Geo replies and flashes a grin. He explains the strange set of events that happened to us, since they left us at the ledge at the top of the death slide. Genji proudly shows off her green stone. Geo also tells them about the earthquake, Genji's injury to her arm, being unable to find a way out, that we had given up any hope of finding a way out and, finally, how we escaped.

"How long have you been back?" asks Jun still warming herself by the crackling log fire.

"It was late last night," I reply comfortably, "we've been here ever since."

"Has anyone been searching for us?" Charlie asks, wondering why they had not been rescued in the same way.

"They tried...but no one could figure out where you were. There's a bloke called Shadrack, he's the Searcher, he searched everywhere he could think of under Holdwood but couldn't find you...we were beginning to think you'd ..." Genji adds but is interrupted when Charlie's mother returns carrying a tray with six large mugs of steaming, milky, hot chocolate and a large plate of biscuits.

"There you go. Warm yourselves up and we'll get you cleaned up before you meet everyone."

Charlie's mother places the tray on the solid wooden coffee table in front of the roaring fire, while taking a long look at the three latest arrivals.

As she leaves the room, she says, "You can clean up when you're ready. You'll be safe here."

"Everyone? Who's everyone?" asks Charlie in a hushed voice when the door is firmly shut behind her.

"You'll see! Have your hot chocolate first," I suggest not wanting to alarm them.

Once she has had time to warm herself and eat most of the chocolate biscuits, Imp quickly recovers her strength and colour.

We are all extremely relieved to be back safely together and slowly, as we chat, we piece together what happened to each other.

Eventually, the conversation turns to the stones.

Charlie, Jun, Geo and Genji reverently hold their stones in the palm of their hands and slowly move them close together. As they do, the stones glow brighter than ever before. Cautiously, they move them even closer together, nearly touching. At this point I have to shield my eyes, and the air around them begins to fizz and hum, very reminiscent of the time when Imp placed the necklace on the rock in the den.

At that moment, Mr. Taylor charges into the room.

"What do you think you're doing?!" he exclaims angrily, "Do you want *them* to find you?! Put those stones back in your pockets quickly. How can you kids be so silly?"

Obligingly, each stone is immediately returned to its owner's pocket and we look at each other in complete dismay.

Charlie asks Mr. Taylor what we are all thinking, "What exactly is going on?"

As if in answer, there is a fierce, piercing screeching from the grounds outside Holdwood Manor. Charlie, Jun, and Imp instantly recognise the haunting sound from earlier when the three hovering creatures leapt up into the sky above the cliff edge - but this time the screeching is even louder, engulfing and surrounding the whole building.

Startled voices from a nearby room reverberate down the hallway to us.

"We have been discovered!"

"They know exactly where we are."

"How did they find us so quickly?"

"Damn kids!" curses Mr. Taylor, quickly leaving us and rejoining the other strangers back in the front parlour.

Looking out of one of the enormous picture frame windows, we can make out a massive, dark swirling cloud encircling the entire Manor, blocking out any remaining daylight, drowning the whole place in complete darkness.

"The Black Mist with more of those creatures!" Charlie shouts out over the noise, "It must have followed us!"

Charlie's mother rushes into the room, "Quickly children, move away from the windows! You can't afford to be seen! Come... Quick! This way!" she instructs as she shuffles us swiftly away from view, hastily closing the heavy curtains behind her. She marches to the paneled wall opposite, presses a petal from a rose flower decorating the wooden panel and the whole section slides silently across, revealing a dimly lit passageway leading deeper inside, into the heart of Holdwood Manor.

"Wow. Cool! I never knew..." Charlie's voice fades as the volume of the swirling screeching swells and fills the air again.

"Quickly! No time for gawping! Quick! To the Meeting Hall!"

In stunned amazement, we follow her along a narrow passage way. She clicks something unseen, behind us and the panel wall section closes firmly behind us.

The incredibly loud screeching is instantly cut off and silence fills the passageway. As my eyes adjust, I notice that all the stones are glowing, now even more noticeable in the dimly lit passage way, as if they know of each other's whereabouts and are, somehow, working together – feeding off each other and getting stronger, brighter.

The short passageway leads us downwards and then opens out into an unexpectedly large hall. The high walls are wooden clad and majestically covered with series after series of magnificent and elaborate carvings. Most are ancient in style, depicting stories from centuries gone by; wild bears, hunters with spears, chariots, stone circles, alters and sacrifices, many battles, swords, guns, burning, smoke, and fire with splashes of light thunder bolting through the air. There are many strange looking creatures and shapes that I don't recognise. It feels as though this room has stood here forever and its timeworn history has been painstakingly recorded on its walls in every detail. It is likely that Holdwood Manor had been built around and over this hall over many generations. I am surprised that Charlie had not known about it.

The splendid room is mysteriously lit by a shimmering light

emanating from a raised oval shallow pool of cool, milky-white water commanding the centre of the room. Around the pool, stand several large, intricately carved, chairs turned inwards encircling the pool but facing each other. It could easily be a place of peace and thoughtfulness or, equally, a place for heated argument and disagreement. Even though the carved wooden walls of the room dully reflect the pool's cool pale light, it still maintains an earthy warmth. It is a room full of contradictions.

"Quick! Take a seat, each of you!" urges Charlie's mother who is fussing and clearly concerned.

Obediently, we sit on the first huge wooden chair that we each come to. They are surprisingly comfortable. Together we take up most of the grand chairs, but there are still three more empty chairs and, I notice for the first time, that the fourth remaining chair across the pool from me is already occupied. In the cool shimmering light, a hooded man is sat, silent and watchful.

We face each other in an uneasy silence. Charlie's mother has already deserted us, leaving us alone with the stranger in the room.

Still, the stranger remains annoyingly silent. Waiting. Waiting at the other end of the pool. His eyes are hidden in darkness under the shadow of his hood though it is clear he is watching us intently – as if, for the first time, he is doubting himself.

The silent intensity of his gaze is painful, and Geo can't stand it any longer.

"Hi, my name's Geo!" he spouts out hopefully and waits for a reply, anything to break the icy silence.

"I know who you are," returns a hoarse voice at last, "I also know what you are…"

Charlie immediately recognises the voice of the hooded man. It is the same man who had nearly knocked him over, when he opened the door on the night of the meeting.

The pause seems endless.

"You are the Blue stone Holder…you are *all* Holders, some with…some without."

Geo continues, more confidently, "What's a Holder exactly? I mean, what do they do exactly?"

"Do?! Do! ... Do nothing yet...Hope! Yes. Hope that you will never have to do battle." As he speaks, he looks directly at Geo and slowly removes his hood, revealing his worn aged features, though the intensity of his perceptive gaze does not waver for a second.

"Battle?! How can I ... we do battle? I don't know how to fight," Geo replies honestly, thinking there must be some sort of mistake.

"You are all chosen...you are all Holders...you will learn to fight."

"Who chose us?" I ask cautiously joining the conversation.

"A force from deep within the Earth, a force way beyond comprehension or understanding, you are all chosen...you are the new Holders," he repeats annoyingly, as if we should know what he means, "You each sit on one of the great seats of the Holders who have passed before you."

"Geo, Blue Holder, look at your chair – it bears your colour. Look into the pool in front of you – see, see the Blue Holders who have gone before you..."

We all look deep into the milky water in front of us. In the pool, we each see countless reflected images, of battles, heroics, faces of both the slain and the victorious, flashing past. The images match exactly with the stories carved on the walls of the Meeting Hall. Each of us sees different faces and images of deeds gone by, places gone by and times gone by.

One thing is the same for each holder, the faces they see are fierce and battle hardened...something none of us are.

"What if we haven't got a stone? How can we be Holders?" I ask looking at Imp.

"Did you see anything in the pool?" he replies, seemingly ignoring the question.

We all did. Imp looks very pale, even allowing for the lighting from the pool.

"Then you are Holders. Your stones will call you when the

time is right, just like the others were called."

That was enough for Genji.

"Well I wasn't called! I never even got a text!" she says defiantly, "I don't want to be a Holder. Anyway, what happened to the other Holders? Are they all dead? Why can't they just come back? Who-ever-they-are can have their stones back!"

As she speaks, she pulls out her green stone and places it on the narrow shelf surrounding the pool in front of her. The stone glows comfortably, as if it is at home.

"You are a Holder for a reason, chosen by Earth forces greater than all of us. You will meet the challenge. You are chosen." replies the hoarse voice with remarkable patience.

Genji works out quickly that it is a pointless argument with the same answer each time.

The hooded man's tone softens as if his previous doubts have been lifted and he is speaking as a friend. "I am Alfide. If I can, I will help you. We are all here to help you."

Leaning forward, Alfide continues speaking intensely in a low voice as he reveals the secret truth that he, and the others, guard with their lives, "Hidden throughout the world are segments, parts, of the Earthcode. With the fully completed Earthcode, it is believed to be possible to alter all life bound to Earth. Once used, the code will force Earth itself to destroy all living things, plants, and animals, and start all over again... like a reset button, I suppose... All the life we have come to know on Earth will die. Everything would start again. Nothing will be the same. There are those who wish this. *We* must not allow this to happen!"

A long thoughtful pause follows as we each take in the enormity of what has been revealed and wrestle with the consequences of such destruction to everything in the world we know; our families, our friends, each other and even the trees in the woods holding up the tarpaulin of our den roof.

At last, Imp challenges the sanity of what Alfide said, "Why would anyone want to destroy every living thing on Earth? What have the Holders got to do with it? What do Holders do?"

Slowly, Alfide runs his index finger across the old scar on his face, deliberately and thoughtfully, and then replies, "You stand between two forces and two brothers. You choose, for the Earth itself, which you want to help...make the wrong choice and victory will surely belong to my brother, Maulum, who already is regaining strength and rebuilding support. You have already heard some of his followers this very night. Maulum believes that, when he finds all the segments of the Earthcode, he can introduce the code like a virus and rebuild a new world, one that he alone can command. He is prepared to destroy Earth, our Earth, in order to do this. He has tried many times before, but he needs the full Earthcode...You will have heard of the Black Death... and Bubonic Plague when he used rats to spread only a part of the code. Imagine what he could do if he ever finds a better way to spread the other code parts or, a thousand times worse, if he gets the complete code! From the safety of this little island, I understand that you may not be very aware of what else is happening across the rest of the world; even as we speak, people are dying from deadly viruses - I am certain it is his, or his followers, work. With every day, they are getting closer and closer, becoming stronger and stronger, more and more dangerous. My brother will continue to search for the rest of the Earthcode as soon as he is able. I am convinced Maulum now believes he has found a new way to release the Earthcode across the entire world, something he has never been able to do before. Believe me, he has tried before...many times. We cannot afford to underestimate him. The danger to every living thing on Earth is very real!"

"He must have found a way out, escaped," he mutters under his breath, "or found help from somewhere."

"Your fore-bearers battled long and hard to defeat him and imprison him, and, like a festering wound, he will never forgive the Holders for that...ever."

"What do Holders do?" Alfide repeats Imp's question thoughtfully, "They stay true to their path and do not falter, using all their skills and gifts to defeat him and his followers before they defeat you, us, and every living thing. You have many people who will help you, some who have battled alongside previous holders. They will train you when they can and, of course, you have me – if anyone knows my brother...I do and, I can assure you, you must not take on this task lightly... that will be the pathway to certain doom...be certain of that!"

Noticing the look of concern and fear in our faces he encourages, "But do not fear, you will prevail, be sure of this...it is you that will hold the balance. Our fate and that of every living thing on the earth, rests with you."

The new Holders stare, across the milky pool, at each other in dismay as Charlie's mother walks back into the meeting place.

"Now, now Alfide! Don't worry, my dears. Just know, we've defeated Maulum before...we'll do it again!" she says warmly.

"Yes, but each time he gets wiser – we must be ready for anything, leave nothing to chance and we must be as cunning as he is...and more! I feel that we are moving into the dangerous days. For the very first time *all* eight known stones have called their Holders and *all* the Holders are together. Grave times!" Alfide continues defiantly.

"Yes, yes, that's enough for now!" she moves closer to Alfide and quietly says, for his ears alone, "We don't want to scare anyone...do we?"

He grunts and stays silent...a painful silence as he ponders the enormity of the undertaking that they face.

"You must be exhausted, it's time for some sleep I think...You can all stay here tonight, I've already contacted your homes to let them know where you are and that you are safe. Boys go with Charlie and girls you follow me, I'll show you to your room. You'll be safe here...a busy day tomorrow...c'mon..."

She fusses over us kindly like a mother hen protecting her young chicks.

We leave the fine Meeting Hall and step out of the dark narrow passage way back into the stillness of the drawing room. It is difficult to judge exactly how long we were sheltering in the Meeting Hall. In the huge fireplace, the fire is still burning strongly but the large log that had been at its heart is now only the size of an orange now. There is no wild screeching anymore, just an eerie, empty silence. On our way across the hallway, we pass the wide-open door of the front parlour where I catch a glimpse of many more strangers now, chatting and planning. They ignore us, too engrossed in what they are doing, as we file passed and climb up the wide carpeted stairs of the old house to our bedrooms.

As we get ready for bed, I can't help noticing that Charlie is very quiet. Maybe he is wondering why his parents had not told him about the secret passage way and Meeting Hall.

In contrast, Geo hardly stops talking, he is so excited, "Did he say the eight stones? There's only six of us! What d'you think he meant?"

We have no answers.

Once in bed, Charlie is still deep in thought then, as he looks up at the ceiling, he asks, "Those creatures must be some sort of bird to be able to hover and fly like that. What do you think?"

"They're no sort of bird I've ever seen before even if you include extinct ones," I reply very sleepily.

"Maybe they were around before even dinosaurs, before anything else… either way it doesn't matter, they are obviously not on our side!"

A few minutes later, a tired restfulness falls over the room. Geo begins to gently snore.

Just before Charlie finally drifts off to sleep, he yawns and asks a good question which hangs, unanswered, in the air as I finally fall asleep, "I wonder why?"

MORNING

~~~

The morning comes too soon for everyone except Geo who bounces out of bed and flings open the thick curtains revealing the day. Judging from the brilliant sunlight that pours into our bedroom, it is at least mid-morning. I shield my eyes and roll over to go back to sleep just as he calls out, "Wow! Look out there! What a mess! Hey, Charlie, I hope your garden doesn't normally look like this!"

Charlie sleepily crosses the bedroom and looks out of the window. He whistles in amazement and shock.

With this, and still blinking in the strong bright light, I stiffly struggle to my feet. Every muscle is complaining, I ache from head to toe and feel as if I am easily one hundred years old, maybe older, but I can't resist seeing what all the fuss is about.

I join Geo and Charlie at the bedroom window. Down below us is the aftermath of last night's dreadful battle, laid out before us in all its devastation. There are strange circular blackened patches scattered across the once beautifully manicured lawn, each about half a metre in diameter, as if the creatures had dive bombed and splatted themselves on the ground leaving a thick black tar like goo behind. Most of the ornate rows of trees which line both sides of the long curving driveway, up to Holdwood Manor, are either burned black or splintered in two. Other trees look as though they have been sliced across horizontally midway up the leafy green canopy; the sliced off tree tops litter the garden grounds several metres away from their trees. Statues and other stone garden ornaments are toppled randomly.

Clearly, last night, a ferocious battle took place here.

"Who did this?" I ask as I survey the wreckage below sleepily.

"Where have you been?" Geo tuts sarcastically, "Did you not hear that shrieking?"

"That's not what I meant!" I continue, "I know who or what *they* were, but *who* was fighting them from *here*?!"

"That's obvious," replies Charlie, trying to piece together the picture of what must have happened, "We passed loads of weird looking strangers in the front parlour last night didn't we? They looked ready for a fight. It was as if they were expecting an attack - as if they do that sort of thing every day. I bet they have beaten those creepy things before!"

It seems to me that Charlie imagined this is just a routine thing, a day in the life of a Holder.

Geo is beaming with excitement and ready to go.

I'm not so sure, and anyway, I don't have a stone, yet.

Thinking back to the images that I saw in the pool in the Meeting Hall. I remember there were glimpses of bloody battles past. Sometimes, there were ancient armies fighting alongside the Holders. Other glimpses revealed just the Holders together, sometimes even just the one solitary Holder but always fending off the shadowy silhouettes and other dreadful looking creatures.

Just then there's a banging on the bedroom door which quickly swings open, making us all jump.

"Just as I thought! Not even ready! C'mon, you lazy bones, breakfast is ready!" Imp chirps happily showing no signs whatsoever of yesterday's ordeal.

Encouraged by the warm smell of toast, wafting from downstairs, it doesn't take us long to get ready for breakfast.

THE ERUKE

~~~

We see debris is scattered everywhere when we finally venture out into Holdwood Manor gardens after breakfast. I'm keen to investigate the black, sticky patches. Charlie's mother escorts us and is happy to answer our endless supply of questions.

She also has some news from the mainland. I can tell that she doesn't want to worry us, but the most recent news from the mainland cannot be ignored. Up to now, I know very little about what is happening at home, away from the island but, after yesterday's meeting with Alfide, I suspect it is not going to be good news, whatever it is. I remember that my parents were worried enough to send me here to 'safety' as the situation worsened in the streets. I wonder if they would be so keen now. Now that I am on the front line in the battle to save the Earth!

As Charlie's mother speaks, it dawns on me that I have already heard bits and pieces before; about infections and viruses that are spreading worldwide but I had no idea how serious things have become.

"All movement between infected areas has been halted, as a precautionary measure," she explains, turning to me she continues thoughtfully, "it seems you are the lucky ones." nodding to Geo, Imp, and myself, "Had your parents delayed…well, who knows where you'd be!"

"Lucky?" questions Imp doubtfully as we walk around one of the black patches of goo, burned into the otherwise beautifully manicured lawn.

It becomes clear that Charlie's mother thinks it is very important that we know exactly what is happening, "As you can imagine, the 'Virus Free' people, who are living in places where the virus has already taken a hold, are worried that they might become infected too. They are scared. Naturally, they are leaving their homes for the safety of a virus free zone, frantically trying to escape. Some areas have already been swamped and whole armies are being drafted in to keep them out, and to defend each country's borders. Innocent people are being killed just for trying to get away from the virus. These are desperate times... desperate times," she pauses for breath, "the situation just gets worse; now, across the world, there are very few countries left which are truly free from the virus. Those that are, understandably, are doing what they can to protect themselves, that's why nothing, no-one, can travel in or out. You were very lucky indeed!"

"And what are all the world leaders and governments doing at this point in time, you may ask?" she asks us rhetorically and pauses, "Well, they continue to do nothing, apart from sending out occasional messages saying that they have the best scientists working on the problem and that they are very close to a cure. They say a breakthrough is expected *any day now*... but, of course, there's been no breakthrough...well how can there be?" she asks, as if we know, "How can there be a breakthrough when the evil is *far* beyond anything they can imagine?"

"At least now, on a more positive note, while *he* is focusing *his* attentions and revenge on you, the Earth may still have a chance to save itself...you need him to keep his eyes firmly focused on finding you."

We look at each other, all wondering how this can be a good thing.

"Ah, Alfide, the children wanted a closer look at the marks our enemy left behind after yesterday's battle," Charlie's mother spots Alfide marching towards us.

"Good. The more they know the better they can prepare!" he replies seriously while still approaching us from the direction of the Manor's imposing front door.

He slows and, without a word, he walks with us until we reach a shaded, wooden trellis enclosure. It is roofed by inter-twined over-hanging vines and overlooks a line of four more fallen stone statues; just their stone base pillars remain, defiantly standing. Alfide purposefully sits on a carved wooden bench and shakes his head as he absorbs the full extent of last night's foul destruction before him.

"You must have many questions," he adds after another short thoughtful pause.

In the light of the new day and with his hood down, he no longer looks as daunting as he did yesterday in the Meeting Hall, although I imagine that could change at any second.

Boldly Geo asks the question, "Why did those bird creatures attack us? What have we done to them?"

"They were deceived a long time ago, by my brother, into thinking *we* are their enemy...they know no better now and do Maulum's bidding without question... they are lost to us."

"What... I mean, who are they?" asks Genji still none-the-wiser.

"The Eruke are part of the Earth, just like every living thing on Earth... each with our own 'Earth-soul' but for some reason they can't share the Earth in peace with other 'Earth-souls'. Maulum uses that knowledge to make them fight for him. He has given the Eruke direction and they are grateful for that – without him they would go unnoticed; void of purpose, lost."

"So, it's your brother!" scowls Imp with force, "What is his problem?"

"As with many families, there's always one who has to have it all - whatever the consequences to others – even his own family, but you will see this for yourselves soon enough..."

As I sit and listen in the deceptive warmth of the morning sun, I can't help feeling that the world around me, has chilled and darkened. Without doubt, it is about to change even more than I could imagine. My parents were smiling when they waved me goodbye but, from what Alfide says, it is very unlikely that they would still be alive, but I refuse to believe that. I would know if they are dead, wouldn't I? I know that I would.

By the looks on their faces, the others are feeling the same way. For Genji, Jun and Charlie, their families are here, fussing about, but even they are so busy that they have hardly spoken to us since our return. Mr. Chen has been conspicuous in his absence although Mrs. Chen assures us that he is just very busy organising 'things' but she can't disguise the concerned look on her face. Also, it is strange he has not been seen since last night's battle. Charlie's father came to check that we were all alright after last night, but we have not seen him since either. He said that they had to prepare...prepare for what...I have no idea.

MAINLAND

~~~

Back on the mainland, in a cramped, faceless, second floor flat, a young woman sits on an old dusty couch with the TV remote control in her hand. She flicks between the few remaining channels, trying to find something less depressing to watch but there are only news channels now, each reporting more disruption, more riots, and more deaths.

"I'm sick of this! Bad news, bad news and *more* bad news! What sort of a place is this to start a family?" she complains to her husband.

"Don't worry my sweet, it'll all work out for the best, I'm sure," replies the young muscular man from across the sparse room, as he pulls the threadbare curtain across the window to shut out the darkening outside world.

He sits next to her and looks at her beautiful but still frowning face in the flickering light of the TV. He thinks how pale she looks; how much she has changed since the start of the rioting and the outbreaks of sickness. Everyone has changed but she seems to be struggling more and more as each day passes.

Kia switches the TV off in disgust, leaving just the dim shadeless bulb to light the room with faded shadows.

"Mum said that we ought to leave and head off somewhere safer."

"Safer? Did she say where that was?" her husband, Paul, replies sarcastically, instantly regretting it.

"Anywhere would be better than this."

"I don't know, my sweet, all I hear is that the same things are happening all over; there's nowhere safe to go now."

"I'm sure we'd find somewhere, if we tried. We might find somewhere not spoilt by what's going on... have you already forgotten our old dream, to sail away and start a new life together? Let's do it!"

"You know I'd love to, my sweet, but I don't think we'd be allowed to sail anywhere right now."

A comfortable silence fills the room.

"Mum sent some potatoes over, she queued at Jacob's farm to get 'em. Jacob told her that at least a third of his crop has already been stolen; dug up, by 'wrong uns', before they were even ready to come out of the ground."

"Desperate times, my sweet."

"Oh Paul, what sort of world are we living in?" Kia asks thoughtfully, not expecting a reply, "You know Reverend John, the old vicar from St. George's Church? He died. They say he was purple with blotches and covered with oozing spots the day before."

"Who says?"

"I don't know. My mum..."

"Your mum this, your mum that..."

"She's just worried... that's all."

"I know, I know. Sorry my sweet. Don't get yourself upset, remember what Doc Brown said," retracts Paul as he hands her a tall glass of weak blackcurrant juice.

Paul will have to get more water tomorrow. If he gets up early enough, he should be close to the front of the queue at the water tanker truck...if it turns up. Nothing can be relied on anymore.

He is worried too; they are all worried.

"I'm fine. Stop fretting."

"It's my job, my sweet," trying to sound lighthearted, betraying the desperate anguish he feels inside.

"I bumped into poor..."

"What now!" he cuts in finding it difficult not to get annoyed. There is only so much bad news anyone can take.

"Don't be cross, dear...I haven't seen you all day... just catching up..."

The ceiling light flickers off and back on.

"That's worrying, yesterday that's what happened just before..."

The lights flicker once more and then stay off permanently, leaving the couple in an awkward blackness.

"...just before the power was cut!" Kia finishes her sentence.

"I'll get a torch... you rest... you know what Doc Brown said!"

"I'm fine. Stop fretting. You know, Doc Brown didn't look too good himself when I had my check-up...hope he's OK."

"He'll be fine..."

In the darkness, Paul rummages around in a nearby drawer, locates the torch and switches it on.

"Let's get an early night...probably the fuel shortages kicking in, it'll be back on by the morning I'm sure."

Kia yawns, "I could do with a rest... didn't get much sleep last night."

"Here... grab my arm... there you go," he helps her up from the couch.

"I *can* walk you know... I've just got a sore back, that's all!"

"I know my sweet, I know, watch the step..."

ROBBERS

~~~

Thud! Smash!

Paul leaps up off the bed in the midnight darkness.

"Quick! There's someone in the flat, we're being burgled again.... stay here, I'll go and check," says Paul still waking up.

"Be careful, don't get hurt!"

"I will be, trust me!" he whispers back.

How times have changed. He could never have imagined that he would have a large, heavy baseball bat at the side of his bed ready for exactly this kind of occasion.

Gripping the handle firmly in his right hand, he slowly opens the bedroom door and peeks through the crack to see what is going on.

There is another thud as someone trips over the step from the lounge into the kitchen.

"There's a p'ing step there!"

"You'll wake 'em up! Shush!" comes back an anxious reply.

Even though hushed, both sound like young boy's voices.

All Paul can see are two faint torch lights dancing around in the kitchen from cupboard to shelf and shelf to cupboard.

Recklessly, he charges into the kitchen brandishing the baseball bat, ready to swing, with his own torch beaming brightly onto two startled young faces.

"Get out! Before I smash this on your heads!" he threatens.

The two dim torch lights immediately swing around to reveal the scary burly man brandishing the baseball bat.

"Don't hurt us, Mister!" cries out the first boy who cannot be more than ten years old. He looks terrified, although it is difficult to see through the layers of dirt on his face.

"We ain't stealing nothing! We just need food!" the older boy explains through his long, curly, unbrushed hair.

Paul halts in the doorway to the kitchen for a second and slowly lowers his baseball bat. He understands their desperation, he has witnessed firsthand the hard times some of the children are having to endure on the city streets right now. Many children are homeless, orphaned or abandoned or have simply lost their families in their panic to escape the sickness. He wanted to help them, but he has so very little to give them. Instantly, he takes pity on them.

"I'm not going to hurt you," he says with a lump in his throat, much to their relief.

From behind him comes a voice, "Paul what's going on? Are you alright?"

"I'm fine my sweet, fine. Come and see our young visitors... our very young and very hungry visitors."

Two very scared, dirty faces peer back up at Kia as she rounds the kitchen doorway.

"Oh my God! Look at you! What a mess! What are you doing out at this time of night? Where're your parents?"

"Don't have no one no more. House got burned in the rioting. Mum and dad got very sick...we stayed as long as we could...but they said there was no point in staying any longer and we should go before we got sick too."

The youngest's eyes well up as he chokes back the memories and his tears.

"Here...eat!" Kia says, quickly changing the subject, "Pass the last of the bread Paul, will you?"

"This is Paul, my husband, and I'm Kia. What do you call yourselves?" she asks in a kindly voice.

"This 'ere's Jack 'n I'm Nick," Nick answers for them both between bursting mouthfuls of bread.

"Do you want any jam on that bread?"

"Jam! Sure! Thanks, Missus!" Jack finds his voice and munches enthusiastically at the food relishing every mouthful as if he is eating Christmas dinner. He can't remember the last time he tasted jam or ate fresh bread for that matter. Since the last safe house burnt down, they have been scavenging, surviving off thrown-away scraps of food from bins but now *everyone* is eating from bins so now they must steal food to live.

"You can stay, if you want to, you'll be safer here," suggests Kia surprising Paul.

"Thanks, but nah, there ain't no where's safe no more, Missus, even here...we're going up North...s'posed to be OK up there," he says appreciatively but keen to be moving on.

He looks around to see if his brother has finished eating.

"C'mon Joe, better be off now while it's still dark."

"Here, take this," Kia quickly packs some cans of food, biscuits, and the carton of orange, she has been saving for an emergency, into a shoulder bag for them to take with them.

Nick gratefully accepts the bag and turns to go but stops, turns back and silently gives Kia a grateful hug. She leads them to the door stepping over the freshly smashed glass from the broken pain.

"Here, take these fleeces too, for the cold nights."

"Thanks, Missus, sorry about that," says Nick pointing his torchlight at the broken window and the glass on the hallway carpet.

"Don't worry, have a safe journey...be careful. Look after your brother."

"I will! Bye! Thanks for everything."

They close the door behind the children in silence, each thinking their own thoughts. Paul takes her hand and they walk back to the kitchen in the torchlight.

Paul feels as if a huge weight has been lifted from his shoulders.

Unwittingly, the surprise visit from the two children has helped him make the decision he has been putting off for too long.

"That's it! We're leaving my sweet!" he says, "Getting out before it's too late."

He gets no argument from Kia.

"Let me say goodbye to my mother before we go."

"Ring her when we get on the boat. There's no time for a visit. Smart kids those. You were right too. We've got to get as far away from here as we can. Now's best. More chance if it's dark; might get out of the harbour without being spotted!"

"What about food and water?" asks Kia being practical.

"Already packed that on board…"

"You had this planned all along!"

"Just in case my sweet, just in case!" he smiles happily, "As quick as you can, put a few things in that back pack and we'll go. We can catch the early morning tide if we're really quick!" Paul sounds excited, he loves the sea and has always wanted to sail away to find a better life; they both have, it's been their dream, but this is not at all how he had imagined it would happen.

Like lightning, they each pack a small rucksack with a few essentials and, before they know it, they're threading their way along the plank walk into the marina, their way dimly lit only intermittently by clouded moonlight. There is a guard, asleep, in the security hut to the left of the pathway which leads to the moorings where 'Vita Nova' is birthed. She's not far from the end of the jetty which, luckily, is very close to the harbour exit to the estuary.

Deftly, Paul jumps onto her wooden deck and then helps Kia climb safely on board.

Kia clings to the metal safety rail which runs around the perimeter of the deck for a few seconds while she catches her breath; the fast walk has been a strain on her back. She breathes the sea air in deeply. She feels tired.

With amazing speed, Paul has the boat ready to set sail. He unties the moorings, keeping noise down to a minimum and allows the weak harbour current to silently drag 'Vita Nova' away from its moorings. Skillfully, he raises the main sail leaving it flapping loosely so that they don't pick up too much speed too quickly. If he approaches the exit too quickly, he knows he'll be unable to steer her safely past the harbour wall and out into the open waters.

With just the light of the moon to guide him, he steers silently and steadily. He is about to gather the main sail and let it fill with the thin breeze, when he notices the faint silhouette of another boat sitting on the water directly ahead of them, between them and the harbour exit and their escape. Fortunately, the tiniest crack of dawn sunlight brakes through the darkness on the distant horizon, signaling the imminent arrival of the new day and giving just enough light to make out the detail of the smaller boat ahead. Though not absolutely certain, Paul suspects that it is another small sailing vessel trying to escape the mainland before daylight. Noiselessly, both boats sail out of the comfortable protection of the harbour and into the open water which greets them with a cold spray of salty sea.

"We're out of the harbour now, my sweet! Better ring your Mum before we get out of signal range," he calls to Kia as loudly as he dares.

'Unable to connect to the Network at present, please try again later' the message is the same every time Kia redials.

"She'll understand. I know she will. We can tack along the shore line and try to call again when the light is better, failing that we can call her when we stop to replenish supplies," Paul tries to cheer Kia up.

"It'll be daylight soon. We need to be out of view from the mainland. Why don't you have a rest below?" he encourages seeing that she looks exhausted.

"Stop fretting, I'm fine, just aching a bit, probably from all that rushing about. I'll go down and organise a few things." Kia yawns and rubs her lower back.

Paul knows this part of the sea very well, he has sailed it since he was a child. He fondly reminisces that just here, his dad would shout out, 'Watch out for the sandbanks!' With that he makes a small adjustment to the heading and checks the main sail is taught. As far back as he could remember, Paul has loved the open sea. He shared his dream of sailing to a new life with Kia when they first met, and she has always been keen on the idea too. Only now, with the dawning of the new day, does he wonder if they both really know what their new life will have in store for them.

After a while, he notices that it has gone quiet in the cabin below, so he tethers the steering wheel and climbs down into the galley to check everything is OK. Kia is asleep. Her open diary is lying next to her; she has written a few lines in her journal and fallen asleep, pen still in hand. Paul gently lifts the pen and moves her diary away. As he covers her with the quilt, being careful not to disturb her, he notices a cluster of red blotches on her arm. Lovingly, he leans over and kisses her forehead and creeps silently back up on the deck.

Paul continues to steer 'Vita Nova' into the open sea with a very heavy heart. He blinks away the salty tears in his eyes.

His worst fears have come true.

He left it too late to leave.

The blotches on Kia's arm mean that she has the sickness, she will be dead by the end of the next day.

There is no cure.

There is nothing he can do.

SHADRACK

~~~

Shadrack, the Searcher, is relaxing in an old red leather armchair. He is looking, thoughtfully, into the leaping hypnotic orange and yellow flames of the log fire which is gently burning in the hearth, comfortably warming the large old room. It seems a shame to disturb him.

"Come in! Come in!" he greets us cheerfully, "Sorry that I didn't introduce myself properly before...I was...shall we say... otherwise engaged!"

The Searcher pauses again before continuing, "Takes it out of you, you know!"

"Yes, that's right. Help yourselves to a chair. Sit down. Make yourselves comfortable."

We sit down and admire the transformation from Shadrack the Searcher into Shadrack the man. He is a large framed, like-able, rosy-cheeked man, very different to the pale, worn out, wide-eyed, scary person Geo, Genji and I met when he saved us from our cavern prison in the rocks deep below Holdwood.

"So, you're the new Holders, are you? How wonderful! Pleased to meet you all at last!" smiling pleasantly as he spoke.

"Sir," I say, "we nev..."

"Just Shadrack, just Shadrack... I haven't been knighted yet!" he interrupts jovially.

"Shadrack, we never got the chance to thank you for saving us from the cavern."

"You sure saved us, there was no way out," Geo adds dramatic-ally, "then Blam! Buzzing and fizzing and here we are!"

"Do you mind if I ask how you did that?" Genji asks.

"You can ask but I can't really explain it! It's just something I do, that's all. Good thing too! You'd got yourselves into a right pickle!" he chuckles but then remembering the ordeal, he becomes more serious. Briefly, his eyes harden at the memory. He clenches his left fist determinedly, "The hardest bit was *finding* where you were. I thought I'd lost you," he says nodding towards Charlie, "I hoped that you had found your own way out...otherwise...well, let's not worry about what might have happened!"

There is a short thoughtful silence and I remember how desperate we were.

"Anyway, much more importantly...tell me all about *your* adventures! Tell me, how did you know where the entrance to the caves was? We've managed to keep it hidden for years." Shadrack relaxes again and one by one we tell him our parts in our search for the stones. The room is buzzing with excitement. He is especially interested in the strange Black Mist with the evil smell, that escaped when the hole was initially opened. Though he says nothing more about it, I notice his mood briefly darken as it is mentioned.

It is Genji who first notices the smell.

Again, she sniffs the air as we talk.

Then I notice it, an acrid smell of electrical burning.

Suddenly, there's sharp flash of blinding green light emanating from the dark corner of the room, furthest away from the fireplace. It is as if the wooden paneled walls are alive and bubbling with energy. Crackling with power, the pencil beam grows in strength and size until flashing green fingers of light branch out from the dark corner in all directions, lighting up our surprised faces.

"Get back!" commands Shadrack, quickly leaping up and standing between us and the threatening fingers of light, "Make sure it doesn't touch you!"

Immediately, we all move away, toward the opposite side of the room. The sparkling light spins like a surgeon's knife slicing through the empty air, examining, and feeling its way around the room. After a few intense seconds, the beam falls back to its corner. Still spinning, like an unwieldy bobbin on a vertical spindle, it starts to create a human shape; difficult to see at first but, as it solidifies, it becomes more and more lifelike and threatening. With an abrupt swish and a final crackle, the green energy evaporates leaving behind a crumpled dark shadowy figure who stands eyeing and evaluating the room and us.

We stand motionless, spellbound.

Unflinching and ready for battle, Shadrack stands as a barrier between us and the dark presence in front of us.

"How dare you come here!" challenges Shadrack aggressively, as if he knows exactly who, or what, he is speaking to.

"So, these are your new recruits, eh?" sneers the voice, ignoring Shadrack's challenge.

"What do you want?" challenges Shadrack again, unable to conceal his loathing.

"Don't look much, do they?" the voice sounds more threatening and the dark figure menacingly edges towards us.

"Don't you move another step!" confronts Shadrack standing his ground defiantly.

The door flings open and Charlie's father instantly joins the Searcher in front of us. "Go back to your hole!" he threatens.

"Not very polite, are we?" jeers the voice then, referring to Charlie, it continues taunting, "Keeping it in the family I see?"

"What do you want?" asks Charlie's father, disregarding the remark, standing firm, and showing the same hatred that Shadrack showed just seconds before.

Alfide quickly joins the two men and faces the dark figure which is looking bigger and even more menacing.

"I have an offer," it says changing its tone, as if it is offering a gift to an old friend.

The dark figure shifts uneasily at the unexpected sight of Alfide and waits.

"Speak it then and don't waste my time!" Alfide commands with authority.

"Lord Maulum, your brother, wishes to grant you a pardon,"

the dark figure replies, this time, less certain of itself, "in return you will give him the stones you have stolen from him."

"A pardon! Huh! Now give this message to my brother," spits out Alfide as if the mere mention of his brother makes him angry, "Tell Maulum to stop spreading his evil viruses and go back to his prison where he belongs, maybe *then* we can talk."

"Fools! You know he will never accept those terms!" splutters the dark figure angrily, already beginning to shrink and fade back into the shadowy corner of the room.

"Then you are wasting my time! Be gone!" Alfide dismisses his brother's messenger with a wave of his hand.

The dark figure fades and vanishes into the darkness.

Shadrack immediately turns to face Alfide and mutters, "I don't like it! He managed to get right into our midst. Now he knows who the new Holders are!"

"It was never a secret. Better, now the new Holders know something about what we are up against." Alfide calmly answers, "More importantly, *how* did he know they were here?"

"You don't think...?" Charlie's father cannot believe what he is thinking. He can't bring himself to believe that there might be a traitor amongst us. Everyone is handpicked. Everyone is completely trustworthy and has demonstrated this time after time, battle after battle. The idea is ridiculous.

"Who can say, maybe it was luck," Alfide replies doubtfully, before leaving.

Throughout the entire strange event, we all stood like statues, unmoving, watching uselessly from the safety of the other side of the room. Charlie's father and Shadrack turn to us and kindly beckon us to sit back down again.

"Hardly the hero Holders who will save the Earth, are we?" groans Geo who is disappointed with himself.

"We need to find out more and find out what to do if something like that turns up again," adds Charlie optimistically, looking up at his father for some hopeful sign.

"There's a first time for everything. No need to worry. In the meantime, I suggest you try to recover from your ordeal and rest. You will need all your energy! You've had a lot to take in and in such a short time," sympathises Charlie's father.

"Make sure you get an early night," he adds, as if he knows that this will not be the last that we hear from the dark presence.

MORE ERUKE!

~~~

I am abruptly and rudely awakened by the, now scarily familiar, shrilling shrieking sound that signals we are under attack again. More Eruke! My heart pounds against my chest walls as I quickly shrug off the groggy veil of my deep sleep and blindly search in the darkness to find my clothes. The noise increases, getting louder and louder with every second like an approaching thunder storm; it feels as if it is rapidly approaching us from all directions. Ignoring the thumping in my chest, trying not to panic, I get dressed. I can just hear Geo and Charlie's voices over the terrifying din. At last, Charlie finds the light switch and flicks it on just as the door flings wide open.

"As quick as you can! Don't bother taking anything with you! Go down to the Meeting Hall. Quickly!" Charlie's mother is still dressed in her ruby robe with matching fluffy slippers. She holds the bedroom door wide open and quickly we file past her onto the upstairs landing. Immediately, we are joined by the three disheveled girls. Hurriedly, we run down the broad stairway towards the main hallway. Charlie leaps down the last flight of stairs in the rush, taking the lead. We follow him to the dimly lit parlour. With ease, he locates the hidden panel to open the concealed passageway door. His mother is only a few steps behind us.

Suddenly, there's a frightening hissing sound like something flying through air at speed, towards us. The sound of smashing of glass follows, as a large framed man crashes through the window. He lands with a deadly thud, crumpled, face upwards, on the parlour carpet only metres from my feet. I am frozen to the spot. The blackened charred body looks as though it has been blasted, through the window, by a nearby cannon. His dirty blood-smeared, scarred face tells a story of hard-fought battles and it is set with ruthless determination. As he falls, his left arm flops loosely towards me revealing his large, clenched fist. His fingers are curled tightly as if holding onto something that he will never release. Each finger is blooded and blackened. Surprising even myself, I move forward toward the body. There's an unpleasant smell of thick smoke about him. As I draw closer, I realise I know him, or at least I have seen him before. I have seen him standing, side by side in battle, alongside my Holder in the pool in the Meeting Hall. His face had been crystal clear, but the Holder's face was blurred; impossible to make out.

'What could have happened to this most valiant man and where is the Holder?' I think as I slowly kneel next to the body.

Unexpectedly, there is an eerie gasp of rasping air expelled from the dead man's throat as his head lurches and falls sideways to face me sending cold shivers down my spine. I feel his bloodshot eyes staring blindly at me, not recognising, just questioning; as if he is willing me to understand something. But I don't. Even in death, the man is formidable. Reaching out to the tightly enclosed fist, I carefully uncurl each charred finger, one by one. There, in the palm of this dead man's hand, is the golden glow of an amber stone! My heart leaps as I pick it up. I wipe the blood off it.

Suddenly, I'm brought back into the deafening, furious battle raging around me and I am grabbed roughly from behind by Alfide. "You have your stone, now make sure you live long enough to use it! Go! Follow the others quickly before ..."

Urgently, he pushes me into the passageway; his angry words are abruptly cut off with the closing of the panel door between us.

There's a familiar cold silence in the narrow tunnel. Without a word, I hold out my hand and reveal the amber stone to the others. It glows comfortably in my palm, as if it has arrived home.

Like before, we follow Charlie's mother down the tunnel corridor into the safety of the Meeting Hall. Strangely, naturally, we sit in the same chairs as before. She leaves us alone with our thoughts in the Meeting Hall. Ritually, we all place our stones on the ledge surrounding the pale pool in front of us. The only one of us now, without a stone is Imp, but not for long.

Directly in front of Imp, from within the cool water of the milky pool, there's a faint white glow of a new stone. It is as if her stone is answering the combined call of all the other stones. We stare in silent awe. Imp stands up from her chair and leans over, reaches deep into the pool, and pulls out her stone, it is clear in appearance but with a cool white florescent glow. Calmly, she dries it on her top and sets it on the ledge surrounding the milky pool in front of her chair.

We each have our stone.

We are chosen.

We are the Holders.

"We could re-make the necklace!" notices Geo, his relief and guilt resurfacing.

"A bit late for that!" Jun replies abruptly, remembering how we had all got here.

I remember how Geo 'borrowed' the old lady's necklace, Imp accidentally opened the deep shaft in our den, the necklace disappeared in an electric flash and the Black Mist was released from the depths. Originally, we had set out to find all the stones so that we could remake it and give the necklace back. Now, the necklace could be remade, that is true but that is no longer an option. There is a dreadful battle raging outside and people are dying. There is an evil brother, hell bent on destroying all living things on the Earth with deadly viruses or worse.

"You know, I think it was no accident that you took the necklace," I suggest pointing to Geo but not judging him, "What if you were meant to take it?"

Imp continues for me, "Maybe the old lady had been protecting the stones all this time but when she died…"

"Yep, when she died, she needed to be sure the stones got to where they belong. What if Maulum had found them? Who knows what might have happened?" chips in Jun, excitedly adding her thinking.

Geo sat silently, thoughtfully. Clearly it had not occurred to him that he might have been meant to find the necklace all along! Looking back, with hind sight, that does make some sort of sense.

"So, it was a good..." he starts.

Imp could see what Geo is thinking and abruptly cuts him off, "No, it was still wrong to take the necklace! You were just lucky this time."

"Yeah but, if it hadn't been for me..." Geo stops himself mid-sentence as he realises what he is saying; would he rather swap being a Holder under the constant threat of attack from hideous screeching black creatures, for a calm lazy summer's day by the den in the woods? Tricky!

"It's no use talking about what might have happened... what are we going to do *now*? Now we've all got our stones," Charlie adds thoughtfully.

"Why are there these extra seats?" interrupts Imp, pointing to the spare seats around the pool.

Geo airs his thoughts on the matter, "Yesterday, Alfide said that there are eight known stones. There are only the six of us. Then he said that for the first time they are all together. It doesn't make sense."

"We've all got our stones," Charlie repeats, ignoring the interruption, "so what do we do now? We can't just sit here! We should be helping fight those... 'whatever-they-ares'."

"It's useless! Pointless! We've all got our stones, true, but what do we do with them?" says Genji looking at each of our dimly lit faces around the pale milky glow of the pool.

"I went through that wall in the tunnel," Geo adds as a matter of fact, trying to be upbeat about their situation, "that might be useful!"

"True, but you couldn't get us out of the last dead-end cave, could you? If Shadrack hadn't found us, we'd still be there, or worse!" Charlie replies firmly, "What's the point of being a Holder if you can't do anything?"

Geo has no answer this time.

No-one does.

A frustrated silence falls over the Meeting Hall.

Down here, there is no sound, no clue of the fierce battle that is being fought around us. We are completely sealed off and utterly removed from what is happening.

Absent-mindedly, Imp allows herself to look deep into the pale pool in front of her. She is drawn into the visions that the pool offers her. At first, she sees sunny scenes of rolling hills and forests, but then there comes a darkness crawling out of the heart of the Earth. It is only a small shadow at first, but it grows and grows until there is more darkness than light. What she sees next make her cry out "No-o-o!" She turns her face away, releasing her eyes from the spell of the pool and breaking the gloomy silence in the Meeting Hall.

"What's up? What did you see?" Geo is concerned for his sister.

Simultaneously, Charlie's father dramatically arrives in the Meeting Hall looking wind swept and exhausted. His cloak is half burnt and ripped at the front; it is smoldering and a short plume of smoke wafts around him. Then he realises his cloak is still alight. He quickly brushes away the smoking embers and pats down the front of his cloak to make sure the flame is completely extinguished. He still looks composed, even though he has obviously been in the thick of the battle.

"Another battle is won!" he cheers and punches the air with his fist, "A famous victory!"

Charlie has never seen his dad like this. Ever! Up to a few days ago, he was a typical, boring, everyday dad but now he is this battling, cloaked person trying to save the world. Charlie can't help admiring his dad for this but when he comes around the pool, checks Charlie over for injuries, and gives him a cheerful hug in front of the others, he looks like he could die of embarrassment.

Geo grins.

"C'mon Holders! No time to sit around. Let's get you organised and kitted out. I see you've all got your stones now! Good! Follow me. This way to the chamber of staffs!"

Charlie's father taps the wall of the Meeting Hall and, with a tremble, the wall loses its form. "Follow me!" Charlie's father walks straight into the wall which ripples like a stone dropping on a still pool of water, as he passes through, "Come on!"

We are left behind, stood together staring at the wall, with only the shimmering entrance to guide us through.

"Follow me!" says Geo, obviously feeling that he should lead the way because he is the only one of us who has done this sort of thing before.

I follow next with my brain screaming at me, 'Bad idea! Don't walk into a wall!! It will hurt!!'

Walking through the shimmering wall is the strangest feeling, it feels like I am pushing my way through thick duvets filled with jelly, which suck at me as I move and then, as I try to step out to the other side, it holds me back like glue as if it doesn't want to release me. I half expect to be covered in sticky jelly when I reach the other side, but I am completely jelly free when I finally squeeze through. I step into the narrow, high roofed chamber of staffs where Charlie's dad is waiting. One by one the others join us, each one checking that they aren't covered in jelly as they step into the room.

The chamber is lit by what appears to be a floating cloud of light, suspended above us. Against the wall opposite, there are several rows of wooden staffs in a variety of colours and sizes, all lined up very neatly, in wooden racks.

Enthusiastically, Charlie's father picks out a wooden staff and holds it horizontal so that he can look down its length. He expertly admires the workmanship, as if in recognition of how much effort has gone into producing such a fine staff.

"What about this one? No?" then he puts the staff down and picks up another, checks it as before, "This one?"

Dumbly, we look at him, and at each other, thinking that the wooden staffs are fine but what would we do with them?

As if he understands, Charlie's father surprises us all and, from his cloak pocket, takes out a glowing orange stone. He walks over to the opposite corner of the room and selects an old worn looking but still splendid wooden staff. He returns, back to where we are standing, and demonstrates what to do. Holding it vertically upright, with one end firmly fixed on the ground, he places his orange stone carefully on the top of the wooden staff. Amazingly, the top of the staff splits apart and grows flexible fingers which claw around the stone clasping it firmly with a cast iron grip. The staff and the stone seem to become one.

"You're a Holder too!" Charlie says - as the penny drops - in disbelief. Everything adds up now, he tries to make sense of it all and it does make sense... The Meeting Hall is hidden deep within his family's house... Holdwood and the caverns are on his family's grounds...

"Why didn't you tell me?"

"Not the sort of thing you go shouting about, is it?" replies his father happily, "Now find a staff that suites you. Think about the height. You don't want one that's too heavy for you. You'll know when you find the right one... the stone will fix tight on the end."

Charlie's father stands back and watches us as we rummage through the long lines of wooden staffs, not really knowing what we are supposed to be looking for.

There is one distinctive staff made from a dark, almost black, wood. Imp homes in on it straight away.

'Perfect,' she thinks as she tries it out for size.

"Ah! Dalbergia Melanoxylon, African blackwood! A fine choice, hard...quite heavy though," exclaims Charlie's father showing off his knowledge of wood.

Undeterred, Imp holds the staff firmly between two large notches which together form a perfect gripping point for her hand. She places her clear white stone gently on the top of her staff. Immediately, the wood splits and black fingers grow around her stone. The stone and the wood become one just as had happened for Charlie's father. The stark contrast between the black wood and the white stone is striking. Imp is obviously pleased with her choice of staff and proudly joins Charlie's father and observes the rest of us selecting ours.

I find a golden coloured staff which closely matches the golden amber glow of my stone. It's a solid, sturdy staff with an elegant curve in it, perfect for holding. It feels right and true.

"Old reliable, eh? Oak! Good choice!" encourages Charlie's father.

I'm happy with my choice and join Imp in the centre of the staff room. Testing the firmness of the oak and stone combination, I cover the clasp and the stone with my hand. Unexpectedly both the stone and staff vanish! My stomach turns. What have I done?

'Not again!' I think back to when the necklace vanished on the rock in the den, but this is different - I can still feel the clasp in my hand, like a ball, I just can't see it!

"That's it," says Charlie's father enthusiastically, "now twist it, and put it in this leather pouch."

He hands me a small, brown leather pouch with a reddish leather pull strap attached. Imp immediately copies my actions herself. She covers the clasp with her hand and, just as happened to me, her staff and stone disappear completely from view, but I can see she is still holding something. She twists the clasp about quarter of a turn and holds an invisible ball in the palm of her hand, the staff appears to disappear! She places the invisible ball carefully in her leather pouch, as instructed.

Following her lead, I turn my clasp, feel the weight of the invisible ball of wood and stone in the palm of my hand, and cautiously drop it into my pouch.

"To get your staff and stone back just do the opposite!" adds Charlie's father enjoying the moment of our discovery.

Straightaway, I test it. I put my hand in the leather pouch and feel inside for the ball. The invisible but solid weight of the ball confirms it is still there. Awkwardly, I try to locate the invisible clasp. I twist it in the opposite direction and then drop my hand away from shielding the glow of the stone. Instantly, the staff re-appears, my staff, solid and true, as before! It feels good to hold.

One by one the others choose theirs and join us test pouch-ing their staff and stones. We are beginning to enjoy ourselves, briefly forgetting the earlier terrifying moments that had forced us to take refuge in the Meeting Hall.

Our playful mood is broken when Alfide joins us abruptly in the staff room. Impatiently, he announces that there's a gather-ing in the Meeting Hall and that we are expected. He turns and leaves us as quickly as he arrived.

THE JOURNEY BEGINS

~~~

No one notices us arrive, one by one through the shimmering wall, as we return to the Meeting Hall. A heated discussion is already in full swing and the mood is ugly. Everyone looks exhausted and battle worn.

"We are all in grave danger. Whether by luck or foul means, we have been found out. There's no point in wasting any more time, they have to leave here now!" says Jennifer, flashing her green eyes threateningly, searching for anyone who dares to disagree.

I recognise her voice from before, when Shadrack saved us from the dead-end cavern.

"Oh yes, and where would they go exactly?" asks Charlie's mother, trying to remain calm but obviously concerned for Charlie's safety.

"It doesn't matter! Now that *they* know that the new Holders are here...they will be back in even greater numbers... you know that! Then there's the Black Mist... who knows what else they've woken up down there!" Jennifer continues, getting more agitated.

"At least here, they are protected!" Genji and Jun's father joins in the discussion.

Genji and Jun are pleased to see that their father has returned safely from his mysterious outing.

"And how long can we keep protecting them?" replied Jennifer, taking a more reconciliatory approach.

"If they leave here, they will be even more vulnerable," adds

Charlie's mother.

"They need much more time! They must learn their stones," continues Genji and Jun's father, in his quiet but forceful tone.

"We *have* no more time! Tell them Shadrack!" Jennifer rounds fiercely on Shadrack.

"I'm afraid Jennifer is right. I sense they are preparing to attack once more," Shadrack shakes his head dejectedly, "I do not think that they are going to give up on this now. They think they know where the stones are!"

"How many more attacks can we withstand?" Jennifer feels that she is winning the argument.

"We can last out here for days unless *he* joins in the attack as well," Charlie's father appears confident.

"All the better if my brother does, but I don't believe he has the strength yet, even he is not that foolish! No, he is committed to finding the remaining segments of the Earthcode...he needs those more than he needs the stones," Alfide's words ring true. He looks dark and threatening; war-like, not at all like the person we spoke with in the gardens before.

"Then there is no need for them to leave," says Charlie's mother happily.

"You are right... except for one thing...we need Maulum to think that the new Holders are already trained and able to fight. We need him to believe that they are ready for battle, already prepared to beat him in the search for the Earthcode. If we can force him to commit all his efforts to this, maybe *others* can damage him closer to home. Either way, he will have less time to concentrate on completing the Earthcode. He must never complete the Earthcode! That would surely be the end."

"What are you saying? What do you suggest we do?"

"I think they should go to the Nix and ask them to help. It's been some time but I'm sure they will help," replies Alfide with authority.

"The Nix? What can they do?" asks Jennifer.

Alfide answers decisively, "They can shield them from the prying eyes of his watchers and, if nothing else, they can give them more time to learn their stones."

"There is much to do!"

"Before we do anything, shouldn't we consult the new Holders themselves?" asks Shadrack as he motions toward us. The grave look on his face leaves me in no doubt that we are in a dreadfully desperate situation.

We have stood in silence and listened intently to every word. Imp found the words for us all. She is the youngest but also, often, the most perceptive.

"We are ready to do what needs to be done!" she answers boldly.

"But, my girl, do you really understand what we are asking you to do?" this time Jennifer is full of genuine concern.

"No. Not really, but I have a good idea what will happen if we don't," Imp replies.

It is the right answer and no one in the room could argue with her.

"I will take them as far as the Nix. You can manage here without me. There's been so little news from the mainland; I need to find out what is going on. As soon as possible, I will leave for the mainland and make contact with the others, and warn them to prepare the way, if they are still able," announces Alfide.

"Then you must leave straight away and travel light, speed is of the essence! I will personally speak to your families and explain what is happening. These are desperate times, I'm sure they will understand. You must try to leave undetected, that way you will have the advantage," agrees Mr. Chen.

"We need every advantage we can get!" approves Charlie's father.

"Then it's settled. We will stay here as a decoy and delay the enemy for as long as possible. We will join up with you again as soon as we can, if we can!" says Mr. Taylor who had remained in thoughtful silence throughout the discussions and unnoticed up to this point, "There's just one more thing... The new Holders will need transport, a boat of some description, ideally one that will go unnoticed, and they will need someone who can steer a course to the mainland when they finally leave the Nix. There's no other way to get there at the moment. I'm assuming that you," nodding towards Alfide, "will be taking a different route."

Alfide signals yes back, "After visiting the Nix, I will travel north. The new Holders may choose another direction."

"Charlie's an expert, he can use the 'Lithos' if needed, she's moored up in the harbour," says Charlie's father with obvious pride, "he's been sailing since he was a young lad, he can handle any boat!"

Charlie's shoulders rise and his head goes up in pride but that is short lived when his mother says, "But he's only a boy!"

"I know a thing or two about boats," announces Shadrack calmly and then diplomatically, "not that Charlie will need any help, but just in case. They will also need a guide to find the segments of Earthcode."

"That's settled then, Shadrack, you come with us and then take them on to the mainland. Now we must use this time wisely, we will travel light and find what we need as we go; take only what you must. We will leave first thing in the morning!"

With that Alfide closes the meeting and crosses the room to talk to Shadrack to make further arrangements.

Charlie's father is more upbeat, "I wish I was going with you! It seems I'm stuck here, missing out on all the fun, yet again!"

"He's only a boy!" hisses Charlie's mother in his father's ear.

"A young man ready for adventure, I'd say! Alfide will make sure they're ready and Shadrack is the ideal companion. This is what we've been preparing him for...yes, he still has much to learn but...have faith my dear, have faith!"

THE NIX

~~~

None of us sleep much. Genji, Jun and Charlie are still coming to terms with the fact that their own parents are linked to everything that is happening. So much to take in, so much has happened already, but we all know that this is only the very beginning of our journey. I am as excited and as ready to get going as the others, although I can't help feeling that there has been some big mistake and I should not really be part of all this. I wonder what my parents would say. I bet Gramps would be smiling...this would be right up his street.

At last, we are packed and ready to leave the security of Holdwood Manor. Stepping outside, it is still dark with only a glimmer of daylight on the very distant horizon, hinting at the arrival of a new day. I breathe in deeply, filling my lungs with the cool fresh air, preparing myself for the unknown.

All are there to wave us off; parents, Mr. Taylor, Jennifer and even the others who have only recently arrived and have not been introduced to us.

Then I spot my Gramps' old friend who has also come to see me off too, "Here, take this." He says and hands me a medal. "Your Gramps would want you to have this. He would be so proud!"

Imp and Geo are excitedly speaking to a lady that I don't recognise, but I guess is their Aunt.

"Good luck! We'll catch up with you soon," Genji and Jun hug their parents, "remember to use what you have learnt."

Charlie's father comes over to Charlie who is standing with

Geo, Imp, and me.

Formally, he shakes our hands and wishes, "Good luck! Learn your stones and do your best!"

Charlie's mother bear hugs Charlie and then, noticing us, waves us over and we all join in.

"Now you've got everything; your pouches with your stones and staffs, your cloaks, good shoes..." she continues through the check list that we have already checked several times before, but we don't mind, it is just good to be fussed over.

"Take care!" even Jennifer respectfully acknowledges the danger we are heading into.

More daylight begins leaking from the far-off horizon as once more we gather together, at last, ready to leave.

No more words are needed.

Alfide pulls up his hood and wheels round with his cloak spinning with him as he marches off, leading the way.

Hastily, with Shadrack guarding the rear we snake away, leaving Charlie's house behind silhouetted in the early morning haze of dawn. A fine white blanket of sea fog gives us perfect cover from any prying eyes. There's a buzz of excitement and trepidation about us; each marching silently, in anticipation of what might lie ahead. In single file, we weave down a narrow pathway, hidden from view on both sides by steep sheer rock faces. They are thickly covered with wet dark green moss. Seamlessly, they blend with the leafy woods which we are about to enter. Unfortunately, the sea mist has not managed to penetrate the thicket, so we stay out of view by keeping to seldom used pathways in the densest parts of the woodland.

It is hard work, but Alfide marches determinedly and confidently onwards, never once turning back to check that we are keeping up with him - his head held low, as if he, too, is deep in thought. He doesn't share our excitement.

Leaving the woodland behind, we are engulfed once more by the sea mist. The secret pathway twists and turns, rises and falls, completely disorientating us. There are many forks and crosspaths. The chances of us ever being able to retrace our steps, gets more remote with each new stride forward. By now my cloak is soaking, not only from the mist but also from constantly brushing against the lush waist-high bracken, still heavy and wet with the fresh morning dew. In places the bracken has overgrown and covered over any signs of a pathway but Alfide doesn't waver at all and holds his pace.

Eventually, as we tire and the bracken gives way to open, grassy scrubland. An unnerving stillness surrounds us. This is compounded by the sea mist which has silently thickened around us, reducing visibility down to a few metres in all directions. We must be moving closer to the edge of the land. Breaking the silence, a single squawking gull, not far ahead, confirms my suspicions.

Prompted by the gull's cry Alfide's pace slows for the first time, as if he is remembering something. He lifts his arm from under his cloak and signals for us to halt. We stop obediently, still in single file on the pathway, still unable to see beyond each other in the dense white mist. He is listening intently but there is no discernable sound. He turns and hoarsely whispers and waves us off the pathway, "Quick, get off the track. Someone is coming!"

'How could he know that?' I think as I stare dumbly back at Alfide. I know I haven't heard a sound.

Imp tugs at my cloak, urging me to move quicker with her. We don't need to move very far off the pathway, as the impenetrable sea mist immediately surrounds and engulfs us, each of us is hidden in our own personal cloud.

Only metres away from the track that we were following, we wait in an urgent silence. Imp holds tightly to my cloak to help keep her balance on the large uneven stones underfoot. The shroud of silence seems to last for an age. We stay motionless, frozen to the spot. I hardly dare to breathe just in case I miss any sound, any sign of who else is on this secret track. But there is no need. A mist covered, invisible cascade of heavy footsteps and rustling of cloaks and clinking equipment crashes past us. Whoever it is clearly doesn't feel the need to travel quietly and undetected. They pass right in front of us, crossing from left to right. We stay silent and unmoving, until the last of the strange travelers' sounds fades into the distance and, once more, the eerie silence returns.

"Who, or what, were they?" asks Geo breaking the silence.

"Didn't sound very pleasant!" says Genji.

"What do you mean 'didn't sound very pleasant'?" questions Charlie, "How can they not sound 'very pleasant'?!"

"Quiet!" Alfide hisses, "There will be time to talk later. We must move on and make the most of the mist's cover!"

With that he returns to the pathway and we continue our silent march. Abruptly the trail starts to fall away, descending ever more quickly. Before long, I hear the soft sound of distant waves gushing, rushing, and refreshing the beach some way ahead of us. I picture us resting at the water's edge and dipping my hot, tired, aching feet in the cool, soothing sea water but, instead of continuing down towards the rolling sound of the sea, Alfide halts once more. I stand behind him, silently expecting to have to move off the track and hide again. I strain to hear approaching travellers but there is no sound. Again, Alfide wears the frowned expression on his face, as if he is remembering something long past.

"Follow, but be as silent as you can be, I am not sure if we will be welcome here."

Alfide turns and squeezes sideways into an extremely narrow vertical gap sliced between two tall sheer rock faces. He slides his whole body along the rock face with difficulty. I follow immediately behind. The rock is smooth with no cracks, no hand holds to help pull myself through, and I am already on tip toes wriggling awkwardly trying to squeeze deeper into the gap. My cheeks are squashed against the rock so tightly I think that I might suffocate.

Then Alfide vanishes. One second, he is struggling to get through the narrow space, a fraction of a second later he's not there, gone. He must be much more nimble than I thought. I am surprised at the speed he has made it through to the other side.

I judge it to be at least another five metres to the other end from where I am. I struggle even more, keen to do my best to keep up with our guide.

A moment later, the rock face that I am pressing hard up against softens in to liquid; I have nothing to push against and tumble forwards, passing into the rock face itself which melts away as I fall, before solidifying again behind me. I land on my hands and knees, sprawled on a hard rock floor in a small cavern where Alfide quickly helps me up to my feet.

The cavern is dimly lit by a fused rainbow of flickering colours, giving the wet walls a golden radiance. As my eyes are adjusting to the light, Charlie lands spectacularly, stumbling forward as he falls through, exactly where I landed. Alfide pulls him up to his feet and out of the way, next to me. One by one, the others tumble in and are moved aside quickly so that no one lands on top of anyone.

Shadrack smiles as he stands up and brushes the dust from his trousers with his hands. "Why don't they have a front door like everyone else?" he mumbles and chuckles at his own joke.

"Where are we?" asks Jun.

"We are entering the home of the Nix..." as he speaks their name there is an impossible gush of cold fresh air in the enclosed space, "...if they will let us," explains Alfide, for once, with uncharacteristic uncertainty.

"Why wouldn't they?" asks Genji still dusting herself down and adjusting her clothing after her unexpected entrance.

"It has been many, many years since we last had any contact with the Nix..." again the cold rush of fresh air, "Old friends should keep in touch more..." his voice drifts off as he becomes thoughtful but he finishes the sentence, not speaking to us, but to whoever might be listening, "but there never seems to be enough time!"

Alfide walks over towards the centre of the space. The light burns noticeably brighter as he reaches the middle of the cavern, our shadows dance across the gleaming rock walls as he moves. He stops still, standing straight and tall as if he is ready to greet an equal, and stares directly at the bare cavern wall in front of us and waits...and waits...

I look across towards Geo and Charlie who are still nursing their knees after their fall into the cavern. Imp is very quiet and matching Alfide's gaze exactly, they both seem to be looking through and beyond the cavern wall.

Genji and Jun huddle together whispering in each other's ears but stop after a withering glance from Alfide.

"Come on old friends...don't let us down in our time of need," mutters Alfide under his breath, a flicker of doubt crosses his worn scarred face.

Another whoosh of cold, refreshing air fills the room and then blasts us as if we are stood on the edge off a powerful storm. Each of us is covered by a fine, silvery cloud of gentle, bright, light droplets, which hover and fizzle over us, as if welcoming us home.

My arms and face tingle as the silvery droplets burst open on my skin. After a few seconds, I feel rejuvenated, refreshed and very alive, as if I could run a marathon... twice! I look around at the others who are smiling, any feeling of tiredness is lifted, and our many bruises vanish into distant memory.

"Thank you for your warm welcome old friend!" even Alfide is pleased and looks years younger, "Your help is much needed, unfortunately sooner than we expected!"

I follow the direction of Alfide's steady gaze but there is nothing there until the cavern wall opens up into a sparkling, short, tube-shaped tunnel. Alfide steps forward into the tunnel, we follow behind. Both Alfide and Imp had somehow seen, or sensed, what is beyond the tunnel, but it had been invisible to me.

We find ourselves standing in the largest underground cave that I have ever seen! It is bigger than several football pitches put together. Floating above, are hundreds of interlinked clouds of sparkling dots, with intermittent flashes of light, bouncing around from one cloud to another. As we enter, they crackle in unison, as if sending messages to each other.

Directly in front of us, the sparkling clouds start to shift and take on the shape of a girl with long sparkling golden hair, floating on a glittering cloud of her own. Occasionally her form dissipates, and reforms as wavelike ripples spread across her.

She speaks softly but as if many different voices are talking together, "Welcome friends of old and welcome to you strangers! I trust you come to us in peace, although we have long sensed troubled times beyond our walls."

"Thank you for welcoming us, your kindness is most gratefully received," replies Alfide courteously, relieved that the old friendship is as solid as ever; knowing that not even that is guaranteed any longer.

"We have sensed your troubles. Sickness and darkness sweep across the world. This does not bode well my friend and, more concerning, we also sense that you are at the heart of it, one way or another."

"These troubles will eventually affect us all. No one and no thing will be able to avoid it this time," replies Alfide referring to something that must have happened in the distant past that I have no knowledge about.

"You will be safe here, as before, our walls are strong, even your infections and diseases cannot pass."

"I hope you are right, but this time Maulum believes he can find the complete Earthcode and, with the completed code, you know he will destroy *all* living things." As Alfide speaks there is another ripple of flashing lights as the Nix communicate with each other.

"He knows that we have new Holders and he will not rest until either he is destroyed, or we are!" Alfide's voice is strong and convincing.

Another ripple of communication passes through the ever-shifting cloud of the Nix.

Sensing that his grim message is understood, Alfide continues, "All I ask is that the Nix help us, by protecting the new Holders while they learn their stones and prepare for the battles ahead. Maybe, when you see fit, you may choose to help us more."

The glowing and flashing continues for some time before the girl answers, "Never let it be said that the Nix do not help their friends in times of need. You are welcome to stay here as long as it takes. We welcome the chance to talk further with you. Come."

As she speaks, the cloud splits apart forming a pathway through the centre of the cavern. We follow her as she leads the way deeper into the heart of the cavern. We walk within arm's reach of the ever shifting, communicating cloud of the Nix. Unexpectedly, another larger open area unfolds in front of us. It is lit by millions of twinkling points of light suspended in more clouds of Nix high above us. Even the knowledge that we are somewhere deep inside tons of heavy rock, does not take away the fresh airy feeling of a clear night sky, lit by thousands of distant bright stars. There's a small gurgling stream running from left to right and the water sparkles as it reflects the lights above.

"Rest here for a moment. I must let the Nix know everything about my brother. I am not convinced they really understand the danger," orders Alfide kindly.

Shadrack and Alfide leave us alone to explore the open underground expanse.

"I could get used to this," says Geo cheerfully, moving towards the stream. He kneels down, cups his hands and scoops up some water to drink, "Mm! Best water I've ever tasted! Try some!"

As if a thirst button has been pressed, we all realise how thirsty we all are and guzzle back scoopfuls of the cool revitalising water. Afterwards, the water sloshes in my belly as I move. Satisfied at last, I lie down on the surprisingly comfortable rock floor, and watch the thousands of twinkling lights high above me, they are not fixed but flicker out, move, and reappear somewhere nearby as if they are alive and playing tag with each other.

Imp walks over and sits down next to me.

"What do you think about this place? And the Nix?" she asks

me in a hushed voice, although there is no one else close enough to hear.

"What do you mean?"

"Well look about you...this place...it can't be real can it? I mean, it feels real but..." her voice trails off thoughtfully.

"I don't know, after what we've been through... with the stones...those creatures..." my answer also trails off lazily.

I am completely relaxed for the first time.

Genji and Jun join us. Genji picks up a small lose pebble and flicks it carelessly away from us. Her arm is completely re-covered, and she sits next to me, "I love this place, it feels so... so peaceful!"

"Yeah, makes a change," Geo joins in and jokes, "what d'yer think Charlie, should we stay?"

Charlie comes over and sits with us, frowning. "I'm not sure about this place," he says, "it doesn't feel right."

"What d'yer mean doesn't feel right? Feels right enough to me," replies Geo, "and I feel great...never felt better!"

"Yeah, I know, that's the problem."

We sit in an uncomfortable silence before Geo says, "Well, whatever the Nix are and wherever we are...I vote we should make the most of it. Let's 'learn our stones' like Alfide said we should!"

He bounces up, undoes his leather pouch and rummages for his invisible stone. In one action he turns the clasp and releases his hands from around it and there he is, standing holding his staff, with his blue stone glowing brightly as if he'd done it hundreds of times before. Above us, the clouds of the Nix respond by freezing still, as if acknowledging the presence of something powerful, before ignoring it and continuing with their game of tag.

"OK then, what are you going to do now?!" asks Imp mockingly.

"I don't know, maybe if I wave it around?" He starts to wave the staff from side to side.

Nothing happens.

"What about pointing it at something?" suggests Genji. "That might work!"

Obligingly Geo points it at the trickling stream.

Nothing happens.

"What's the point of having a stone, if it doesn't do anything?!" says Geo disappointedly and, in his frustration, he bashes the base of the staff on the ground.

With that, the entire fabric of our surroundings vanishes briefly before immediately, returning to normal. What we see is very, very strange. It is as if we are contained in a bubble which has just burst but then, instantly, reformed. Just for that fraction of a second, we were still standing in the small cave that we had fallen into earlier. But within a flash, we are back by the trickling stream.

"Did you see that?" I check.

"We're still in the cave where we fell through the opening in the rock!" says Charlie excitedly but not knowing exactly what this meant.

"We can't be! Look around you! We're here!" replies Genji. "Didn't you see what happened?"

"What?" Jun asks, wondering what all the fuss was about.

"You know!"

"Know what?" she asks again perplexed.

"Just for a second, the whole place vanished, and we were stood where we were, just before we met the Nix!" says Charlie impatiently.

"Oh! That's weird! I never saw anything. My eyes were closed!" replies Jun.

"That's alright, I'll do it again!" says Geo with indulgent enthusiasm.

"NO! That will be quite enough!" booms Alfide's voice and turning to Geo. "Can't I leave you for two minutes without you causing chaos? Remember we are guests here!"

"But *where* is here?" challenges Charlie.

Alfide strolls over to the stream and drinks deeply, before turning around and answering.

"Here is where we are. The Nix are not always physical like you," as he speaks, he realises none of us understand what he's saying. Alfide pauses and tries again, "They share our earth. They are part of it, but not. They are not tied to flesh and bone bodies like you and me, but they live together as one, mostly, keeping themselves to themselves. They have given us desperately needed shelter for a brief time, for which we are very grateful. Do not dishonor them by playing fools in their world! They have no need for us but have often helped us, even saved us, in years gone by. At last we may have a chance to repay them by helping them save themselves!"

Shadrack moves next to Alfide at the stream's edge.

"I was only trying to 'learn my stone'," complains Geo, feeling he has been unfairly accused, again.

"That, at least, is good but we must learn slowly, together, before you destroy everything around you! I am afraid, it will take time," Shadrack adds sounding much more understanding than Alfide.

"All I did was hit my staff on the ground because nothing happened when I pointed it or waved it!"

"Nothing will happen, unless *you* make it happen. You were annoyed which is a powerful thought and feeling, your stone simply amplifies your feelings which you, unwittingly, then released when you hit your staff on the floor," explains Shadrack patiently.

"Think of your stone as something that feels what you feel. The power of the stone comes from the Earth's own life energy. If you can combine the two and focus them together, there are few limits to what you can do. As with all things, this knowledge must be used sparingly and with care. Every time you use part of the Earth's life energy, you also take away energy that the Earth, itself, needs to remain a living world, teaming with life."

We are all surprised to hear that there might be consequences for *using* the stones.

"You must also learn to defend yourselves, fight and survive in preparation for the battles ahead of you. Shadrack has trained many new Holders in his time but we have so little time, most of what you will learn will have to be learnt as we go along. You must always keep your wits about you!" adds Alfide.

"Can I move that pebble using my staff and stone?" I ask keen to learn.

"Why would you want to?" challenges Alfide, "Why not get up and pick it up yourself?"

"I thought it might be good to start small and work up to bigger things that I can't carry myself."

"Alfide, let the boy learn!" encourages Shadrack cheerfully, "OK, get your stone and staff ready."

Seconds later, I am standing in front of the others holding my stone and staff. My heart is beating fast and I clench my staff to help steady myself. I don't know what to expect.

"OK, now *feel* the pebble and at the same time imagine a part of you wants to move to the stream."

My face contorts with lines of concentration. My whole body tenses up as I focus on the defiant pebble. Nothing happens.

"How do you do it?" I gasp in annoyance, "It won't budge!"

"Don't worry it'll come. You're trying too hard...and remember to breathe!"

"Use your senses, *be* the pebble," Shadrack repeats softly, close to my ear.

I can see the pebble. I can imagine it moving towards the stream but still nothing is happening. The pebble refuses to move.

"Relax, you're focusing too much on what you see, *be* the pebble."

Taking a deep breath, I try again. At first, I think the pebble shifts slightly but then I doubt it.

"Don't even look at the pebble! You know what it is; it knows what it is..."

I have another attempt, this time with my eyes closed.

I don't see the pebble move.

I don't see it rise up off the ground.

I don't see it float through the air across towards the stream.

I don't see it settle gently by the stream ... but it does!

The others watch with wide-eyed disbelief as the pebble moves through the air, seemingly by itself. It is their cheer that confirms that the pebble is now by the stream.

I open my eyes, I know exactly where to look for the pebble... I sense it!

"There you are! Not so difficult was it?" encourages Shadrack.

Then, feeling confident that I now know what to do, I pick up the pebble and take it back to its original position, to prove to myself that I can do it again. I am relieved when the pebble moves exactly as I imagined it. Next, I start to play, making the pebble hover and float around in front of us.

"Now you're just showing off!" accuses Geo itching to try himself.

The others join me and, after a shaky start, there are pebbles of all shapes and sizes, crisscrossing the cavern and bouncing off each other in a sort of mid-air pebble fight.

"What about something a bit bigger?" I ask Shadrack, keen to test the limits of my new-found skill.

"It's doesn't matter what size the rock is, it is the same sense, but you do need to channel more Earth energy. Sometimes it's easier if a few holders work together. It's also safer, just in case one of you gets distracted as can often happen in the heat of battle."

"I'll do it with you!" says Imp eagerly, just as hungry as me to learn the new skills.

"Me too!" Charlie stands next to me with his staff and stone at the ready.

"Three will be more than enough! OK...see that boulder over there," Shadrack points to the large boulder across the cavern by the far wall. The boulder is impossibly large, even if we all push together, we would never have been able to budge it, "agree where you want to move it to, then, when you're ready... move it!"

Imp suggests that we move it to the middle of the open space in front of us. With that in mind, working together to feel the boulder, we move the impossible boulder across the 10 metres and settle it down in front of us! Half in disbelief, and half in amazement at our achievement, we look at each other. My legs are a little shaky. "Phew! That was hard, much harder than before!" I whisper to the others, taking in a deep breath.

"You will improve with practice but remember, once you have learned what to do, only use the knowledge when you *have* to, use it sparingly," instructs Shadrack, "Now let the others move the boulder back and then we will rest."

The others are also desperate to have a go, to prove that they can match us.

They stand in a row and start. At first the boulder doesn't move, even a millimeter, but, just as I begin to wonder if something has gone wrong, the boulder suddenly launches high above us like a rocket, almost touching the cloud of Nix which immediately parts, scattering either side to avoid being hit.

"Geo you're trying too hard! Relax!" exclaims Shadrack.

Quickly, they manage to control the boulder which gently glides down towards the ground and into position.

"Phew! That was close! Don't know what happened there," Geo says out of breath.

Genji and Jun look at each other and start laughing.

Straight away, Geo realises they'd played a trick on him; together they were holding the boulder on the ground against Geo as he was trying to raise it, so at first it wouldn't move, then they released it, that is when it catapulted straight up into the air!

"Very funny. Ha! Ha!"

LONG-LIVEDS

~~~

As we rest Alfide returns. He's been in more secretive discussions with the Nix and seems genuinely pleased with the progress we have made.

Feeling the mood is right, Jun decides to ask Shadrack, "How come you and Alfide haven't got a stone and yet, can do the same things with your staff, as if you had a stone?"

"That's simple!" answers Shadrack cheerfully, "Practice, practice and more practice! I dare say that you wouldn't need stones yourselves if you had had as much practice as we've had!"

He smiles warmly and nods towards Alfide.

"Some of us have been around for a long, long time!" adds Alfide.

"'Long-liveds', that's what some people call us," Shadrack tries to explain, "Alfide and I have lived many, many years, hundreds of years in fact...so you pick up a few tricks along the way!"

"Hundreds of years?! That's cool!" says Geo enthusiastically.

"So how come you don't die like the rest of us?" asks Charlie not convinced. He can see they are obviously old, but hundreds of years old?

"There are quite a few of us, though not as many as there used to be, we like to keep ourselves to ourselves," explains Alfide, "I believe the Earth allows us to live, like the Nix, so that we can be caretakers of the Earth... a little point Maulum seems to have over looked!"

"So, how old are you exactly?" quizzes Jun.

"How old? Age is something we don't usually bother with, it has no real meaning, we don't really measure it like you do," Shadrack tries to explain, "old enough shall we say!"

"Wow! Can anyone be a 'Long-lived'?" asks Geo keen to put his name down.

"The Earth itself chooses its own caretakers... whether they want to be or not... a bit like when it chooses the Holders," replies Alfide solemnly.

"Well it didn't do a good job choosing your brother, did it?" Imp observes.

"He was not always like he is now," says Alfide regretfully and stands up and walks silently across to the stream.

Imp looks across at Shadrack, "I didn't mean to upset anyone, it just that it doesn't make sense to me!"

"Imp, there is no need to be sorry, you are not to know how close he and his brother were... and you're right, it doesn't make sense... unless you understand that the Earth itself is always in a state of constant battle to evolve, survive and keep the life it supports alive against incredible odds in the wider universe," Shadrack pauses, trying to find the words to explain to someone who has lived so few years, "Sometimes out of a struggle comes something good, like a hero or a change for the better...it's a tough one...don't judge too harshly, would be my advice!"

Sensing that the mood in the cavern has darkened, Geo tries to change the subject, "What else do we need to learn before we're ready?"

"Trust me, you will never stop learning new skills Geo. We have only scratched the surface of what you need to know; the tip of the ice burg. You will have to learn as you go along. Unfortunately, we don't have much more time."

"By the way, what time is it?" I ask, not really bothered but realising that I have no idea whatsoever, what time of day or night it is.

Shadrack answers me very vaguely, "As you might have guessed, time has little meaning here. The time is what the time is."

TEAM SKILLS

~~~

Alfide is sat, cross legged, on the ground. In front of him he has four differently shaped smooth black stones each the size of a clenched fist. He deftly stacks them on top of each other. Without looking up, he speaks to us all, "Often balance can mean the difference between success and defeat; if you are off balance, your aim will be poor whatever your weapon or, worse, you may fall and, within seconds, the enemy will be upon you. This will help you improve your balance."
Before us, is a raised balancing beam, formed from the rock itself. Unlike the straight gymnastic beams, this also has an 'S' shape and an undulating zigzag line, looping back to the start.

"Easy!" Jun and Genji agree and walk across to the challenge, keen to show off their athletic prowess. Jun is first to go; she starts very quickly and has no problems at all. Genji is as good, if not better!

"Good!" cheers Alfide, "Now, carry each other...remember you are a team."

The girls look at Alfide with dismay but rise to the challenge and Genji tries to carry Jun around the balance track but topples by the 'S' bend.

In the end we all try. A few hours pass by with only minor success.

Sensing that we are getting frustrated and about to give up, Alfide stands upright and moves to the start point with Shadrack on his back. With his eyes firmly shut, he focuses on the raised beam of rock beneath his feet and steps onto it.

Slowly at first, he moves, step by step, along the beam; it is as if he is feeling his way and somehow using the Earth's energy to keep them in balance. He comfortably completes the trail.

I watch in disbelief but can't help being impressed. Shadrack and Alfide are definitely a team and clearly trust each other completely. I guess they have needed to rely on each other many times before, in much more dangerous situations in the past.

Charlie is the first to take the challenge, this time with me on his back. I hold on tight so that his arms are free to hold his stone in front of him. He closes his eyes and focuses on the raised beam in front of us. I close my eyes too and imagine the beam. I feel the unsteady movement as Charlie takes us one step forward, then a second, then a third, then a fourth. I hold on firmly. A fifth step... a sixth step. I know we must be getting very close to the 'S' bend. A seventh step, an eighth, a ninth, a tenth. I am hardly breathing. Then we fall, fortunately only our pride is injured.

Two by two, we each test our balancing skills on the raised rock beam.

One by one, we improve until eventually we have all navigated the whole trail successfully. It feels as if we have achieved something important. It is not the balancing itself, it is knowing that we can trust each other and work together.

Later Shadrack shows us how to control the amount of light that our stones radiate; how to change its intensity from a dim glow to a powerful bright beam that could instantly dazzle or blind. Using very similar feelings and thoughts, we also learn how to vary from a gentle warming to burning with sparks.

My confidence grows and grows with each new challenge but Alfide's mood seems to get darker with each success.

Eventually he gathers us together and solemnly announces, "Tomorrow, you must leave the protection of the Nix. I will leave straightaway. Before I travel to the mainland as planned, I must go back to warn the others about the news of the enemy, that the Nix have shared with me. The Nix have noticed that there are many more unwelcome strangers arriving on the island, than we thought. They are using the secret pathways freely and their numbers are increasing by the hour. We nearly ran straight into a small group of them coming here, you may remember... the Nix think they are building an army! There can be only one reason for this."

"To attack Holdwood Manor!" says Geo excitedly.

"They must believe that we are still there," I add.

"Exactly," Alfide continues, "They will soon discover that you have moved on when they attack. There is no time to lose. Events have overtaken us. You must continue with your journey, travel to the mainland with Shadrack and start the search for the Earthcode segments in earnest."

"But what happens if we are spotted and *we* get attacked?!" said Genji full of concern, "What will we do?"

"Shadrack will make sure you remain safe. You will be able to travel for some time without being spotted. You already have the advantage; remember *they* think you are still at the Manor... that is why they're preparing an army to attack it and that is why I must leave, to warn the others! Remember, once you leave the protection of the Nix, use your stones wisely and only if you must! Avoid drawing attention to yourselves at all costs."

Looking around at everyone's stunned faces, it is clear no one feels prepared for this.

"The others and I will join with you as soon as we can," he says as an encouraging afterthought.

"How will you know where we will be?" asks Genji.

"We will know! Don't worry," replies Alfide, "that's the least of your problems."

Moments later, Alfide is stood in his dark cloak ready to leave. He quickly shakes hands with each of us and encourages us solemnly, "You are the Holders, you have been chosen... now prove your worth and get those Earthcode segments before Maulum does! Good luck."

With that he turns and walks back, the way we arrived, into the tunnel pathway and through the shifting cloud of the Nix. Briefly he stops, faces the Nix, mutters a few words and is gone. In acknowledgement the Nix sparkle and fizzle, as a goodbye.

We stand together, alone.

MOVING ON

~~~

The next day, although even that is not certain, we are excited and bristling with energy as we prepare to leave the home of the Nix.

"Make sure you don't leave anything behind!" fusses Shadrack over-protectively, "Check you have your stones and staffs in your pouches."

We pack up the very few possessions we have and are ready to leave. We leave the huge underground cavern the same way we entered, seemingly days ago, and find ourselves back in the smaller entrance that we had fallen into when we arrived. The whole cloud of the Nix seems to compress itself into the small space with us and then the girl with the glowing golden hair appears from within the cloud, once more in front of us.

"Going without saying goodbye?" she pointedly asks Jun and Genji, possibly joking but it is difficult to be certain.

"Oh no, we want to say thank you for all you've done for us!" they reply together.

Shadrack politely takes over, "Thank you again for your hospitality but, as you know, we must be on our way. Troubled times ahead of us I'm afraid."

She turns to Shadrack and simply says, "Good bye, old friend, you will be missed."

"And you Imp, the youngest and yet also unusually gifted we sense, what do you have to say?"

Imp bows her head politely but says nothing.

"I feel *we* will meet again," she adds before moving on to

speak to the rest of us.

Majestically, she shimmers and withdraws a few metres before proclaiming, "We would like to give each of you a gift that we hope you will never need."

As she speaks six translucent discs like flattened air bubbles, the size of a large coin, form from within the Nix cloud and appear floating in front of her. She hands one to each of us except Shadrack.

"Press this healing disc on any wound and, while the Nix survive, our spirit will help heal whatever the injury is. Use it sparingly otherwise it will lose its potency but even that will return with time."

We each politely accept the unexpected gift. I notice that when I look at the clear, yet silvery, surface it reflects a rainbow of colours as if it contains part of the cloud of the Nix themselves. It feels hard as rock but with no weight to it at all.

Finally, the time comes to leave.

"Be safe, be strong and you will succeed!" she says as a shimmering exit way appears in the rock face, "Be weak and you will fail!"

"Good bye, old friend," says Shadrack bowing before turning to go.

One at a time, we pass back through the rock which finally solidifies behind us and vanishes, leaving us with a sense that, at last, we are moving forward and starting our journey.

Imp walks beside me. "What did she mean by that? 'I feel we shall meet again.' Did you hear what she said? She said it to me, no one else...me! Why do you think she said that?"

"Maybe you'll meet her again?" I reply sarcastically, immediately wishing that I hadn't.

"But why just me, not all of us? Does that mean that we will get split up?"

Imp is, no doubting, a brave soul and she is an integral part of the team. The idea that we will ever split up is not good news. The more I think about it, the less I like it too.

"Why don't you see what Shadrack thinks she meant?" I suggest avoiding having to answer.

Imp pauses thoughtfully. "Did you hear how she said goodbye to him?"

I shake my head, I clearly had not been paying attention.

"She said 'Goodbye old friend, you will be missed', it sounded so final...like she doesn't expect they'll ever meet again. What do you think she meant?"

I shake my head again, "Maybe it's just the Nix's way. I shouldn't worry. We've got a long way to go." I know I'm changing the subject, but I have no answers for her either.

We walk on, silent in our own thoughts.

The day is gloomy and dark, the smell of recent rain is in the air. The open scrubland is soft and squelchy under foot as we track back to find the pathway that we were previously on, before visiting the Nix.

Before long, Shadrack leads us out of the low bushes onto more rocky ground, trekking downward towards the sea and stopping every so often to check for any signs of more unwanted travelers.

We are no longer safely shrouded by the thick sea fog which had given us such useful cover before. However, now at least, I can see clearly where we are heading. Our pathway drops rapidly through a steep, narrow valley which extends down to the sea further below.

Passing through the gorge is extremely risky. Several points along the valley are only wide enough for the pathway itself, making it impossible to see very far ahead and providing no cover, if we need to hide from the enemy. Fortunately, we pass all the way through without hindrance although we have a minor scare when an unstable rock, high above us, breaks away from the rock face and tumbles down, partially blocking the pathway behind us.

Our mood lightens when the sky brightens, and the sun burns through the thinning clouds. The salty smell of the sea air grows stronger and the cry of the gulls becomes louder, as we walk towards the coast.

Climbing to the top of the line of sand dunes, which hug the sandy deserted beach below, we are greeted by a warm, incoming sea breeze and the calming sound of rolling waves. We rest half way down the seaward side of the first sand dune we come to. It is sparsely covered with patches of knee-high blades of grass.

"We'll rest here and then we'll have to risk the coastal pathway, back to the harbour. By the time we get there, it will be close to nightfall. We should be able to board your father's boat and sail out unnoticed, if we are lucky," says Shadrack as he sits down next to Charlie, who already has his boots off and is rubbing his hot feet.

"I'm going to dunk my feet in the sea!" Geo says excitedly.

"Make sure no one sees you," reminds Imp, concerned about her brother's recklessness, "Remember we need them to think we are back at Charlie's."

"There's no one for miles! You coming too?"

"Just try and stop me!" I have already taken off my boots and fold my cloak on top of them.

The water is not as cold as I expected, nevertheless the relief to my tired feet is like being back at the Nix's cave. I roll up my trouser legs and wade further out. Geo roars with laughter when, unexpectedly, a large incoming wave catches me, soaking me up to my waist. Charlie joins us and we have a water fight, splashing each other until we are all completely soaked.

PLAGUE

~~~

From the sand dune, the others are looking out to sea, past us, at something they have just spotted on the horizon.

"There it is again!" exclaims Jun who was the first to notice it.

Between waves, about 300m further out to sea from where we are splashing, bobs a solitary sailing boat, being buffeted by powerful waves slamming it from side to side. Occasionally the tall sail mast tips so far over, it looks as if the boat is about to capsize before springing back upright in anticipation of the next wave which obligingly crashes into it. Once more the boat is lifted high onto the next wave's white crest before being dropped back down like a child bored with a toy. The main sail flips and flaps ferociously, like a wriggling snake in the gusting wind. As it creeps towards our bay, more sheltered by the hilly Eastern peninsula, the main sail falls lifelessly, without direction, in the lighter wind

"I bet it's broken away from its harbour mooring during a storm or something," Genji surmises.

Shadrack looks carefully for any signs of life on board but can see none and relaxes.

From the sand dune, Genji waves and shouts down to us, to attract our attention. It is Geo who spots her frantic antics and works out where she wants him to look. He sees the bobbing sailing boat straight away.

Charlie and I follow his gaze too.

"Probably slipped its mooring!" speculates Charlie knowledgeably.

"That boat would be perfect! No one will miss it and it looks in reasonable shape," says Geo thinking he has solved our transport problem.

"Better see what it looks like up close, before we can be sure."

"Why don't we use our stones to bring it in? If we work together..." I suggest.

"Remember what Alfide said about only using them when we *really* need to." Charlie replies responsibly.

"Yeah but... it's a long way out."

"The tide's bringing it towards us and the water's not that deep here anyway," continues Charlie and pointing to a row of jagged rocks, "Mind you, if we don't try something quick, it'll probably smash into pieces on the rocks over there!"

"I'll go!" announces Geo.

"Me too!" I am already soaked.

Together, we wade further out into the sea. The movement of the waves and water churns up plenty of sand and mud; it doesn't take long for my feet to disappear entirely from view. The shallow ripples of the seabed feel unpleasantly soft, squelchy, and slippery under foot. Eventually, we are shoulder deep in the murky grey-brown sea, being buffeted backwards from the constant crashing of incoming waves. With each couple of steps forward, we are swept back one step, not helped by the extra weight of our clothes. Meanwhile, the power of the sea continues to usher the still silent boat relentlessly closer towards us, ever closer to the dangerous rocks.

Already on my tip-toes, I judge the distance between us, and the boat has more than halved since we first spotted it, but I can go no further out if I want to stay standing. Fortunately, it looks as though the boat will be brought the rest of the way to us by the incoming waves. So we wait, awkwardly treading water to hold our positions.

20 metres...

15 metres...

10 metres...

5 metres...

At last, I start to swim as fast as I can, to breach the remaining distance to the boat. However, close up, the boat is much larger than I expected and, even now, with the boat in the calmer beach waters, it is still being tossed around easily by each rolling wave, making it very difficult to reach. Quickly, I swim up as close as I dare and try to push myself up, half out of the water, to grab hold of one of the white balloon shaped buoy fenders which dangle on short heavy-duty ropes at even intervals along the side of the boat. Several misses later, I catch hold of one with both hands and hold on for dear life. I try to pull myself out of the water, but a large wave must have struck the boat from the other side. The boat tips over me, forcing me underwater as the boat rolls, pushing me deeper and deeper under the hull. Completely disorientated, I hold on with every shred of strength I possess, in the hope that the boat might try to right itself and drag me back to the surface. I can hear the rushing of trapped air bubbles escaping past my face from the underside of the boat. Not a second too soon, I feel the sharp tug of the fender wrenching at my hands with such a powerful pulling force that I very nearly lose grip. I feel like my arms are being pulled out of their shoulder sockets. With huge relief and gasping for air, I am thrust back above the water's surface. Wasting no time, I grab again at the thick wet rope holding the fender and, with a final surge of effort, pull my legs and feet out of the water. Holding firmly onto the metal storm rail which protects the perimeter of the deck, I haul myself onto the slippery wooden deck. As I attempt to stand triumphantly, another wave crashes against the side of the boat with such force that it nearly throws me back into the water. Just in time, I grab onto the storm railing and regain my balance.

Taking a second to gather my thoughts, I decide to try to steer the boat away from the rocks and straight onto the beach. Steadily, I track along the edge of the deck using the storm rail as my guide. I make my way towards the steering wheel at the stern. Feet apart for better balance, I hold onto the steering wheel and, for the first time, quickly look around me. There's no sign of Charlie and Geo but my focus changes to the rapidly approaching rocks that Charlie had previously pointed out. I have never steered a boat before but have no time to worry about that. Without thinking, I undo the tether which had held the steering wheel locked, and urgently turn the wheel again and again until it wouldn't turn any further. The main sail is still hanging loose and flapping vigorously in the sea breeze. Instinctively, I feel that I am solely reliant on the power of the sea current to change the boat's direction. She responds surprisingly quickly, too quickly, because I have steered the boat too far. Before I can react, the bow faces outward to sea. Unfortunately, the bow now is slicing through the oncoming onslaught of rolling waves taking very little power from them. More gently this time, I turn the steering wheel port-side and the boat obligingly starts to turn with each wave pushing its weight against the rudder until the boat is painfully, slowly, cutting a course away from the dangerous rocks and towards the beach.

Meanwhile Geo and Charlie have waded back towards the beach and they are knee deep in the water, ready to help me land the boat.

As I steer the boat unsteadily towards the beach, I am extremely grateful that they are there to help when the keel finally bites into the sand and mud of the beach bed with a slow crunching sound. The boat suddenly lurches and jerks to a halt. It is only because I am holding onto the wheel that I avoid being tossed overboard under the impact.

Without hesitation Charlie leaps onto the wet deck to inspect the boat.

"Well done! Brought in like a true sailor!" he blusters as he searches for the catch to unlock the anchor. The catch clunks open and releases the chain holding the anchor. There's a satisfying splash as the anchor pierces the water, "There you go...the tide's still coming in... that should hold position for a while!"

Enthusiastically, he unwinds the cable holding the main sail up the tall mast and pulls down the flapping sail fixing it securely to the boom as if he does this sort of thing every day. For the first time, the deck falls silent without the flapping of the main sail.

At that moment, I decide to investigate the cabin below deck, but I can't open the hatch door, it is as if something heavy is blocking it from behind. I give it another shove, this time with my shoulder, and the door moves inwards a few centimetres. I shove again and the door opens further, allowing a shaft of daylight to pass through and, with a final push, there is just enough room for me to squeeze through. Once inside, to my horror, I discover what was holding the hatch closed. Leaning against the back of the door is a body.

"Charlie, there's a body in here!"

I look more closely at the man.

"He's got red and purple marks all over him!" I gasp not really knowing what to do and feeling sick.

"Don't touch it whatever you do! He might still be infected!" he advises me unnecessarily and shouts to the others who are wading up to the boat, "Finn says there's a body in the cabin!"

"Here, let me see," Charlie struggles to squeeze his larger frame through the narrow hatch opening.

I start to search around for clues about what had happened. I sweep back the curtain covering the opening to the first sleeping cabin. What I see makes me turn away and throw up in the galley sink right next to me.

"What is it?!" Charlie asks, noticing me propped up against the sink.

"Look in there!" I gulp and vomit again.

Charlie pulls the curtain back for himself.

Lying on the bed is another body, this time a woman. Her face, arms and legs are covered with purple blotches, her fingers are blackened. There are livid bulges either side of her neck which are caked in dried blood and yellow puss. The putrid smell of rotting flesh hits Charlie, as it did me, making him close the curtain and gasp for air.

"I think we'd better get out of here!" I say, "This is not good."

"Do you think this could be have been caused by one of those viruses Maulum has released?" Charlie asks in a detached way.

For the second time today, I have no answer.

From the other side of the hatch door is the sound of rummaging as, one by one, the others help each other climb up onto the boat's slippery deck.

"What's going on in there?" shouts Geo pushing at the door.

"I'd stay out there if I were you. There're two bodies in here, one's covered with red and purple marks... the other's purple with blotches everywhere...and it smells evil in here too!" I shout back trying not to be sick again.

Unable to resist, Geo sticks his head through the narrow gap in the door way and looks down at the man's body still half propped up against it.

"Ugh! See what you mean! What d'you reckon happened to him? How long d'you reckon he's been like that?"

Shadrack nimbly climbs on board with an improvised sack made from his own cloak full of our boots and cloaks that we had left abandoned on the sand dune and on the beach, tied to his back.

"Perfect! What a stroke of luck! We can sail from here and be on the mainland before we..." as he speaks, Shadrack notices our worried faces staring back at him, "What's wrong?"

"There are two bodies below!" Imp says pointing to the half open hatch door, "Covered in spots and blotches!"

"Right," replies Shadrack confidently, "Don't you worry. Now then, let's have a look and see what's going on."

Heavy-handedly, he shoves the door further open and the man's body slips further down again and slumps head first to the side with a dull thud.

Shadrack takes one look at the corpse, "Just to be safe, make sure you don't touch anything! Looks, to me, like the signs of a plague of some sort! I've seen this sort of thing before... a long time ago..."

"And here, there's another one here!" I point to the cabin trying to conceal my panic. I am very relieved to have Shadrack here at last.

He looks behind the curtain at the poor woman's body, "Yep, that's the plague for sure! She's probably been there for several days, him... more recent I should say. Not nice...not nice at all...I wonder where they came from...wouldn't surprise me if they're from the mainland...s'pose it was only a matter of time."

"Plague!" says Geo quickly moving away from the body slouched only inches away from where he is standing.

"Doubt if you can catch it off them now but best not to touch them...just in case," recommends Shadrack.

"Well, that blows out using this boat to get to the mainland, doesn't it?" says Charlie with disappointment in his voice.

"It'll be a bit tricky, but we can still use her. We can lift the bodies out and give them a decent burial on shore...with a thorough clean she'll be fine," Shadrack says thoughtfully.

"But you said we better not touch 'em, just in case we catch it too!" I remind him.

Three faces peer in from the relative safety of the door hatch.

"Oh! I get it! USE the stones...like with the boulder in the Nix's cavern. We can use the stones!" Imp explains to our disbelieving faces, staring back at her head, poking through the hatch door opening.

Then the penny drops.

"Great idea, sis'!" says Geo showing his brotherly pride in his little sister.

"S'pose we could. Can we lift up a person or a dead body?" asks Charlie uncertainly, looking for confirmation from Shadrack.

"It's just the same although they're a little bit more... 'slippery'... harder to feel but you'll be fine. Now, I'll go with Jun and Genji back to the beach," Shadrack points to the girls, "we'll have to do this in stages. You stay here and lift the bodies off the boat and across the water, half way over to the beach then we'll take over and put them in their resting place."

It is a gruesome task, but it is also a very good and quick solution to our problem. We need to get to the mainland undetected and, with some effort, we can get this boat ready to set sail with the next tide.

Shadrack wades back to the beach, treads half way up the nearest sand dune and points his staff directly into its side. The sand directly beneath his staff crackles as he heats it up to a blistering temperature, the silicon glows orange with the intense heat and starts to flow like heavy lava. Like a master glass sculptor, he forms the molten sand into a large hammock shape which solidifies quickly as he allows it to cool.

This will be their grave.

We stand in the boat with our stones and staffs poised.

"On 3, 1... 2... 3!" Charlie takes charge.

It's a very wobbly start but we manage to lift the man's heavy body through the hatch door and then hover him, suspended, above the deck before lifting him several metres across the sea surface. I can feel our control and energy fading just as the others on the beach take control of the body. They slowly transport the body over the sand and reverently lower it into the glass grave. The woman's body is much trickier, probably because she has started to putrefy. As we float her past us, the sea breeze wafts the rotten stench back across to us making me gag, nearly losing control.

Eventually they both lie, side by side, together in their shared glass grave. Shadrack solemnly seals the grave and allows the loose sand higher up the dune to cascade and tumble over the grave, completely covering it.

Quickly we return to the boat to prepare her. Genji and Jun must swim the last few metres as the tide has already started to come in, significantly raising the water level. Shadrack helps them onto the boat before climbing on board himself.

The gentle rocking of the boat with each new wave indicates that the boat is floating and is no longer grounded on the sea bed, only the anchor holds us in position.

Time is of the essence, we need to be ready to set sail soon.

Shadrack goes down below deck and finds a large bottle of bleach under the sink in the galley. Carefully, we use the bleach to wash down and disinfect the entire galley including the sleeping cabins; we use so much bleach that the strong smell seems to permeate everything. I prop open the hatch door to let the fresh sea air in. At least that smell of death has gone.

Meanwhile, Imp and Geo go carefully around the living quarters and collect together the few personal possessions that they find, give them the bleach treatment, and put them on the galley table dry out. Other than an assortment of clothes and some canned food, there is only a mobile phone, an mp3 player, a diary, a pair of spectacles and, most importantly, a large rolled up map. Charlie is extremely pleased when he spots the map and he unrolls it flat on the table.

"I think we are here," he points knowledgeably at a part of the coastline, "the mainland is North North East."

He pauses briefly for thought and asks Shadrack, "Where should we make land?"

Shadrack comes over and checks the map with Charlie. While they pour over the map, Imp picks up the diary and Geo switches on the mobile phone. Both search for anything that would reveal who the man and the woman were and where they had travelled from.

Unsurprisingly Geo found that he can't get signal for the phone. He starts to flick through recent calls. The last number called was 'Mum' other than that he finds nothing useful.

Imp however reads the cover page at the front of the diary.

"Her name was Kia Dobbs, 18 Jute Road, Estmouth."

"Estmouth eh?" echoes Shadrack.

She flicks to the last diary entry and reads it out aloud for us all to hear, "We've done it! We've set sail to start our new life. Sooo exciting! I can't wait. I think it was seeing those two poor starving boys that finally convinced Paul. Couldn't get hold of Mum, will try her again tomorrow but I doubt I'll get a signal. I'm so tired all the time and my back is killing me. Doc Brown said I should take it easy, but he didn't look so good himself. I must have knocked against something getting on board, got a row of bruises down my arm. Oh well. Anyway, will write more tomorrow. NEW LIFE HERE WE COME!!!"

Imp stops reading, we are all silent, a black silence.

"That is *so* sad," gasps Genji, "poor Kia!"

"What a way to go," agrees Charlie.

Quietly, Imp withdraws and sits alone in the corner while she reads more of the diary to herself to find out more about the couple but when I look around a few minutes later she has tears streaming down her cheeks.

"There's nothing you could have done for them, Imp... remember it's Maulum who's doing this. That's why we have to fight him!" I try to comfort her.

"All they were trying to do, was escape the street rioting, the spread of the sickness and start a new life together... it was their dream! That's all!" she sobs once more.

"I know, I know! We'll get him, don't you worry!" I reply feeling anger in my belly.

VITA NOVA

~~~

The tide has already turned. We know if we don't leave soon, we will be grounded again.

Shadrack and Charlie are busy preparing 'Vita Nova', to ready her to set sail. Both look very comfortable on the deck, issuing orders to the rest of us. I help bring up the anchor while Genji hoists the main sail. Before long, we are heading out to sea with Charlie at the helm and Shadrack trimming the sail.

Wordlessly, we watch the Isle of Sarro slowly shrink and disappear from view. Briefly, I wonder what is happening back at Charlie's place. How large was the invading army? Would they be able to fight them off? I take comfort in knowing that Alfide has gone back to warn them. Wrapped up in their own thoughts, Genji and Jun stay next to me at the stern railing.

Surprisingly quickly, we are out on the open sea, surrounded by deep blue swelling and crashing waves in every direction. Holding tightly onto the metal handrail, I try to take in the vast openness around me. A sense of smallness comes over me as I see how massive the ocean is and how far away from home we are, even the sea gulls abandon us to return to land.

~~~

That night I struggle to sleep. My bed is a hard, narrow bench that is fixed along one side of the dining table. I hear and feel every thud, every roll, and every pitch, the boat makes as it labors through the storm as it lashes down on us for most of the night. I could have slept in the cabin where we found the woman's body but that would have been worse.

Charlie and Shadrack share watches throughout the night, strapping themselves securely to the deck with strong belts, just in case a rogue wave catches them and washes them overboard.

The weather is much less threatening by first light. The sky glows a faint orange against wispy white clouds giving a warm glow to the new day. In contrast, Charlie looks exhausted when he swaps watch with Shadrack. Despite protesting, Shadrack tells Charlie to have a longer break this time. Charlie drags himself onto the bunk and falls asleep within seconds. The rest of us tiptoe about the cabin while he sleeps, though I think he would have slept through any amount of noise we could have made!

Up on deck, Shadrack appears in a cheerful mood and is keen to give the rest of us a chance to steer the boat. He makes regular adjustments to our course to keep us on track.

"Land ahead! I think!" Jun shouts out.

I turn to face where she is pointing and, sure enough, there is the dark outline of the mainland, in the distance.

ON LAND

~~~

C harlie steers us skillfully up the estuary, keeping a watchful eye for any ripples and shadows in the waters ahead which would indicate dangerous mud banks or, even worse, hidden rocks. We spotted the mainland hours before but Shadrack and Charlie decided to wait, just out of view of the mainland, for the high tide so that we will have the best chance of avoiding being beached when we approach the coastline.

Shadrack thinks he remembers a suitable secluded cove further down the inlet, where we will be able to land safely and, if his memory serves him well, we will be able to disembark unnoticed too. He has already warned us that there is a very real chance that we might get shot at, to deter us from landing; he explained that the people are likely to be very scared that newcomers might be carrying the virus. Some governments had even resorted to extreme measures to protect their coastlines from any unwanted visitors, such as sinking boats before they have the chance to land. Desperate times, desperate measures!

Not a single living soul is in sight, as we carefully creep up the ever-narrowing estuary. We sneak, undetected, into the isolated cove. Shadrack is right. It is exactly as he remembered.

With the anchor down, gripping the cove seabed, we climb, one by one, off the boat, still very concerned that we might be discovered. To our horror, the beach pebbles scrape and crunch loudly with every single footstep, as we cross the short distance to the shelter of two overhanging rocky outcrops where we regroup. If there is anyone nearby, the unavoidable noise would have easily given us away! But there is still no sign of life.

"There's an old farm barn up over that ridge, or at least there *was*! I think we should take shelter for the night there," suggests Shadrack who seems pleased with our progress so far.

Leaving the boat behind, we start the long trek upwards, away from the coast. It's a relief to have firm land underfoot again. We stick to a single narrow rocky track until we reach the bottom of a rolling hillside. Here the lush green grass stretches for miles ahead, rising and falling gently - unlike the stormy sea we had just endured. We follow the most direct route to reach the top of the hill, only to be greeted by yet another hill, and then another!

Finally, in the late afternoon, we arrive at the timeworn wooden barn. Part of the badly rusted, corrugated metal roof has been blown off and the patchwork of wooden planks making up the barn walls, are mostly rotten, green with age and neglect. There is no barn door to open as we step inside. I search around the barn trying to find somewhere dry to sit, disturbing a few pigeons They flap their wings at us and coo indignantly, in protest.

Shadrack sighs as he walks toward the only dry corner of the barn. He is remembering better times when the barn was in its heyday. "Before we make ourselves too comfortable, we need to find food. Go and check the bushes for berries and see if there's anything edible in the field. Remember, we don't want anyone to know we are here. Keep quiet and go in pairs."

Charlie seems to know exactly what he's looking for, but I haven't a clue. Under some nearby trees, he finds some straight leafed plants that smell like onions but leaves them in favour of fistfuls of berries on the adjoining hedge. The best discovery, however, is the carrots that the others find; the whole field must be full of them!

We arrive back at the barn with our forages and Shadrack seems pleased, "Yes that will be plenty."

"I'm getting cold!" moans Jun as the sun dips lower in the sky.

"Me too!" agrees her sister.

"Let's light a fire," suggests Geo reaching for his stone and staff.

Before Geo has time to take them out of his leather pouch Shadrack warns, "Better not to have a fire, there's a lot of wood about but more importantly the light will be seen for miles around. We don't want to attract any unwanted attention."

"What about warming up something, like those stones from the tumbled down wall we climbed over?" suggests Shadrack patiently.

"I'll go and get some of the bigger ones! I'll need help, they look heavy."

"Too heavy if you ask me!" I add.

Geo reaches for his staff and walks up to a large stone. His stone begins to glow with energy as he concentrates. A few seconds later, the first stone from the wall, is floating across the barn threshold to where Genji and Jun are sitting. Another follows, then another, until there are five large wall stones, in an untidy circle, on the ground before us.

Together, we heat the stones gently using our staffs and, although it takes several minutes of intense concentration, the result is more than worth it. The stones dimly glow orange, radiating warmth throughout the barn, keeping out the chill of the evening.

"Shadrack I've been wondering, how did Amelia end up with the necklace?" Imp asks as she munches on some carrot and a few of the berries that Charlie had found.

"Good question. The long and short of it is that she volunteered to be the key bearer. Her job was to make sure that the key was hidden from those who wanted to release the Black Mist, at least until the stones themselves called the new Holders. You see, we can never know *when* a Holder will be called. And Amelia did a good job too. I think, somehow, she must have known that you were being called." Shadrack stops and eats another delicious berry.

"As you unwittingly discovered yourselves, the necklace was

the key to the underground caves. Years before, the stones that you found there, were hidden inside and, later, when Black Mist was finally captured, it was decided to seal that in the caves too."

"So, what about Jess?" adds Jun with a yawn.

"Well, I don't know about Jess. All I can think is that she found a way into the caves not known to us. She could have been searching for the stones. I'm sorry, I can only guess."

PRISONERS

~~~

At first light, we leave the uncomfortable run-down barn behind. Shadrack guides us across an old stone style into the adjacent field which is completely overgrown with thigh-high grass and weeds. No farmer has tended the fields about here recently. We thread our way along a narrow, uneven, stony pathway which weaves westward and deeper inland. In places, the pathway is extremely overgrown with nettles and briars, confirming its lack of use.

"Do you think they're all dead?" asks Geo, prompted by the fact that we have not seen a single person since arriving on the mainland, "I mean since we arrived, we've seen no one at all! It's weird."

"We are trying to keep it that way too," Imp impatiently reminds him, "that's *why* we're keeping to the track and getting scratched to pieces!"

"I was thinking that!" I agree with Geo and speculate, "What if there's no one left alive on the mainland?"

Over hearing, Shadrack points out, "We'll be coming up to a small village soon. You'll see for yourselves then. Be warned that those who live there, will not welcome us with open arms though."

"Ow! That's the millionth time I've been stung by these stupid nettles!" Jun curses from the middle of our single file. Angrily, she stops to count how many sting marks she has, "1, 2, 3, ...4, 5, ...6, ...7, 8 ..."

"Watch it! I nearly walked into the back of you!" complains

Genji who is walking behind Jun.

"Will you stop moaning, you two?!" Charlie hisses at the sisters.

Suddenly, Shadrack stops dead in his tracks.

Blocking his way, directly in front of him, stands a very large burly man, dressed in camouflage dark green and browns. He is pointing a hand gun directly at us.

"Who are you? What do you want? Where are you from?" he questions gruffly, his thick dark curly hair falls half way over his eyes, making him squint as he speaks.

"They're not from 'round here!" accuses the second person, who is much thinner and shorter than the first. He fidgets nervously with his sheathed machete hanging menacingly from his belt.

"Well, talk!"

"Your friend is right... we are not from 'round here... we are travelling to the next village. There is no need for the gun," replies Shadrack calmly.

I can see Geo slowly reaching for his leather pouch.

I can feel myself wanting to do the same but then I think, what would I do exactly? So, I remain still.

Shadrack glances sideways towards us and, unnoticed by the strangers, minutely shakes his head, warning us not to do anything.

Reading his signal, Geo holds fast.

"What do you want there?" quizzes the imposing man suspiciously.

"Food and shelter, if possible."

"Ha! Are you mad?! No one's going to help a stranger... you might have the sickness for all we know!"

"Look at their arms! Covered with marks! Don't go near them," panics the other man, as he edges away in frightened alarm.

"Merely stings off these nettles and scratches from the briars...nothing more!" answers Shadrack coolly dismissing any concerns, "You have nothing to fear from us."

"I'll be the judge of that!" comes the stern reply.

"Has the village of Meade escaped the sickness?" continues Shadrack quietly, "We have some skills in medicine if you need help."

"There's no cure! You know that. He's lying!" says the smaller of the two untrustingly, looking very agitated.

Shadrack notices the large man pause for thought. Pressing home his advantage, Shadrack continues, "As you can see for yourselves, my friends and I have no sickness, yet we have travelled many miles, surely if we have no skills in medicine, we would have fallen down to the evil virus that has swept through these parts."

"True, you appear to be free of the sickness, but we have been tricked before! We could use your skills in medicine, but the risk is too great. No one would stand for it!"

"Has the village of Meade lost its courage of old?" challenges Shadrack again.

"It is not about courage, traveler, it's about fighting an invisible enemy which has a deadlier strike than even this gun!" the larger stranger waves the gun in the air to emphasise his point.

"A place where we could be quarantined maybe?" suggests Shadrack persevering, "You know that if we show no symptoms after seven days then we are clear."

"Don't believe him! No one can heal the sickness," whispers the friend.

"We are already heavily down in number; we could do with help to fight this sickness. If he can do what he claims, he could save what is left of the village."

"Can we afford to take the risk? If he lies and they are carrying the sickness that will surely finish us all!"

"We already have too many with the sickness...if we don't try something we are surely finished anyway! The way I see it, we have more to gain than lose!"

Shadrack remains still and silent, sensing a change of heart within the companions before him.

"Why are you prepared to enter our village knowing that we

have the sickness, why would you help us?

Shadrack replies rhetorically, "Surely you would help us if we were in need...if you could?"

"I still don't like it!" the second voice says still full of caution.

"I don't think we have much choice," the larger man empathises with his cautious friend, although he has reached a decision. "Very well, you can stay at the old station house on the village outskirts. It has been vacant for weeks now. You will remain there for a week. If you are clear of the virus, we will know by then. If you are clear, you will be made welcome in our village."

"I am Johnson and my, rightly, very wary friend is Bren. You will excuse me not shaking your hand! Walk behind us and we will lead you to the old station house. You will find a well for water there, and I will make sure some supplies are left outside for you and your friends."

"Thank you... that will be more than ample. In return, we will do what we can to help those infected... bring them to the house and if they are not too far gone..." he pauses and wonders if he is pushing his luck too far before asking, "Is the old village wall still standing? I would very much like to visit it again!"

"That wall will stand forever...long after we've gone, that's for sure!" Johnson jokes as he replaces his gun in its holster and leads the way down the track towards the village.

Only fifteen minutes later, we arrive at the outskirts of Meade, at the Old Station House which, in bygone times, had been home to the Station Master and his family, back in the days when the railways had penetrated every corner of the mainland. The village itself is still another kilometre further down the narrow straight road cutting through flat farm fields on each side. The now rusting railway track stretches north-south into the abandoned station nearby. It is completely overrun by dense briars intertwined with weeds and thistles. Even in its heyday, the railway had not been widely welcomed here. The villagers of Meade liked things just the way they were; most had no time for 'city types' and kept themselves to themselves.

Johnson explains to us that the house had been bought recently, by a family from the city who were in the process of making extensive renovations, many of which are still half finished. Fortunately, the new windows and door have been installed so the house is habitable.

"Bren reckons it was them who brought the first sickness to the village. They were from the city, you see," explains Johnson.

Pointing to the long thin rounded mounds of earth at the end of the garden, Bren bends over and whispers from a safe distance, "That's where they are now."

A cold shiver runs down my spine.

"Who buried them?" asks Shadrack interestedly.

"Me and Bren 'ere, that's who!"

"How come you weren't struck down with the sickness?"

"I'm not rightly sure. Bren says we can't catch it. I hope he's right but plenty of others 'ere have and I still keep my distance."

"Some people are immune to the sickness?" Shadrack says thoughtfully, more to himself than anyone else.

"We will need your help to bring the sick to us. How many of them are there?" asks Shadrack taking control.

"Only 'bout twenty now, maybe less...Sissy's lass looked in a very bad way when I saw 'er last."

"The sooner the better then! Time is of the essence." Shadrack replies, "We need to hurry! We'll set up some beds for the sick."

With that we enter the Old Station House. The decor is very modern, in contrast to its traditional rustic shell. Shadrack checks out the facilities, turns to us and asks us to search the house for sheets, blankets and mattresses, anything that people can rest on.

"Shadrack, I didn't know you knew medicine," remarks Charlie when he is certain Johnson and Bren are completely out of earshot.

"Oh, only a few things that I've picked up on my travels...I always carry my medicine pouch with me...but, my friend, it is you, not I, that will be doing the healing!"

We all look at him in disbelief, jaws dropping wide open.

"What? I don't know anything about medicine!" replies Charlie.

"You don't need to know anything about medicine; you just need to know how to use your healing gifts from the Nix! I will mix a sweet tasting potion which will give our patients much needed energy...but you will heal them."

"But...but what if we catch the sickness! What if the Nix healing disc doesn't work against this sickness!" questions Genji, not liking this plan at all.

"It will. Trust me! And now I'm convinced that you too are protected against the sickness too. I should have known."

"How are we protected?!" asks Jun doubting Shadrack.

"I believe the Earth power that chose you to be a Holder will also protect you." explains Shadrack excitedly, "Now! There's no time to waste with chatter, we must get ready!"

"But what if you're wrong?" Imp checks.

"Trust me."

Within the hour Johnson and Bren arrive with a horse drawn cart carrying the first of our patients. We assist each person down from the old cart and up through the garden gate to the Old Station House. Bravely, Genji and Jun help them slowly walk the rest of the way into the front room, which is now a hive of activity. It looks more like a small hospital ward than a front lounge. The settee cushions are spread on the floor to give extra bed space. Red faced Geo found some air-beds but couldn't find the air pump so he is blowing them up himself.

In the kitchen, Shadrack is busy brewing his medicinal potion in some large aluminium pans that he had found under the sink.

The youngest victim brought to us is only eight years old, at the most. He's plastered with the tell-tale bruised purple blotches and is mumbling incoherently to himself. He is very hot to the touch with sweat dripping from his forehead. It takes a determined effort for me to hold him upright. I am reluctant, not because he is heavy, but because each time he coughs his saliva globules splatter over my arm, making me feel as if I will definitely catch the deadly virus despite Shadrack's assurances. I notice a lump on his neck, just as the woman had, back on the boat. It looks painfully red and sore. With relief, I help him lie on some cushions and Shadrack gives him his sweet potion. I take the Nix healing disc from my cloak pocket. It is difficult to know exactly where to start. In the end, I decide to place it on the seething lump on his neck. Immediately the redness fades and the lump reduces in size. I notice the healing disc glowing and a rainbow of colours dance within it as it works its healing power. Moving down the boy's body, I hold the disc over the worst looking areas, livid bruise after bruise gently fade and vanish leaving behind only pale blemishes on the skin's surface, as a souvenir of the deadly illness. Eventually, his high temperature drops and returns to normal. When he looks up at me, I notice a brightness in his eyes that wasn't there before.

"Where am I?" he weakly asks in bewilderment as he tries to push himself into a sitting position.

"Take it easy," I say and pass him his cup of Shadrack's potion, "Drink this medicine, it'll give you energy. Give your body time to recover, you caught the sickness...but you'll be fine now." I sound much more confident than I feel.

Unfortunately, there is little that could be done for the last man to be brought off the very same cart. He is writhing in pain. His hands are black with bruises. He is sweating and delirious. His staring eyes are wide open and unblinking but unseeing. Shadrack rushes over to help Genji and Jun in their joint attempts to try to revive him. All three work desperately to save him but, in the end, he dies...they are too late. The virus had too tight a grip on the poor fellow. Genji and Jun are tearful, but they bravely blink away their tears and escort the new batch of patients off the next cart, into the make shift hospital and start all over again.

In the end, only two out of the nineteen patients die. Johnson and Bren unceremoniously remove their bodies for immediate burial to minimise the risk of any further disease spread. It seems cold and heartless, but everyone is too exhausted to help.

We are lucky that there are no more arrivals because the healing power of the Nix discs has seriously reduced; for the last few patients we have to work in relays as the healing power of the overworked Nix healing discs becomes less and less effective, as more and more healing energy is drained away.

Shadrack's sweet potion is a hit with both the patients and us, its fusion of berries and secret spices gives us energy and keeps us going, without interruption right through to the final patient.

UNDER ATTACK!

~~~

"**P**repare for an attack!" shouts Alfide as he crashes through the backdoor of Holdwood Manor foregoing all pleasantries, "The Nix have sensed an army is being amassed on the island nearby and some even passed by *us* before we arrived at the Nix. They're using the secret pathways!"

"How has this happened?" worries Charlie's mother.

"I don't know," replies Alfide, equally perplexed.

"Send a message out to all who can help, every last person you can muster, and get them here!" commands Charlie's father.

"Hold it! Wait! On second thoughts, we don't need to win *this* battle...we need to win more time, to *delay*, to give the new Holders a head start," reminds Alfide thoughtfully, "Better to save our energy for a battle of our choosing and let the enemy waste time gathering their army together here. Let them waste their resources."

"Remember also if *we* are delayed much longer then we won't be able to catch up with the new Holders for some time. Who knows what might happen to them!" says Charlie's mother.

"What about setting a trap?" suggests Mr. Taylor with a seldom seen deviousness.

"What sort of trap?" Jennifer is intrigued.

"How about multiple layers of defense, like pealing an onion to its core. Let them think that they are winning inch by inch, layer by layer, and then when they're deep inside the building...

BANG!... No building. No enemies!"

"That's a bit extreme, isn't it?" says Charlie's mother, thinking that she would rather not have her beautiful home blown up.

"Carmella, can you come up with a better idea?" challenges Mr. Taylor.

"Do we have to blow up the house? Surely not! Even the Meeting Hall?" she continues.

"I'll take care of the Meeting Hall," says Alfide, "There will always be another house. I suspect we won't be back here for some time and we need to strike the enemy hard. Even better if they think we were all destroyed here too!"

"I'll set up an outer perimeter which will trigger as soon as they start their attack. You set up rings of sensors around the outside of the building to make it appear that we are still inside defending it," he orders enthusiastically revealing each step of his battle strategy, "We will make it appear as if we have retreated deep into the Meeting Hall, they won't be able to resist tracking us down the passage way...that'll be the perfect place to set off the final and deadly explosion!"

MEADE

~~~

The seven days of our quarantine would have dragged by if we had not had the company of the revitalised villagers, now fully recovered and itching to return to their friends and families. Luckily, there are no more reports of further sickness in the village.

We find out very little about the wider world outside of the village of Meade. The feeling in the village was that as long as they keep away from the city folk, they will be able to survive. We do discover that, for weeks, there has been no reliable electricity supply, no fuel, no phone connections, and no contact beyond the village walls, except for the occasional crackly nonsensical radio broadcast.

Nothing.

Fortunately, the villagers are largely self-sufficient; they grow their own food and drink fresh water from an underground stream. True, they would have preferred to have fuel for the tractors and cars, but they consider this a small price to pay, to be safely isolated from the city and to keep the risk of contracting the deadly sickness to a minimum.

I hide my increasing concerns about my own family, from the others. I already know deep down that it is extremely unlikely they have fared much better than anyone else in the city; it doesn't look hopeful.

Finally, late in the afternoon, having completed our quarantine, we briskly walk the final kilometer, all together, into Meade village. Johnson and Bren cheerfully lead the way. Bren is a completely different person to the scared agitated man we met on the track, at gun point, a week ago. They have already told the rest of the villagers about our amazing success but as we approach the first row of grey sandstone crofters' houses, we are greeted with extreme caution and kept at a healthy distance. Some villagers even stay inside their single-story houses, peering at us from behind half drawn, twitching curtains. Understandably wary, the fear-gripped villagers want to see for themselves that none of our patients show any symptoms of the sickness whatsoever. Nervously watching, they allow us to enter the village. Grey fear is etched across each villager's face as we walk down the main road into the village. Like Johnson, I notice some have guns.

My heart is beating quickly in sympathy with them, but I know a wrong move here could result in death.

Silently, we continue walking on into the heart of Meade village, down the middle of the narrow main road, towards the cobbled stone market place.

The heavy air of tension is broken abruptly when Ned's mother spot's her son.

She is overwhelmed with joy. Instantly she can see that he has made a full recovery – up to this point, she had not dared to believe that it was true. She thought she would never see her boy again. But there he is looking as healthy as ever! She rushes over and gives him a hug, checks him over and announces to the other villagers that he has never looked better. At last, there is an encouraging cheer from the other villagers and then, much to my relief, we are all warmly welcomed.

The villagers are friendly, and we immediately feel at ease after the tense standoff.

As if in sympathy, the sun breaks through the clouds, helping to lift our spirits. We are offered food and drink which we gratefully and politely accept. While we chat happily with the very relieved villagers, Shadrack stands a few paces apart from the crowd. He is lost in deep thought, remembering past people and places. He notices the imposing, weather worn Celtic sandstone cross in the centre of the market square but, more importantly, he notices the old village stone wall, still standing tall, marking the boundary of the village. It is in a better shape than he remembers; whole sections of the wall have been completely rebuilt since he had been here last.

There are many battle sites scattered across the mainland. The battle of Meade had been one of the fiercest and most ferocious battles. The main encounter, the last stand against Maulum's vast army, had taken place on the rich flat grassland just beyond this section of the village wall. Only a low grassy mound in the middle of the otherwise flat field, bears the dreadful memory of what had happened here; it is the burial mound. Hundreds had lost their lives in the bloody battle, a lump comes to Shadrack's throat as the dreadful memories flood back; there had been too many dead, too many to bury in individual graves.

The victory had been extremely costly but even now the fight is not over...the war remains unwon.

"Are you OK Shadrack?" I ask noticing his thoughtful distant gaze.

"Tired, that's all," he avoids my question, "See that grassy mound beyond the wall, that's where we must go, tonight after dark, when there are no prying eyes. That's where we will find the first segment of Earthcode."

"What will it look like?"

"You'll know. It's more like a memory, a thought, than a thing. You'll see soon enough."

Johnson comes over to speak to us. "Some say that Meade village has stood here forever, longer than that wall itself! When were you here before?"

A large black crow circles above us before settling on the wall. It reminds me of the Black Mist swirling around our heads in the den.

"Oh, a long while back," Shadrack evades the question, turning away throwing a bread crumb for the crow to eat, not wishing to encourage any unwanted interest.

FINAL STAND

~~~

For the last time, Alfide walks solemnly down the dark passage way leading to the ancient Meeting Hall. He ponders a while as he surveys the ancient wooden carvings, before walking across to the pool in the centre of the room. He carefully scoops up some of the milky water into a small glass bottle and replaces the top, sealing in the liquid. Emotionlessly, he returns to the Meeting Hall entrance, turns, and faces back to face the milky pool. He pours a small pile of white, sand-sized creatures into the palm of his hand. He raises his hand up to his mouth and forcefully blows the tiny creatures into the air. As a cloud they swarm like locusts around the old Meeting Hall. They greedily start to eat everything in sight, like thick acid eating through metal. Before long there is nothing of the Meeting Hall left - just the dark hollow cavern in which it had once stood. Like well-trained soldiers marching back from duty, the tiny white creatures return to Alfide's palm and he billets them back in a soft leather pouch. Finally, he loads the entrance of the now empty cavern with explosives, setting the final trap, before turning back to help the others prepare for leaving.

~~~

The last night is miserably damp, with dark black clouds soaking up any hint of moonlight. Carmella Boyd silently closes the backdoor behind them for the last time. With a sigh in her heart, the happy memories flood through her mind. She remembers fondly the many, many years spent in this old house and, even though she has always known they were only caretakers, it had still been her home, where they had raised their son. She turns her back on the Manor, knowing deep down, it is for the final time. Charlie's father feels it too and puts his arm around her shoulders as they creep away together into the black night and steal silently, undetected, across the enemy's line which already surrounds most of the Manor grounds.

When the escaping party finally reaches the edge of the woods they stop still, sensing an abrupt change about them. Except for the fine drizzle of rain, the night is unnaturally quiet. There are no sounds of nocturnal animals or even scratching insects; just a hushed, unnerving silence. It is as if the whole place is holding its breath...

Then the battle begins!

Creatures of all shapes and sizes flood toward Holdwood Manor, from every direction like black rats escaping a sinking ship for dry land. Looking on through the fine rain from a distance, it is not the suddenness of the attack that surprises them, it is the sheer ferociousness and sustained intensity. The attacking army is much larger than they had imagined, despite the warning from the Nix. The charging roar is deafening even from the edge of the woods where they stand.

Mr. Taylor hears, with immense satisfaction, that the first perimeter defense has automatically activated around the grounds, exactly according to his plan, temporarily stunning the onslaught into silence but within minutes the threatening screeching noise returns, this time with even greater venom. They make the most of this distraction and weave their way through the wooded hillside, using only the dimmest of lights to guide their way. Without slowing, they constantly listen for clues about the raging battle back at Holdwood Manor.

Several minutes later, a screeching cry of celebration filters its way down to the fleeing marchers. The attacking creatures have at last taken possession of the Manor. Now they will be urgently searching through the rooms for the people and the Holders, sensing victory is near.

Finally, it comes; the loud howls of anger as the attackers find themselves trapped deep inside the abandoned Meeting Hall cavern realising, too late, that they have been deceived. Seconds later follows the shocking explosion that reverberates around the whole island, briefly lighting up the night sky around the grounds.

A thin, half smile works its way across Alfide's face. They have gained some more time for the Holders.

TRESPASSERS

~~~

L
ate that evening, we secretly leave Meade village behind us. We walk past the village wall in single file, the slow line of faintly glowing stones are hardly discernible even against the pitch-black dark of the country night sky.

We reach the grassy burial mound.

Shadrack has already told us what to do before we set out. We walk part way up the mound and form a human ring around the mound, keeping equally spaced, then we each lie face down on the already dewy damp grass.

This is the moment we have all been dreading.

I close my eyes and hold onto my staff and stone which glows nervously echoing my feelings.

"Now we need to wake the dead and ask them to let us pass!" Shadrack announces, "Have no fear! They are our friends! They fought and died to keep their segment of Earthcode safe for this moment. Have no fear!"

Without warning the grassy ground that I am lying on squelches, softens and gives way. I am being sucked into the earth, squeezed slowly through the soil and deeper into the earth itself. My heart pounds as I think I might suffocate. I can sense the others are still with me, falling. I sense the awakening of old souls that have been resting here, undisturbed for hundreds of years, pale shadows of past lives making way for me, parting, allowing me to pass through their personal permanent resting places, as I sink deeper and deeper into the earth mound. Then, as if the dead have fully awoken, the shadows unexpectedly start to block my fall as if they are trying to stop me dropping any further. They reach out towards me, but their shadowy ghostlike hands have no effect as they try to grab at me. Unrelenting, I continue to slowly fall ever deeper, deeper, and deeper into the earth until I pass even below and beyond the grasping arms of the dead.

Here, embedded deep down in the heart of the mound, is a large smooth mound shaped rock; it is as if the earth mound above has shaped itself on this centre stone and is protecting it.

Above us float the shadows of the fallen, menacingly trying to reach below, towards us, but unable to move down any closer as if there's an invisible impenetrable barrier, forcing them back.

There is a dark, ill feeling.

This is their place on earth, not ours.

We are the trespassers. They have reluctantly allowed us to pass down, but would they let us pass back up?

Shadrack reaches out and touches the smooth stone at the centre of the mound with his outstretched hand. It is exactly as he remembered it.

Instinctively we follow his lead.

I reach out and touch the stone, as do the others.

Instantly, I am blasted backwards, jolted by a tremendous surge of black energy, shaken, and flung by a powerful wave of destructive force. My arm feels as if it has been completely ripped out of its socket, but I can still feel my hand burning with searing pain. Out of the corner of my eye, I can see Geo and Jun both reeling backwards, as I am, from the powerful blast.

Shadrack looks badly hit and confused. He did not expect this. He falls heavily in a crumpled heap next to the centre stone. Unmoving.

We are hit by another full blast of the black power which slams us even further back again and away from Shadrack.

Realising that Shadrack is in trouble, I struggle to move back downwards to help him. Using my stone, I turn and push myself hard against the blast which rips through my body again like an electric shockwave stunning me and making me feel heavy and uncoordinated. I see Charlie also trying to fight against the blast; he must know Shadrack is in trouble too.

Painfully slowly, I fight my way back down to Shadrack who is still not moving.

I am the first to reach him.

Still struggling for balance, I turn him over so I can see his face. It is bloodied and torn, his hand is charred and blackened, and his arm bowed and impossibly bent back the wrong way. He must have taken the full brunt of the powerful black force and stayed behind to shield us in the only way he could.

With a terrible lurch Shadrack grabs my arm and, trembling, places a marble sized ball of light in my palm, closing my hand around it. His eyes are wild with pain. I look down and it is gone, like a thought.

I try to lift Shadrack up, to somehow take him to safety, but it is useless.

I start to use my stone to lift him to away from the centre stone but, as I do, Shadrack mouths the words 'Black Mist...GO!' before slumping again falling onto the smooth stone at the heart of the mound. With that another blast, even more vicious than the first, propels me backwards and upwards. As if I am riding a tidal wave of black energy, I am cast even further backward with ever increasing speed, launched back up through the cloud of dead souls who, now, seem to be trying to help me; shielding and saving me from the powerful evil force buried deep below the mound.

Distantly, as if in a dream, I feel the fresh dewy grass beneath my burning face before I finally drift out of consciousness.

Later I have a vague memory, a feeling that someone is calling my name.

I remember staring up at hazy grey faces and trying to fight them off me, not wanting them to touch me. I try to scream, 'No! Shadrack is still down there!' but even through my unconscious mist I know he is gone.

Shadrack is dead.

Printed in Great Britain
by Amazon